ECHOES IN THE WALLS

Center Point
Large Print

Also by V. C. Andrews® and available from Center Point Large Print:

House of Secrets
The Silhouette Girl
Beneath the Attic
Out of the Attic
Shadows of Foxworth

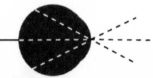

This Large Print Book carries the Seal of Approval of N.A.V.H.

ECHOES IN THE WALLS

V. C. ANDREWS®

CENTER POINT LARGE PRINT
THORNDIKE, MAINE

PROLOGUE

"All of us commit sins in our dreams," my mother once told me when I was a little more than five years old and guiltily described a dream I had about watching Enid Austin fall through thin ice on Lake Wyndemere.

"She screamed and screamed and reached for my hand, but instead of helping her, I put my hand on her head and pushed her farther down in the icy water until she disappeared, Mummy. I saw the bubbles stop," I confessed. My voice trembled. I was afraid God would punish me for wanting it to happen and so vividly envisioning it.

Enid was a girl in my first-grade class who had told others in my class that I was illegitimate. She had told my classmates that I was against the law because my mother had given birth to me without a husband. I had no legal father.

My mother was right about dreams. But I thought that in fantasies, we could get revenge also, brutal revenge, and when we woke up, we would feel satisfied as well as guilty. Wasn't that better than actually doing it?

But it was in dreams where we could do other

immoral things, too. We could steal and enjoy what we had taken. We could trip our mean teachers and other mean adults and watch them fall down stairways. We could see bullies break their arms or legs and enjoy watching them writhe in agony, crying hysterically.

Looking back, these childish dreams seemed silly, but when I was older and the woman in me was beginning to emerge from under the swirling and bubbling cauldron of childhood, I had sexual dreams about Ryder Davenport. I didn't know yet, of course, that he was really my half brother. Even in my daytime reveries, we held hands, we kissed, and we saw each other naked. When I was older, some of my night-time fantasies were so intense that I woke up wet and frightened at my own overwhelming passion.

The kisses and caresses I had envisioned in dreams became real shortly before I learned how we were related to each other. And when I dreamed about them, even after I had learned it all, I understood that there was a deeper part of ourselves that was defiant of rules and laws, no matter what the threats or the consequences. What my mother once told me was ever so true in this mansion. The sins of childhood dreams paled before the bright glow of my adult transgressions and the transgressions of others older than me here. However, not any edict, not any biblical commandment, and not even my mother's deep and painful disappointment could stop me from slipping gracefully and lovingly beside Ryder when in sleep I fantasized being with him. In my dream, we were always already both naked but very innocent. We were like Adam and Eve before the snake.

His kiss began almost brotherly, on my forehead, my cheek. His hands remained on my shoulders. There was space between us but no room to retreat.

Take a breath, step back, Fern Corey, I told myself in my dream.

I should tell him, I thought. *He should know before he goes any further.*

But then he might stop.

Oh, be still, my troubled heart; otherwise, he will step back, and it will end. I will wake up and be alone in the dark, so unsatisfied and raging with frustration.

I swallowed back the words that would condemn us. I didn't care. His hands were moving to my breasts. He was growing harder. My head fell back against the pillow. His lips were on my neck. He was telling me he had the same passion for so long, a passion that had made him ache every morning.

Yes, I thought. *I'll risk hell.*

He moved softly, almost flowed between my legs. I turned to welcome him. The child in me was sinking. It gasped and disappeared. We were so close now. It was happening.

And then I saw my mother in the doorway. Her face was twisted in a grimace of utter shock, her eyes never as big or her lips as twisted.

She brought her hands to her ears, covering them before she screamed. *No!*

And I awoke.

Shivering.

1

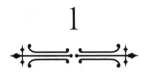

I sat at my computer desk by the window of my upstairs bedroom facing the front lawn, the walkway, and the crescent driveway to Wyndemere House that exited onto Lakeview Drive. For the past few minutes, I hadn't had a single thought. The snowfall had hypnotized me. Every ten minutes or so, it fell in larger flakes that looked more like shavings from a bar of soap. From the way the leafless trees swayed, I could see that the December wind had picked up, too, and I knew it had to be very cold, because it blew in over Lake Wyndemere, a five-mile-long lake that our property abutted on the border between New York and Massachusetts.

I heard the familiar and expected growling sound of the Davenports' tractor. It seemed to vibrate the walls and floors, even in a house as large as this. I gazed down and to my left to see Mr. Stark, the estate manager, come around the left corner of the mansion to plow the driveway. His clothes glistened with the moist flakes that clung to his hat, coat, and pants, causing him to resemble a polar bear at the North Pole. Poking out from under his hat and between his earmuffs, his face was the color of a ripe turnip. Later, I might tease him and call him Rudolph the Red-Nosed Polar Bear.

It had been snowing all morning and now was at its heaviest, fulfilling the weatherman's weeklong promise of a white Christmas. At this hour, surely seven or eight inches had already accumulated. I could barely distinguish the driveway or Lakeview Drive. The sticky snow, which Mr. Stark called the worst kind because it was so heavy, had already turned the hedges into crouching ghosts and made the leafless trees look like gawking white chalk skeletons. Not a car had gone by during the entire time I had been sitting here watching the storm and studying how the flakes struck my windows and immediately changed into tears zigzagging across and down. To me, it was as if the mansion was having a fresh cry. With its history, it had so many reasons for grieving periodically. Lately, I felt like crying along with it.

"We're in for it," Mr. Stark had told me earlier when I saw him having a mug of coffee with my mother in the kitchen. The snow had just begun in earnest. He was leaning against the counter and clutching his mug between his thick fingers as if he was already shivering. He wore a brownish-white cable-knit sweater with its turtleneck collar, which my mother had bought him on his sixtieth birthday. As usual, when he was inside the mansion, he had pushed the sleeves up over his thick, muscular forearms. My mother said he reminded her of one of the Clancy Brothers, her favorite Irish singing group.

"Only he can't carry a note across the room," she said in front of him. He wasn't insulted. Instead, he smiled with delight at being ragged, especially by her. My mother often had the effect of turning him into a little boy again. His eyes would warm, and the sternness in his face would melt and disappear. Years would fall away like red and yellow November leaves.

"Who'd know about that better than your mother?" he asked me, nodding as if he wanted to convince me and keep me from quickly coming to his defense, which I often did. "Someone who herself sings like a canary."

"And didn't earn enough to build a canary's nest doing so, thank you," she said.

My mother was whipping up pancake batter. She had her raven-black hair, the same color as mine, pinned back with two thick ivory combs, and she wore a plum-colored cardigan, a white blouse, and matching plum slacks. It wasn't ever possible to catch my mother looking sloppy or half dressed once she had stepped out of her room. She thought that was disrespecting not only yourself but also those who couldn't avoid seeing you. I saw she had risen earlier to set the table, something I would usually help her and Mrs. Marlene do. I certainly should have been helping this morning.

Mrs. Marlene, who had been in charge of the kitchen and meals for as long as I could remember, was off on holiday visiting relatives, and my mother had assumed all her duties, beginning with preparing today's breakfast for my father, Dr. Davenport; my half brother, Ryder; my half sister, Samantha; and myself. Mr. Stark would eat before us so he could get to work.

Seeing the bed tray set out on the counter, I knew my mother would bring Ryder his breakfast this morning. Over a month now since his return from the hospital and therapy, it was no longer necessary for her or anyone to do that. He was able to get around the mansion on his own quite well, although he rarely went wandering about these days. But he didn't need any special nursing care. My mother enjoyed spoiling him, though. She always had.

"In for what?" I asked, yawning and stretching.

I was still in my lavender-pink matching robe and slippers, an early Christmas gift from my mother because she said my old set was "knackered," which was her British expression for something terribly worn out. She clung to so many expressions like that, expressions that were among the few things that brought a hint of a smile to Dr. Davenport's face nowadays.

His smile would start with a playful light in his sterling-gray eyes, start to ripple down his firmly sculpted cheeks, and then stop and sink back inside to wherever uncompleted smiles lived in frustration. I was sure it was getting crowded there. Even Christmas couldn't free what depression had chained to his walls of sorrow.

My mother always said "Happy Christmas" rather than "Merry Christmas," too. It was her way of clinging to her youth, to the life she had left in Guildford, England, when she came to America to become a professional singer, now well over twenty years ago. She had no real traveling money and had to work as a maid on an ocean liner to get "across the pond." It was a decision that had estranged her from her father, who had forbidden it and had warned that if she left, she would be ostracized by her family.

"Step out of that door and never come back" were words still resonating even after all these years. But she was very determined, defiant, and full of expectations planted in her mind by friends, family, and most influentially her high school music teacher, expectations that wilted even before the blush had left her ambitions.

I often wondered where big dreams for your future went when they died. Was there a cemetery in the sky with big tombs to house Movie Star, Singing Star, Pianist, Baseball Player, Football Player, Doctor or Lawyer, and even Astronaut, all the ambitions people had for themselves, ambitions that never had materialized?

What would be the name on my tomb of dreams? I could sing but not half as well as my mother. I could dance better than most my age, but I didn't see myself doing it professionally. I didn't want to be an actor, either. Nothing in the world of entertainment held any promise as it did for so many of my classmates. I tolerated science and math, sometimes enjoyed history, and did love to read. However, right now, I saw no career for myself as a writer or a teacher, a doctor or a lawyer.

I wasn't supposed to worry too much about it yet. Few my age had specific vocational goals or even seriously thought about it until we were confronted by college plans or post–high school life, but I couldn't help wondering what was out there for me and why I didn't care or wasn't, like some of my friends, full of glorious images of myself splashed on the covers of magazines or visions of myself being rich and living in my own beautiful home. The cover of my magazine, *Fern's Magazine*, was stark white, with a big black question mark at the center.

If you had no ambitions, were you like a kite whose string was broken and was now vulnerable to the frivolous wind?

It was certainly how I felt . . . aimlessly gliding through the days, the weeks, the months since it had all happened, that terrible day, that terrible storm that twisted my heart into a knot.

Would it ever unravel?

"Probably a foot or more of snow by evening," Mr. Stark now predicted, to explain why we were in for it. "And with this wind, drifts that will mount up higher than a twenty-five-hand horse before it's over."

"Oh, go on with yourself, frightening the girl with the unbelievable," my mother said, spinning around on him. She was always protecting me these days, even against horrendous images. "There's no such horse. Twenty-five hands. Pure poppycock."

"Yes, there is," Mr. Stark insisted. "I read about him in the *Guinness World Record Book*."

"You were drinking your second or third pint of Guinness, you mean." She waved the air between them as if she could push his words away. "Nevertheless, after you eat something, you bundle up out there, George Stark," my mother warned him with her eyes full of reprimand. "That sweater is not enough today."

Mr. Stark had been working at Wyndemere since long before my mother arrived, and whenever she was in the mood to tell me about her early days and my birth, she admitted she had needed his daughter Cathy's help caring for me as well as caring for Ryder when I was born nearly three years after him. For over twenty years, Mr.

Stark was her "rock-solid tree, never wavering no matter how strong the wind."

There was almost twenty years' difference in age between them, but it didn't matter how old Mr. Stark was. My mother still treated him as if he was one of her wards, and he usually followed her orders. Whenever he didn't do that, like dressing appropriately for very cold weather, she would bawl him out until he raised his hands in surrender and did whatever she had told him to do. For most of my life, he and Cathy, who had become a nurse working in the hospital where Dr. Davenport was head of cardiology, my mother, and Mrs. Marlene were really the only family I had.

Now, because of the Revelations, Dr. Davenport's and my mother's confessions, I finally had a father as well as a half sister and a half brother. That meant Ryder's and Samantha's paternal grandparents, long gone, were mine as well. What they had inherited from them, I had inherited. I was a member of the family that owned Wyndemere, the seventeen-bedroom house and the grounds of rolling hills and trees that seemed to go on forever. There was a pool and a tennis court and a barn for equipment. The landscaping was elaborate enough to require a dozen grounds people. I knew many girls my age would be envious of me because of the size of my room, the ballroom, and the game room, but I had good reason to wish the truth of my birth had remained a deeply buried secret.

Who would be better off not knowing how she had come into this world?

Me, that's who.

I turned from the window of tears when I heard Samantha come into my bedroom. Since Dr. Davenport's confession that he was indeed my father and since his subsequent divorce of his second wife, Bea, their daughter, Samantha, had drawn much closer to me and dependent on me, even though I knew she was jealous of me as well. I still had a mother, and now I had a father. Everyone, including myself, had yet to openly acknowledge that I had a brother, too, Samantha the most reluctant.

Contrary to what most mothers would want in a divorce settlement regarding their children, Bea requested only holiday visits, and she often missed those, even missed Samantha's most recent birthday because she was on a fashion-buying excursion in Milan, Italy. We already knew she wasn't coming on Christmas, and Samantha wouldn't be joining her to celebrate the holidays. Bea was in London and had sent Samantha's gifts two weeks ago, probably when it was most convenient for her.

When so many gifts arrived, my mother said, "The woman is trying to buy off her conscience."

I understood why my mother thought Bea

should feel guilty. These were the most important years for a mother and a daughter, years that were supposed to draw them closer, not further apart. Like most girls in the eighth grade, Samantha was quite into boys, and the rippling emotions her hormones were stirring brought a daily crisis of one sort or another. I remembered well when it had happened to me, but at least I had my mother to listen to me and advise me.

Especially these days, the moment Samantha's eyes opened every morning, she was gasping with questions about herself. Sometimes one would be half formed and put on pause because she had fallen asleep before she had explained fully what she wanted to know. The next day, she'd come into my room to finish her question or remind me of something that had been troubling her like a bad itch.

"Should my breasts ache when I get my period? Do boys pretend not to see you so they can bump into you and touch you on your behind? Do boys really kiss you on the nipples when you make love? Why do they call it an orgasm? It's such an 'ugh' word. Pictures of organs are so ugly."

She relied on me more and more for insights about sex and relationships, not that I was any sort of expert. I had no special boyfriend and had yet to go on a single date this school year. According to what I heard some of the boys had said about me after I turned two down, I was supposedly too distracted with myself to keep their interest anyway. Later I heard that more than one had said going out with me would be like going out with someone who was deaf and dumb. To kiss me would be like kissing a mannequin. I knew they were embarrassed that they had asked me and been rejected. Their egos were bruised, but what they had said about me wasn't all that far from the truth. I really wished Samantha wouldn't come to me with questions about romance and sex. It stirred up my own longings.

I had retreated to my room right after breakfast. Before the snow mounted too high, Mr. Stark was going to drive Dr. Davenport to the hospital in his four-by-four truck, which he claimed could travel through an avalanche. My mother was worried for both of them, but Dr. Davenport said that he had to put a stent in someone's artery. He hated losing a patient, but "it would be doubly devastating to lose someone close to Christmas."

Despite that, I knew he was a little nervous about getting to the hospital in this storm. He was unusually quiet at breakfast. It was a winter storm that had taken the life of his first wife. The first snowfall surely revived the terrible memories. It had for every year since.

He had barely acknowledged my mother when she returned from bringing Ryder his breakfast, happy to say that he appeared to have a good appetite this morning. On the other hand, I shouldn't have been surprised at Dr. Davenport's lack of a joyful reaction to such good news. Smiles, much less laughter, had become as rare as moon rocks for everyone in Wyndemere, and, I suppose, for good reason.

It had been months since my half brother Ryder's near drowning in Lake Wyndemere. He and I had been caught in a vicious spring storm when we were in one of the Davenports' rowboats. We were battling to return to the dock when Ryder fell out. Dr. Davenport's driver, Parker Thomson, swam to us and brought Ryder up. The storm was still raging. It took a while for Parker to get to him and get him back to the dock to be resuscitated.

Paramedics arrived at the estate as quickly as they could and then took Ryder off in an ambulance to the hospital, where he was given the best follow-up treatment by one of Dr. Davenport's good friends, Dr. Malisorf, a neurologist. He and his wife had been to dinner at Wyndemere often, and their son was friends with Ryder. I was sure it was like caring for his own child. Ryder received the best possible treatment. No one could blame the aftermath on that.

We all learned that Ryder's subsequent health problem came about because he had suffered brain hypoxia. Not counting Samantha, I was the last to be told the devastating news. His brain had been denied oxygen a little too long, and some damage had been done. It had affected his memory most of all.

Consequently, although he was physically fine now, he was still very much a stranger in his own home, and I remained quite a stranger to him, even after all this time and continual therapy. I had heard the psychotherapist, Dr. Seymour, who attended him twice a week, compare his condition to Alzheimer's, but he'd thankfully added that he believed Ryder would enjoy considerable recovery. I wanted so to believe him, but how much recovery Ryder really would enjoy remained, as Shakespeare had written and my mother would often quote, "in the womb of time."

I had rushed through breakfast this morning and was almost finished before my father, who was mentally already in his operating room. That didn't matter. When he was like that, it was useless asking him questions. You'd have to repeat them, and his answers were usually incomplete, his thoughts hanging in the air. If I was too insistent, my mother would flash one of her not so subtle looks, warning me not to annoy him. But maybe my father wasn't thinking about his upcoming cardiac procedure or occupied with thoughts of his patient; maybe he was swimming through his muddled and troubling family history instead, because it was about to be Christmas, and holidays meant you thought most about your family.

Why shouldn't I believe that was troubling him? No one was haunted in this house as much as my father was. Every corner welcomed the shadow of some sad memory, like the loss of his little sister, Holly, because of a heart problem. My mother said that was probably what most drove him to become the specialist he was.

Ironically, unlike Ryder, who had good reasons to be the exact opposite because of his continuous physical improvements, I didn't have a good appetite this morning. I ate as little as I could, which was something my mother was constantly criticizing. We were on our holiday break. Joyful tunes were supposed to be floating around us instead of the imagined deep echoes of ghost-like footsteps and doors opening and closing in unoccupied rooms. Surprises in decorative boxes awaited us on Christmas morning beneath the twelve-foot-high Christmas tree Mr. Stark had brought into the living room, with its neoclassical sofas, chairs, and tables.

My mother, Mrs. Marlene, Samantha, and I had decorated it. Ryder had been brought down to watch, but he had fallen asleep in his chair despite Samantha's incessant chattering, or maybe because of it. We were still hoping to have a holiday dinner; however, as always, anything we did together was totally dependent on Dr. Davenport's schedule. His patients seemed always to have emergencies. When I voiced my skepticism, my mother quickly reminded me that he was the doctor for life-and-death moments.

Despite that, I was often convinced that he had invented emergencies to justify his frequent absences. Holiday happiness especially was locked up along with most of his happier memories in trunks, cartons, and armoires stored in the attic. Something that had once brought such pride and joy, like a picture of Ryder in his baseball uniform or receiving an academic award, was painful for us all to behold now but far more so for Dr. Davenport. Surely, every time he returned from the hospital, the dark-gray stone-faced house with its louvered vinyl black shutters, towering brick chimneys, and gargoyles replicating those on Notre Dame in Paris reminded him of the tragedy that awaited him within.

I knew that was how I often felt returning from school. Parker drove Samantha and me to and fro when he didn't have to drive Dr. Davenport anywhere; otherwise, we'd go on the school bus, which we boarded just outside our driveway. Samantha hated that. She'd have to mingle with the less fortunate.

The moment Parker stopped in the driveway, Samantha would burst out of the Davenport limousine and rush to the front door, eager to get up to Ryder's room first and fill his ears with her school stories, even though it was obvious that they were of little interest to him. I would get out of the car slowly, even reluctantly. Parker would nod, understanding why I was not anxious to face the disturbing reality inside. I hated how Ryder often looked at me with dead eyes.

"What's happened now, Samantha?" I asked, frowning at the way she had burst in on me this morning, not that my doing so would change her behavior. I looked down at the magazine in my lap to show her I wasn't really that interested in what she had come to tell me. She could easily exhaust anyone, and sometimes, before her mother had moved out, I didn't blame Bea for avoiding her every chance she had.

Samantha was much more dramatic at thirteen than I ever was. Everything was a crisis. Her coffee-bean-brown eyes were almost always wide and flooded with some emotion stretched to its breaking point. If she was sad, she was wretched; if she was happy, she was ecstatic. And if she was disappointed, she was sick with frustration. There was no middle ground for my half sister. A boy who smiled at her was either dreamy or disgustingly ugly. Her teachers were usually unfair, resented her for being rich, or thought, as my mother might say, that she was the cat's meow. I often thought that would have to be an alley cat.

Over time, I had developed immunity to her reactions, taking everything she said with "a grain of salt." My mother, who could have been a college professor, told me that expression came from the idea that a grain of salt was an antidote for poison. Of course, that wasn't true, but too often something Samantha said was poison to me.

"Don't think that if you took a grain of salt, you could swallow arsenic," my mother jokingly warned, back in the days when everyone would make jokes.

This morning, after breakfast, even though she couldn't go anywhere because of the snowstorm, Samantha had changed into her new cobalt-blue jumper and leggings with a pair of fur-lined shoe boots so she could parade through the mansion like some tween model in an upscale department store. Yesterday she had gone to her hairstylist and had her dark brown hair trimmed into short sides and a long top pompadour. Two of her girlfriends had the same hairstyle, so she wanted it, and especially these days, whatever Samantha wanted, Samantha got.

She did look older in her new hairdo. Her body was maturing faster than mine had at her age. She had real cleavage and was already a year past her first period. Her legs and her curvy rear end made her look even more mature. She was always talking to me about virginity, curling her lips as if it was a disease when she pronounced the word.

Apparently, there was a group of girls in her class who were titillated with the idea of losing theirs simultaneously, maybe at a special house party. In their way of thinking, it was like an initiation ceremony for adulthood. Something magical would happen, and the mantle of childhood would be lifted away. All their senses would heighten. They especially would see and hear boys differently, and everyone who saw them would immediately stop treating them as adolescents or, worse, as children.

I had done my best to convince her otherwise, explaining that some of the most promiscuous girls I knew in my tenth-grade class, and even juniors and seniors, were quite immature, but she refused to believe it and especially refused to believe that I was still a virgin.

"You're like most adults," she accused in a huff. "You lie to keep us from doing what we want to do, what you already have done."

Sometimes she infuriated me so much that I felt like going into her bathroom when she was taking one of her bubble baths, which her mother had convinced her were important for keeping yourself young and attractive, and pushing her head down under the water until there were no more bubbles. Maybe because of the divorce, Dr. Davenport was reluctant about chastising her or punishing her for almost anything she had done, whether it was being nasty to the servants, especially Mrs. Marlene, or getting into trouble in school.

Whoever had come up with the expression *spoiled rotten* anticipated Samantha Davenport. The little girl who once daintily followed me about, taking great care not to upset me or my mother so we'd let her tag along, had undergone a makeover since what we called the Revelations had occurred and since her parents' resulting divorce and Ryder's troubles.

Occasionally, Dr. Seymour would whisper some excuse for her behavior to me, but I didn't need a psychiatrist to tell me why she had changed. When your mother treats you with indifference and your father seems to be more interested in your siblings, you can't help but rage at everyone and everything and act out for attention. I simply wasn't in the mood to be sympathetic and understanding, especially today, a day before Christmas, which should have meant as much to Ryder as the rest of us but would be just another empty day to him, another day filled with blank pages on which he surely thought nothing wonderful was promised to be written.

Yes, I understood that under it all, Samantha was angrier than she was hurt, maybe even angrier at the world than I was. I was just far better at hiding it or better at not taking it out on others. I transferred my frustrations into something like a punishing fast walk around a quarter of the lake and back, my heels digging into the earth and gravel, my arms pumping up and down like an oil-rig drill. My whole body would ache when I was done. I didn't know if it made any sense to rage at nature, but I often ranted at the lake as if it were a living thing and it had betrayed us, betrayed Ryder.

"Ryder just said my name when he saw me," Samantha said, gloating. "I didn't have to remind him who I was. He even called me 'Sam the bird,' just like he used to. Remember?"

I looked up from the magazine in my lap quickly. Surely, she was just saying that to rile me. Ryder had yet to pronounce my name on his own; he had yet to have that look in his eyes that told me he remembered who I was and what we had once meant to each other. "It's Fern," I would tell him whenever he looked at me with that lost expression. He would nod, but there was nothing to indicate my name had opened a closed door or pulled back a dark curtain, and this after countless hours of conversation carefully guided by my father's and Dr. Seymour's instructions.

Especially during the first few weeks, we were told exactly what to say and what not to say to Ryder and how to behave with him so as never to cause him to feel frustrated and depressed, but it was frustrating for me and at times depressed me

28

so much that I didn't want to talk to anyone, even him. I avoided the opportunities.

"I don't believe you," I said.

Ryder had never looked at her with any special recognition and always had to be reminded who she was, something she was more than happy to do.

She smiled and gleefully performed a pirouette as she came farther into my room. She had been given ballet lessons but had quit; she had also been given piano lessons and had quit. She quit her private art lessons as well. She had the attention span of a fruit fly. My mother once told me Samantha would go through the British Museum in London in less than five minutes and claim she had seen everything worth seeing.

Samantha paused and began roughly handling my dolls on my bottom bookshelf. I had never lost or thrown away one of them since I was two. I had only five dolls, but Samantha had thirty or forty scattered about her walk-in closet and some buried in one of her toy chests. She tried to twist the head of one of mine, and I screamed at her to put it down.

"It doesn't move. You'll break it!"

"Sorry," she said, tossing it back onto the shelf indifferently. "I don't know why you care so much about these silly dolls now. You're too old for them."

"Everything I have has some meaning for me.

That doesn't disappear because you get older. They're special maybe because I didn't have as much growing up as some people had around here."

Of course, Samantha had been old enough to know the little I did have, not only compared with her but compared with other girls my age. Before the Revelations, my mother and I lived in what was known as the help's quarters at the rear of the mansion, where there were two small bedrooms and a small kitchen, all the furniture and appliances looking like they were hastily thrown together from some secondhand thrift shop.

We didn't start our life at Wyndemere there, but we were eventually relegated to it. After I reached the age when I could be left alone, Samantha's mother, Bea, discouraged me from being in the main house and specifically forbade me to use the front entrance. The rule about the front entrance was set in stone for my mother as well. When returning to Wyndemere from anywhere, my mother and I had to use the side entrance where deliveries were made. In those days, Dr. Davenport did not put up much resistance to whatever Bea wanted and rarely came to my defense or even my mother's.

Neither I nor Ryder ever liked Bea. He never missed an opportunity to disrespect her, and our father often chastised him for that whenever

Bea complained to him about Ryder's behavior. How ironic and sad it was now that Ryder couldn't appreciate Bea's fury at learning that Dr. Davenport was my real father and then see and appreciate their subsequent divorce months afterward. Ryder was finally rid of her, as was I, but for him, it had come too late. If he couldn't remember her, he surely wasn't even aware she was gone. My references to her in his presence were few and far between, as my father had ordered. Actually, I wasn't even supposed to mention her name. When I looked like that bothered me, my father told Dr. Seymour.

Taking me aside one day after one of his sessions with Ryder, Dr. Seymour told me that when people were battling to regain their memory, they especially avoided unpleasant recollections.

"It's the mind protecting itself," he said. "It blocks unpleasant memories. He'll recall her when he's ready to recall her, when he can best handle it."

I wanted to say that might be true for Ryder's remembrances of his stepmother, but surely that wasn't true for his memories regarding me. Why wasn't he remembering me—and fondly, too? He was seeing me daily in the mansion, and he was hearing my voice repeatedly when he was present and I was talking to my mother or Mrs. Marlene. Of course, I didn't ask that, despite how much I wanted to. What he was saying about Bea made great sense, though. It helped me understand why he had no recollection of his near drowning, either.

When the Revelations occurred almost immediately after Ryder's near drowning, Dr. Davenport had insisted that my mother and I be moved back into the main house, where she and I had once shared a bedroom. Now, because I was older, I had my own. Dr. Davenport's willingness finally to accept his full responsibility was the straw that broke the camel's back, as Mrs. Marlene would say. Because of what had been developing between Ryder and myself, both my mother and Dr. Davenport had decided the truth could no longer be kept hidden under the shadows in Wyndemere. It was time to disclose another Wyndemere secret.

Nevertheless, Bea thought she had been played for a fool. How could he have kept my mother right under her feet all this time? How could he have still employed the woman he had slept with and impregnated, "breathing down my neck and surely hiding her smiles"?

She knew that Dr. Davenport and his first wife, Samantha, had brought my mother here to serve as an in vitro surrogate mother for Ryder. My mother was desperate for the money after failing to earn enough singing. She was tired of being a waitress and accepted the offer rather than head back to England, where her father would gloat.

Bea tolerated that fact by putting most of the blame and embarrassment on Dr. Davenport's first wife, ironically accusing her of being the self-centered one, afraid to get pregnant and spoil "her dainty little figure." From Bea, I learned that you could be jealous of a dead person.

Bea's one concession was to agree to name their daughter after Dr. Davenport's first wife. Perhaps she had realized that was a demand that Dr. Davenport would not give up, along with other memories and pictures of his first, more beautiful wife that he kept in his home office.

However, whenever she could, Bea ridiculed Dr. Davenport's first wife's memory in front of Ryder and Dr. Davenport, as well as my mother. She pronounced her own daughter's name as if it was a profanity, clenching her teeth. I was too young to remember how it had all begun, of course, but my mother explained that before I was born, she had continued to live in the main house after Samantha's tragic car accident one winter day. When Ryder was just four years old, Dr. Davenport remarried, having chosen Bea, who my mother said was selected more for social and professional reasons than romantic ones. So my mother remained as his nanny.

And then, when Bea gave birth to Samantha, my mother was kept on as a nanny for both Davenport children, but as soon as Bea decided that Samantha no longer needed my mother day and night, we were ordered to move into the help's quarters, and my mother became officially the house manager more than anything else. That way, Bea could blame her for anything that went wrong.

Now, Samantha said, "I'm not lying. He knew who I was. I just came from Ryder's room." She was determined to get one up on me. "I was going to bring his breakfast tray down."

"Sure you were," I said. "You don't even pick up after yourself in your own room. One of the maids told my mother that when she cleaned your room last week, she found a plate with some cookies on it under your bed, where you probably kicked it a week ago. There were ants or roaches or something crawling everywhere."

"There were not!" she cried, grimacing. She thought a moment and then, stamping her foot, added, "I want a new bed now."

That made me laugh. "The doctor bought you all new furniture two months ago because you said your furniture was too babyish."

"It was. I was embarrassed to invite anyone over."

She looked around my room, never sure if she should be jealous or not. Everything in it was as it had been here for decades, except for the mattress, which had been replaced just before I was moved back to the main house. I had no complaints. The classic old set was a dark oak

34

Churchill five-piece poster bedroom set that Dr. Davenport's mother had bought. It was a valuable antique now. The furniture in most of the mansion's seventeen bedrooms hardly had been used. Overnight guests were never frequent. Compared with the much smaller spartan bedroom I had in the help's quarters, my room looked as if it had been created for a princess, at least to me.

Whenever I told Samantha that, she gazed around, wondering what she was missing, what I had that she didn't. Surely, there was something. She thought that way because she took everything she had for granted and always thought she was a princess.

"We'll see what happens when I tell my father about the bugs," Samantha said. "Emma should have told me about the creepy-crawlers."

"I've told you many times, Samantha. You call her my mother or you call her Ms. Corey. It's not respectful for you to call her Emma."

She shrugged. "She never complains when I do." She ran her finger over the bottom right post on my bed and then looked at the tip of it as if she expected to see dust. "Some of my friends think it's funny that my half sister's mother is my maid."

"She's far more than your maid, Samantha. Most of your life, she's been more of your mother than your own self-centered real mother. That's what you should tell your snobby friends, and if I ever hear them say something like that . . ."

"You won't, you won't. Don't have heart failure," she said quickly.

Her expression of fear changed quickly to a sly smile. I never liked it, because whenever she had that expression on her face, I was reminded of Bea pouncing on me for one thing or another. It was gleeful and full of "wicked sauce," as Mrs. Marlene might say.

"I have a secret," she said, "but you have to swear not to tell your mother or my father."

"People who swear to things like that usually get themselves into trouble," I replied, and looked at my magazine to turn a page. Samantha had no tolerance for being ignored. I knew she was fuming, with bees buzzing madly in her stomach.

"You'll get Ryder in trouble, too," she warned.

There wasn't anything better she could say to get my interest.

"Why?"

"I have to be sure you don't tell. I don't want to get into trouble." She focused her eyes sharply on me. It was like playing poker. Who would give in first?

"Why should you?"

She looked away, thinking.

I held my cards.

"I did a sneaky thing," she confessed.

"Did it hurt someone?"

"No," she said.

I shrugged. "So there's probably nothing to tell anyone."

I looked down again, but I wasn't reading anything. I was waiting.

"When everyone's downstairs, I peek in on Ryder sometimes."

"What does 'peek in' mean?"

"I open his door a little more so I can see him. He doesn't know I'm there. I'm very good at it," she added, as if that really was an accomplishment.

"And? So what?"

"I saw him doing things."

Now I was holding my breath. The little demon, I thought. "What sort of things?"

"He was completely undressed, and he was fondling himself. He did it until something happened," she added. "You know what I mean," she said with her licentious little smile.

I felt like I had been slapped sharply across my face.

"That's disgusting!" I screamed, and threw the magazine at her. "Spying like that on your own brother who can't help himself. It's the most horrible thing I've heard. If you ever do that again . . ."

"I won't," she moaned, and started to back away, really frightened of me.

I stood up and took a step toward her. I did feel like pummeling her. "If I even smell that you've told one of your nympho friends any of that, I'll break your neck and dump your body in the lake at night, and no one will know," I said in my most threatening tone. I had my mother's violet eyes, and I could look forbidding whenever I had to.

Samantha paled as if she was seconds away from fainting. Backing up faster and close to tears, she said, "I thought you'd want to know."

"Why would I want to know that?"

"Because when he was doing it, he had that picture of you in the silver frame in his other hand," she said.

Then she turned and ran out of my room.

I thought she had taken all the air out with her.

2

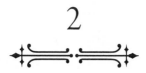

Before the Revelations, mainly because Ryder had wanted me to, I went on a double date to the school prom with him and Alison Reuben, his girlfriend at the time. She was one of the prettiest girls in school, if not the prettiest. I envied her for many reasons, not the least of which was that she was Ryder's girlfriend. He had arranged for me to be Paul Gabriel's date, also a senior and one of our school's baseball stars. Paul was gangly and socially awkward, but I did it to please Ryder. I was only in ninth grade, yet at the end of the prom, I was chosen prom queen, and Ryder was chosen prom king.

Afterward, we had gone to a house party where drugs were being freely used. Ryder, Alison, and I left when Paul got out of hand and forced himself on me, trying to get me to make love to him. My screams brought Ryder to the door of the bedroom we were supposedly using to take a rest from the bedlam in the basement below. Ryder then rushed Alison and me out of the house and home. Unfortunately, Paul overdosed on Ecstasy later that night, and Dr. Davenport, as well as the police and most of the community, found out everything. Paul was saved at the hospital, but he was expelled from school, along with some other students, because of the no-tolerance drug policy. The administration had taken the position that the prom and the after-party were all school-related.

Ironically, the subsequent events, especially Bea's outrage and Dr. Davenport's disappointment in us, drove Ryder and me to become even closer. Since we didn't do drugs, we felt we were being unfairly blamed. At the time, neither of us knew the truth about my lineage yet, so our romance began without any real hesitation. Bea was already on the warpath, making me persona non grata. Because my date was involved with the drugs, she blamed me for damaging her precious reputation. We thought it was solely because of her that Dr. Davenport asked Ryder to "cool it" when it came to socializing with me until things calmed down. Of course, I was soon to learn the real reason he wanted Ryder to do this.

Nevertheless, we were both being somewhat defiant by secretly meeting in my room late at night and eventually going for that row on the lake, which was supposed to be romantic. After the disaster, when both my mother and Dr. Davenport realized what had begun between us, I finally learned the truth about my birth. My mother confessed first, and then Dr. Davenport came to see me to explain how it had all happened. Both claimed that they weren't really lovers in the traditional sense. Dr. Davenport was in great emotional and mental pain after his young wife's accident. He sought comfort, and what happened between him and my mother was unintended. Regardless of their explanations, Ryder's injuries and my realization that we could never be the lovers we thought we would be were devastating facts. It was an avalanche of injustice.

But because of Ryder's condition and my concerns about him, I didn't have time to feel sorry for myself. How could I complain that one of the many secrets in Wyndemere had blindsided me? Ryder's near drowning and the side effects were so much more tragic.

Subsequent events occurred with lightning speed. After Dr. Davenport had moved us back into the main house, I had new status as his daughter, and Bea eventually turned her shock into rage and her rage into vengeance in the form of a bitter divorce. Even though she had given up full custody of Samantha, she left with more than half of the Davenport fortune. Nevertheless, after the turmoil had ended, when I looked at Dr. Davenport, I thought I read his relief. He acted as if the results of the divorce had been a bargain. None of the servants, especially my mother, was upset about Bea's departure. That was for sure.

Mrs. Marlene said, "She was forgotten as quickly as a soap bubble."

Maybe for everyone else it was easy to forget her, but it was not so easy for me. For too many years, I'd had to tiptoe through the shadows in Wyndemere. Bea's condemning brown eyes haunted me in dreams, in which her dark brown hair was always witchy black, streaking down her face and neck like ink. She was tall, almost as tall as my father, with thin, hard features. When she did smile, it looked like it was made of porcelain and it would shatter any moment and the shards would fly off at me. For quite a while after my mother and I had moved back to our bedrooms in the main house, I walked timidly up and down the stairs. If I heard a door slam or someone talking, I immediately froze, anticipating Bea pouncing on me and demanding to know how I dared show my face in these "royal palace rooms."

Although Dr. Davenport had come to me to confess and explain, and although he had swept away any pretense and welcomed—in fact, insisted on—acknowledging me as a real part of the Davenport family, to me he was still an intimidating and somewhat aloof figure. Perhaps I was unfair to judge him so harshly. His only son, a bright and handsome young man, had been significantly diminished and nearly completely lost.

Even without Ryder's serious injury and the guilt Dr. Davenport felt, it would have been difficult for him to suddenly become as warm and loving as a father should be with his newly recognized daughter. In so many ways, we had been strangers for most of my life. I was sure he was trying in his own way, but now those dark shadows that were always so comfortable sliding along the walls of Wyndemere were even bolder. The secrets that were whispering behind and around us most of my life hardly retreated. Confessions and revelations didn't send them rushing back to the dark corners. I easily imagined that empty rooms still echoed with the cries of past tragedies, like the death of Dr. Davenport's little sister, Holly, and his first wife's fatal accident. Sometimes I wondered if we hadn't been better off when my mother and I were relegated to the help's quarters on the other side of a short, dark hallway and stuffed away like some afterthought.

Mrs. Marlene, probably intending to cheer me up once I had mentioned some of this, told me that no one's life is a road of continuous happiness, rich or not. "Being alive means you will suffer; you will be frightened and sad. There are weddings, but there are funerals, too. That's the only promise you're given the day you are born. Endurance," she said while rolling the dough for her famous homemade bread, "fortitude, and perseverance, thank heaven for that."

I cherished her words, but they didn't really comfort me, especially on the day Dr. Davenport finally brought Ryder home. He had gone from the hospital to a clinic for therapy for over ten weeks. It was finally decided that he was ready to come home. I hadn't seen him at all that whole time. I wasn't sure if that was because of what the therapist wanted or what my father preferred. He brought us periodic reports, but there was nothing in any of them to predict or confirm a miraculous recovery, and I was afraid to pursue him too aggressively with more questions. I didn't want him to think that despite the Revelations, I still had romantic intentions and that I hoped when Ryder regained his memory, he would still be in love with me.

Finally, just before we had our dinner one night, Dr. Davenport asked Samantha and me to join him in the living room. I looked at my mother, who nodded slightly. Her eyes told me that something significant was about to happen.

Samantha and I sat together on one of the settees. My mother stood to the right side of us, and Dr. Davenport sat across from us. Seeing him with his perfect posture and his regal air always impressed me. My father was an important man and, despite the Revelations, was highly respected. He did loom in the community as the man who held life and death between his skilled fingers.

"As you two know," he began, "Ryder has been undergoing intense therapy at the Seymour Clinic. Dr. Seymour himself has been Ryder's therapist. When someone suffers what Ryder has suffered, he feels like he's living in a thick fog. Faces and voices might sound familiar, but placing names with them could be difficult, even the names of your closest relatives. What's particularly hard is recalling the recent events, especially the ones that put you in this condition."

"You mean he doesn't even remember almost drowning?" Samantha asked.

"No, he doesn't. And that's why I wanted to speak with the two of you tonight. We're bringing him home tomorrow."

"Oh, good," Samantha said. "About time," she added, with her mother's sour grimace, as if Ryder's absence was his fault.

"Dr. Seymour feels Ryder is ready to reconnect with Wyndemere, and our hope is he will have a quick recovery once he is here," my father said, ignoring her.

"I'll help," Samantha said. "I'll tell him about everything he's missed and . . ."

"You'll listen to me first before you do anything or say anything," Dr. Davenport said sharply. He never had to raise his voice to command respect and obedience. His words were like darts. Samantha sat back, pouting as usual. "We're to follow Dr. Seymour's orders. He does not want you to bring up the accident. What you, we, don't want to do is cause him to feel even more lost. We don't want those memories thrust upon him. He'll remember them in his own way, in his own

45

time. We won't blurt things out. Understood?"

"Yes," I said. Even though he was looking at Samantha, I knew he was saying that mainly for me.

"Good. We'll take everything very slowly. He's still under medication. No matter what he does or says, you don't want him to feel incompetent."

"What is that, exactly?" Samantha asked.

"Inadequate, inferior, helpless, stupid," he rattled off, visibly irritated. "Especially if he appears not to know something obvious about the house, about us. Do you understand, or do I have to explain it further?"

"Oh, yes, I do," Samantha said.

"Okay. We'll be limiting his contact with people who aren't part of our regular household for a while obviously. Do not bring any of your friends here to see him," he told Samantha clearly. "In fact, until further notice, do not invite anyone here for any reason without my explicit permission."

"That's not fair," she moaned. "My friends like to come here. They think it's a big deal to come to Wyndemere. I'll lose them as friends. Not fair," she repeated.

"What's happened to Ryder isn't fair, either," my mother told her. "And if the only reason they're your friends is to get inside this house to brag about it, they're not very good friends anyway."

Samantha held her grimace for a while and then

folded her arms and returned to her usual pout.

"Unless you're asked specifically to do something for him, do not do anything without permission," our father continued.

"Anything?" Samantha asked.

"Anything," our father emphasized. He looked at me. "Until he makes some progress, don't pressure him to realize what his place is in this house. Let him grow to know you in his own way."

"You mean, he doesn't remember who I am?" Samantha asked.

"Don't be surprised if he doesn't. Don't pressure him to remember, and don't make him feel bad about forgetting."

"How can he not remember me?" she insisted. "I'm his real sister," she added. That was something she was fond of saying, especially when I was present. The truth was we were equally his half sisters.

"He'll remember you completely in due time, remember you the way you were before his accident. Dr. Seymour is confident of that."

"Then he won't know Fern's his half sister, either," Samantha said gleefully. "He'll think she's just our maid's daughter."

"My mother is not your maid," I snapped.

"Fern," my mother said, closing her eyes softly and opening them again.

"He'll know everything he has to know in due time," my father said.

I had no doubt in my heart what that meant, the meaning between the lines. He wanted him eventually to know me only as his half sister.

"Okay," he said. "Let's hope for the best and do all we can to make him comfortable."

Samantha bitched to me afterward. Her main complaint continued to be about being restricted in inviting friends. I told her that her middle name should have been Selfish. She was already learning how to rationalize.

"It's selfish not to let poorer girls see Wyndemere. When you're as rich as we are, it's your obligation to be generous, like a queen or something."

"Spoken like your mother's true daughter," I replied. "You're no princess, Samantha."

Wasted breath, I thought. Whatever I said was water off a duck's back.

But who wanted to spend time on that now that Ryder was coming home? Despite how he had sounded, secretly in his heart, even with all his medical knowledge, I believed my father still hoped for something like a miracle the next day the moment Ryder stepped through the main entrance and gazed at what should have been familiar, something he had seen every day, every time he came home his whole life: the open staircase, molded cornices, and red marble fireplace. The hope was that somewhere in Ryder's mind, those electric impulses would awaken the sleeping brain cells and rekindle his memories. It would be the beginning of a real homecoming. With every step he took toward the stairway and his room, he would draw closer and closer to who he was. All would be well again.

Would anything ever be well again in this house? When had it ever been? I wondered, but what really was on my mind was how I should look, how I should dress for his homecoming. If I dressed too fancy, my father would surely think I was trying to stir up Ryder's memories of our aborted romance. And yet if I dressed too casually, I thought I might look like I wasn't excited about his homecoming. And then there was my hair. I had let it grow out since Ryder had last seen me. It was down to my shoulders now. Would that further confuse him?

In the end, I simply brushed it and pinned it back, put on a plain white blouse and a pair of jeans, and didn't even put on any lipstick. My father looked pleased.

Mrs. Marlene, Mr. Stark, Samantha, my mother, and I stood off to the side, watching and waiting for some sign to emerge in Ryder's terribly blank expression. Thankfully, there was no fear, but the emptiness in his eyes drove ice water down my neck and over my heart. When he looked at me, he was looking through me. Not my smile, not my love, and not my urgent and sincere need for him to know me made any difference.

"Okay, Ryder," Dr. Davenport said. I detected some disappointment in the tone of his voice. "We're going up to your room. Mrs. Marlene has made you a Dutch apple pie, your favorite. She'll bring it up with something to drink."

I could see Ryder struggling to remember that it was his favorite or even what it was or who Mrs. Marlene was.

My father nodded at us, and Mrs. Marlene hurried to the kitchen. I didn't know whether I should step forward to say anything, something as simple as "Welcome home."

Samantha didn't hesitate. As if nothing had happened and he had just returned from school, she said, "Hi, Ryder. Want me to bring my checkers set to your room?"

He raised his eyebrows and looked at his father.

"Let him rest a while first, Samantha," Dr. Davenport said curtly.

My mother stepped forward, and she and Dr. Davenport started Ryder up the stairway. He glanced back at me. I thought his eyes were swimming in question marks. It filled me with sadness and anger that I could not provide the answers.

"Checkers," I said disdainfully under my breath. "How stupid. He hasn't even settled in his own room again."

"It wasn't stupid. You were never good at checkers, so you didn't think of it," Samantha told me.

"I always let you win, Samantha, or you would cry."

"Like, that's not true," she said in her favorite whiny voice.

"Let's go play, and we'll see," I said. I was smarting from the fact that she had spoken to Ryder before I had. The truth was I was afraid to speak to him. I couldn't stand his not recognizing me. Despite it all, I was ashamed to admit that I was still feeling sorrier for myself.

Afraid to discover I was telling the truth, Samantha fled to her room and to her phone to tell her girlfriends her brother was back. Who knew what stories she would concoct about him and how he had reacted to her as opposed to how he had reacted to me? Whatever her stories were, she would surely be at the center, hoping they would feel sorrier for her than for Ryder and pity her more than any of the rest of us.

Those early days throughout most of the fall were difficult for everyone. Most of the time, Ryder was kept in his room, or he went for walks with Dr. Seymour and occasionally with our father. Sometimes, when I was home at the time, I would watch them walk and talk, following far behind them. Usually, either Dr. Seymour or our father did most of the talking. Ryder walked with his head down, listening. After they took a number of these walks, I saw them head toward the lake more often. Maybe Dr. Seymour was testing to see how the sight of the lake would affect him. Of course, I was never asked to join them, nor did I dare ask permission to suggest to Ryder that we take a walk. Samantha would surely be tailing along anyway. So, with him mainly in his room most of the day and the evenings, our opportunities to talk to each other were quite limited.

Whenever we were together, there was always someone else present, and even then, I was hesitant about talking directly to him, frightened I might say the wrong thing. Samantha leaped to plunge into any silent moments, mostly babbling nonsense. He would look at her as if she was some strange creature. It was his lack of reaction to almost everything that had to do with us that saddened, even sickened me, whether it was times together when we were growing up here or the prom and its dreadful aftermath.

In the beginning, he was given things to do that didn't really require someone else to assist anyway. Just as during his formal therapy, he was told to do crossword puzzles and sudoku puzzles and provided with many new things to read. Dr. Seymour told us that the purpose was to stimulate his mind as much as possible doing different mentally challenging things or at least things that would seem new to him now. He had to force his brain to work and to form "fresh wires."

When he thought Ryder was ready for it, Dr. Seymour prescribed his having more and more contact with us. Actually bringing him down for meals so he could interact with my mother, Mrs. Marlene, Samantha, and me was preferable to having his meals brought to his room, where he would eat alone or with my mother standing by to be sure he did eat. Samantha usually dominated the conversation at the dinner table, rattling on about something she had done at school or some gossip she had heard about another family. Occasionally, I caught Ryder looking at me curiously. I imagined a search engine on a computer seeking out some subject. He was struggling to understand why I was so familiar to him, I was sure. Or at least, I hoped.

Gradually, our visits with him in his room were increased, but they were always with Samantha present. I avoided all extracurricular activities at school that would keep me there when the regular day ended. Instead, I went directly home with Samantha and most of the time followed her to Ryder's room. Rarely did we find him in the living room or anywhere else in the house, for that matter. Dr. Seymour had encouraged me to mention students in my class and the classes above mine whom he knew.

"A familiar name, an image, could help his memory return. It's like building blocks. Think of it that way," he said.

Ryder's bedroom was the second largest of the seventeen in Wyndemere. Samantha was always upset that her bedroom wasn't larger than his. When Ryder was in the hospital and in therapy, she asked Dr. Davenport to switch her room with Ryder's, claiming girls needed more space than boys. Look at how much room her mother had needed for her vanity and closets of clothes and shoes. Of course, our father adamantly refused.

In fact, Dr. Davenport had moved some new furniture into Ryder's bedroom when he was anticipating his return from the clinic. Besides his computer table, bed, and bureau, he had a settee and two matching heavy-cushioned chairs in dark blue installed. The room was big enough for a sitting area. Whenever the three of us were there, Ryder would sit in one of the chairs or sit up in bed, and Samantha would sprawl out on the settee and talk and talk as if she was the real patient in therapy. I sat in the other chair, waiting for a chance to say something and watching him closely for some sign of recollection.

Sometimes it seemed like he was waiting for us, but most of the time, he looked surprised when we entered. The questions were clearly in his eyes: Who were we? Why were we there?

Competing for his attention now, Samantha always tried to beat me to him. Many times, he was dozing before either of us had arrived, but when she got there first, Samantha deliberately woke him so he would lay eyes on her before he did on me. Those first months of darkness, as I liked to think of them, Ryder really did seem devoid of even the slightest memories of either of us. Even though Dr. Seymour was so optimistic, I thought Ryder would never return and certainly would never remember who I really was and what we once were to each other. Samantha never hesitated to remind him who she was. In fact, she relished doing it.

"I'm Samantha, remember? I'm your sister, Sam the bird."

He didn't speak or nod. He looked at me, and she would quickly say, "This is Fern, Ms. Corey's daughter."

I suppose it was dishonest of me not to describe myself as more and to let Samantha project that she was closer family to him than I was. From the start, I had been unwilling to accept that I was his sister, too. Apparently, neither Dr. Davenport nor Ryder's therapist, Dr. Seymour, had delved into the Revelations yet. I thought they were both hoping for it all to happen naturally, smoothly. Repeatedly, we were told that too many shocks too quickly were dangerous.

But there were some shocks you couldn't prevent.

And they were coming. As Mr. Stark might say, that was as true as spring follows winter.

3

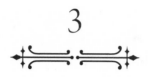

Whenever the three of us were together and Samantha rattled on and on about things she and Ryder had done together, he looked at me as if he expected me to translate what she was saying into comprehensible English. Of course, I had no idea what she was making up and what was true, so most of the time, I would simply smile or remain quiet. We were continually warned that we shouldn't do anything to upset Ryder by making him feel sorry that he couldn't recall something. For the moment, at least, I had to pretend whatever she told him was true. Having an argument in front of Ryder was out of the question. Samantha took advantage of that, often saying things to me and about me in his presence that were denigrating, anything to make her more important in his eyes than I was.

"Fern and her mother used to live in the help's quarters. Her mother is still our maid. Fern still helps out in the kitchen and sometimes with the cleaning, right, Fern? She was brought up poor. She hasn't been to the places we've been. I have lots of pictures of our vacations to show you. Fern doesn't have any pictures of vacations, do you,

Fern? I don't think you and your mother went on a vacation. It was probably too expensive."

"You lived in the rear of the house," Ryder said, digesting the idea. Whenever he said anything about me, I waited with bated breath. What would the next sentence be?

"Yes."

"Where the help was supposed to live," Samantha added. "Her mother is still really just the head maid."

"But . . . you live here, not in the rear of the house," Ryder said. He looked at Samantha.

Go on, I thought. *Go on, remember, and figure it out.*

"That's because Daddy felt sorry for them," Samantha blurted.

Ryder looked at her and then at me. I knew he was looking either for confirmation or for me to tell him something else. The truth was buzzing around inside me. If I began, could I stop? Would I reveal it all with every added question, each question being born out of another factual statement?

"It's smelly back there," Samantha said. "And too damp now."

"You didn't always live in the back of the mansion, did you?" Ryder asked.

I shook my head, holding my breath. It was coming back to him, right before our eyes. What if he blurted out what went on between us?

Nothing could be worse than Samantha knowing all that.

"That was when she was just a little baby. Her mother had to take care of us. She was a nanny, too. A maid and a nanny," she added with a smile. "You played with me. You taught me stuff, like checkers. She had to stay in the back. She couldn't even come through the front door, could you, Fern?"

Ryder looked at me for my response, but I bit down on my lip and waited until we were away from Ryder's room to scold Samantha for making my mother and me sound like we were inches from poverty. Her reaction was almost always to break down and cry, claiming she had no idea I'd be upset. She was developing her two faces. Could such a thing really be inherited?

"I'm just telling the truth. We're supposed to tell the truth," she said, with that face of innocence.

"How can you tell what's the truth? It's a foreign language to you," I said, and walked away from her.

I really shouldn't have been at all surprised. Even as a very young girl, Samantha would fabricate things she had done, seen, or heard. Whenever I complained about it back then, my mother rightly pointed out what a lonely childhood Samantha was enduring. She wanted me to be understanding. Samantha

58

needed to imagine more because she had so much less when it came to a loving family. Dr. Davenport was a workaholic (probably to escape an unhappy home life), and Bea was so into herself, her friends, and social activities that I thought she had to be reminded daily that she was a mother. Ryder was a good brother, but he was much older, and girls needed girlfriends their own age. Bea really never encouraged Samantha to have friends visit and rarely tolerated anyone staying overnight. Actually, she was more discouraging. In her eyes, few families qualified to breathe the same air. She was always threatened by the possibility that something about her life, about Wyndemere, would become the subject of nasty gossip, especially after the Revelations.

In fact, one day before she had begun to sue for her divorce, Bea surprised us all, including Dr. Davenport, by hiring a personal secretary, Darcy Samson, a forty-five-year-old spinster not more than five foot five and at least twenty pounds overweight. She had beady eyes full of suspicions and fears. When it came to serving Bea Davenport, she couldn't kowtow more if Bea truly was a goddess or some royalty. Whenever I witnessed them together, Darcy looked like she was grateful for every word Bea said and every glance she gave her. She nodded so much that I thought her neck was a thick, wide spring.

Bea made it clear to Samantha and later to me

that everything about the family or Wyndemere had to go through Darcy first before it could be voiced outside the house, even on a telephone call. According to Bea, the Revelations had done irreparable damage to her family, the Howell family, as well as the Davenport name. All the servants were told the same thing. Gossip about the Davenports was a capital crime. Nothing was too small or too insignificant to be scrutinized by Bea's personal assistant first and then approved by her.

Dr. Davenport ignored the whole thing. My mother, Mrs. Marlene, and Mr. Stark laughed about it, and then Mr. Stark and Mrs. Marlene had some fun telling Darcy the most mundane things, like Mrs. Marlene saying she was changing the brand of scrub pads or Mr. Stark describing in great detail the shrubs he was replacing at the east end of the mansion. Darcy would take notes in detail.

Sometimes, when I felt like being mischievous, I would encourage Samantha to make up something someone had asked about her mother or Wyndemere, something ridiculous that no one in her class would ask, like if there were any bidets in the bathrooms. When Darcy reported it, Bea cornered Samantha in her room and conducted a questioning that resembled the Spanish Inquisition. I listened in the hallway and for a little while felt sorry for Samantha.

"Who asked this? Why? What were your friends discussing? What did you say? Where were you? Who else could have heard it?"

She fired off one question and then another before Samantha could answer. I heard Samantha start to cry, and then she brought me to laughter when she protested, "I don't even know what a bidet is!"

When they heard about how I was egging Samantha on, both my mother and Mrs. Marlene chastised me, but with smiles bursting out like bubbles that simply couldn't be kept beneath their thin masks of reprimand.

I really didn't have to encourage Samantha to invent stories, however. It seemed to be her second nature. For me, it was only a small annoyance until Ryder was brought home from the hospital. When we were able to see more of him, she practically attacked him with one fantasy after another, always making herself the center of attention and building up her importance to him. No matter when I went and saw him during the day, whether in the living room, the game room, or the kitchen, she was there or arrived moments later, as though she had been waiting and watching for me.

Another month had passed, and I had yet to spend any significant time alone with Ryder, just a few minutes here and there in the entryway, the hallway outside one of the downstairs rooms, or the stairway. I didn't take advantage of any opportunities to do so. I was really afraid, afraid of what I might say or do. He would surely see something in my eyes, something to make him remember what we were to each other and why we went on that boat ride. I wouldn't even dare touch him, not even brush against him.

It wasn't easy. I had to battle hard to contain myself. One night, when I was going up the stairs, I heard music coming from his room. His door was wide open, so I stopped to look in. He was at his computer and was listening to a song I quickly realized was a song we had danced to at the prom last year. He turned to me as if he expected me to be standing there. I saw no surprise on his face.

"I like this," he said. "Do you like this?"

"Yes."

What would he ask next?

"I remember it," he said.

I hadn't heard Samantha come running to my side, but there she was, as if appearing out of thin air.

"I showed you that song," she said. "That's why you remember it."

"Is that why?" he asked me.

"Yes, is that why, Fern?" Samantha asked. She was smiling smugly.

"Maybe," I said. "I wasn't here when she showed it to you on your computer."

He looked at the computer. "Why was it on my computer?"

What else could I say without getting into trouble? Samantha would practically fly down the stairs to get my father. She stood there smiling at me, daring me to get myself in trouble and clear the playing field for her with Ryder.

"I've got homework to do," I said, and walked away, tears glistening.

This wasn't the first time he had said something that could easily resurrect memories of us dancing at the prom or taking secret walks at night when we were both supposedly doing homework. I might just open a dam and get him an avalanche of our intimate memories.

But not yet, I told myself. Anyway, it had to come from him. No one could blame me then. I was always looking over my shoulder, anticipating Dr. Davenport's concern that despite what I now knew about my family tree, that we were indeed blood-related, I would still flame the passion Ryder and I once had found for each other.

Truthfully, it wasn't easy to shift from being someone's girlfriend to being his sister. My mother sensed it. There was concern in her eyes, too. Because of this, I think she, as well as my father, was happy that Samantha was something of a chaperone. My spoiled half sister didn't understand why it wasn't easy for me to show

how much I cared about Ryder, but she certainly welcomed what she saw as my indifference and claimed aloud that she cared more for him than I did.

"After all, he was my brother all my life," she liked to remind me.

One time, I snapped back at her. "Half brother, Samantha. You're no different from me when it comes to our relationship to Ryder."

She started to pout and then said, "But I've been his half sister years and years more than you. For years and years, he's only known you as a servant's daughter. That's what he's bound to think of when he has his memory again," she said with glee. "Why should he think anything else?"

I imagined that thought took all her mental energy. Actually, I was a little impressed. She was not to be underestimated.

Many a night, after I had done my homework and lay in bed thinking, I couldn't help but wonder if Samantha was right, that when and if Ryder began to regain his memories of me, he wouldn't remember me with a young lover's affections. Would he remember me only the way he had before all this had happened? Would I be the young girl he liked to look after but for whom he never dreamed he would have romantic feelings?

And what of those memories of when we were

together, caressing and kissing each other and each thinking of the other as our first real love? Were they really forever lost? Or were they there just beneath the surface, ready to emerge? When and if they did, would they still be as strong? And then, when he learned the truth as I had, when he was capable of understanding it, would that revelation send him reeling back to the empty world his near drowning had created for him? It was how I felt most of the time, caught in an empty world and as good as nearly drowned myself.

Consequently, sometimes I felt like I was tiptoeing around him, trying not to be noticed. It broke my heart to be even in the least way disinterested in him, but always haunting me was the question of whether the last thing you remember before you lose your memory takes precedence over everything else. Ryder's last memory surely was of us clinging to each other in the storm after making so many promises to each other. However, one thing we, mainly me, were repeatedly and emphatically warned was not to mention the accident on the lake during the storm.

I think both Dr. Davenport and my mother were increasingly concerned about this and my temptation to help him remember in great, emotional detail. I could see it in the way they searched my face after they knew I had spent time with Ryder, especially if I was lucky enough to spend a few minutes alone with him.

One time, I walked into the living room, not noticing he was there, actually seated in my father's chair. He was working on a crossword puzzle.

"Hi," he said. Was it my imagination, or was he checking the doorway to be sure no one else was coming in, especially Samantha? "What are you doing?"

"I left a magazine here yesterday," I said, and nodded at the settee where it still lay.

He stared at me for a moment. Something was happening. "You ride a little red bike," he said.

I smiled. "I did. When I was five. You had a blue bike with a horn and a light."

He nodded. I saw my mother standing outside the doorway. I hurried to get the magazine.

"What's the magazine?" Ryder asked.

"Just girls' fashions," I said.

He nodded and then returned to his crossword puzzle.

"How was he?" my mother asked when I stepped out. She practically pounced on me.

I knew what she was really asking and why. Love was an emotion. Did you forget your emotions when your memory had been damaged? When you looked at someone you liked, someone you loved, did you have the same feeling even though you had no understanding of why you would? And if you did, would you express it? Would Ryder reach for me, not knowing himself why he wanted to? And if he did, would I retreat or welcome it? Would that be like taking unfair advantage of him just to please myself?

"Weren't you just in that room with him, Mummy?" I imagined she was; she probably had brought him down to it.

"You heard the doctor, Fern. He could have different reactions with different people at different times. We're supposed to keep track."

"He was no different," I said sadly.

She nodded, but I could see the suspicion. Would I tell them if Ryder suddenly turned to me with a lover's passion? Or would I keep it to myself for as long as possible?

This was, after all, the house of secrets. Why not anticipate another, even one of my own?

I thought family secrets mainly thrived because my father kept them so locked up in his heart. Occasionally, one would burst free. It was like sweeping out another shadow. That happened just before our Christmas holiday break had begun. My father had missed dinner again. He had called to tell my mother that a cardiac procedure had gone longer than he and his team had anticipated. Mrs. Marlene hadn't left yet for her holiday, but he always called my mother, who was still our house manager.

Ryder had fallen into such a deep sleep late

that afternoon that my mother didn't want him awakened, so it was just her, Samantha, and me. As usual, Samantha ran off at the mouth, but my mother only smiled at me and let her talk about her friends, listing those she liked and those she disliked and why. She criticized clothes and hairstyles. I thought she was beginning to sound more and more like her mother. I was happy when dinner was over and I could go help my mother and Mrs. Marlene in the kitchen, something Samantha would never do.

My mother checked on Ryder and then returned to say she would bring his dinner up to him. "I think it's better if he's going to eat alone that he eat in his room. He's somewhat used to it."

"I can stay at the table if you want him to come down," I offered.

I saw she was tempted, but the thought flew off like a frightened bird.

Mrs. Marlene prepared Ryder's dinner for my mother to take up to him. She remained with him while he ate. She said he seemed comfortable with her there. My mother was very cautious about any hopeful comments she might make about him, but I had the sense she thought he was beginning to recall more and more about her. If he was remembering her, wouldn't that mean he would soon be remembering me, the way I wanted him to remember me? I could hope for that, at least.

I still had some schoolwork to do before the holiday break, so I went up to my room to do it. Later, after he had arrived and had some dinner, my father came to see me. Since the day of the Revelations, my father and I had never had another private discussion about my mother and him, Ryder, and me. I was at my computer desk working on a book report when I heard him knock on my door. It was partially opened almost always. I think in the back of my mind, I was hopefully anticipating the day or the night when Ryder would suddenly come to my room, smile, and say, *Hi. What's happening? What's this nonsense about my forgetting who you are?*

It would surely be like everything since the day of the storm while we were on the lake was one long dream, mostly a nightmare. Neither of us would mention it. For me, it would be like Christmas and my birthday all wrapped into one.

"Busy?" my father asked. Even after all this time, I had still not gotten to the point where I would call him Daddy, Dad, or even Father. Perhaps I never would. Whenever I referred to him now, I still called him the doctor or Dr. Davenport. My mother didn't make a point of it, but I could see her thinking about it. Would she ever dare say, *Call him your father, Fern. That's who he is?*

"Just a book report due before we break for Christmas," I told him. "I'm almost done."

"Oh, I can come back or . . ."

"No, it's only going to be another ten minutes," I said.

I was sorry I had even mentioned it. Having him come to my room was special. Most of the time, whenever he spoke to me, either Samantha or my mother was present. Even though I didn't show it, it really bothered me that not much had really changed between my father and me since the Revelations. When I mentioned that to my mother, she said, "Sometimes we are trapped in ourselves, in who we have become. Change is difficult for people like your father."

"But wasn't he very different with you once?" Of course, I meant when he had impregnated her with me, when they had resembled lovers.

"I explained that to you, Fern. He wasn't himself then; he was quite lost for a while. Personal tragedies can do that, but after enough time has passed, it becomes safer to return to who you were. He's a powerful and extraordinary man, but give him time," she said. "Lots of time."

And so I did.

He came farther into my room and gazed around. "When I was in my teens, I slept in this room often," he said.

"Really? Why?"

I thought he was going to smile, but he pressed his lips together like he usually did when he went into a deep thought and then sat in the one other chair I had. It wasn't very feminine, and I doubted any other girl in my class or in the entire high school would want to have it in her room, although it was comfortable. It was a matching Churchill nailhead leather chair, the leather the same shade as the dark oak furniture.

"I used to have different feelings, reactions to the different bedrooms in this house. Some were so cold, off-putting, that I didn't even like looking into them. Of course, my mother talked about people, members of the original family of Wyndemere, the Jamesons, dying in some of them. She didn't make it up to keep me from wandering where I shouldn't. The real estate agent who sold the house to my father was obligated to reveal if someone had passed away in the house.

"But no one died in this room," he quickly added. If he thought that might bother me, he was right.

"So why did you like sleeping in here?" I asked.

He sat back and closed his eyes. It was rare for me to catch my father unaware that I was there and available for me to observe him closely when he closed his eyes to rest or fell asleep on a sofa or in a chair in the living room. It was his eyes, after all, that were the most intimidating thing about him. Maybe it was because of the intense concentration he needed to operate on someone's heart and arteries, but I never saw him look away or down when he was talking to anyone. And it was equally difficult for anyone to look him in the eyes for too long. I imagined that was especially true for a patient who had disobeyed an order. I recalled even Bea shunned looking directly at him, and she was mean enough to stare down Satan.

But sitting back, relaxing, his eyes closed, my father was suddenly vulnerable to me. I could stare at him more closely. Now in his late forties, he had just the faint outline of gray in his pecan-brown hair. He was still quite attentive to his diet and still exercised as regularly as he could. I wanted to go with him on one of his jogs along the lake, especially on weekend mornings, but I was afraid I wouldn't be able to keep up and he'd be sorry he had agreed. Because it was too cold for that now, he ran and exercised in a gym near the hospital. We couldn't be sure when he was doing that. Except for informing my mother when he wouldn't be at dinner or when he would just be late, he didn't reveal much about his schedule. My mother said he was a very dedicated physician. She had no doubt that he spent way more time than any other doctor in the hospital or with his patients in his office at the hospital.

His face was always closely shaved and smooth. He had just a tint of rose in his cheeks, but he seemed to have a habitual tan despite spending most of his time indoors. His lips were firm and straight, his nose Roman. I was sure many a movie actor would like to have his looks. I imagined dozens of nurses had crushes on him and just as equally imagined that if he had noticed, he had ignored them and not given any of them a reason to hope. He was always aware of his surroundings and especially of other people. Maybe he didn't like being surprised, no matter how small the surprise might be.

Everything he did was precise and careful. When I was very young, I was fascinated with the meticulous way he ate, occasionally dabbing his lips with his napkin. My mother had often told me to observe Dr. Davenport's posture. Now that I thought about it, thought about those early days, I realized how much she wanted me to emulate and respect him. Maybe she anticipated the day would come when he would tell me in the simplest way, *I am your father.*

And I would think, of course. I had somehow always known that.

"I have this cousin on my father's side," he began now, his voice softer. He sounded younger, too. His eyes were open, but he was looking across the room and not at me. "When she was your age, she was as pretty as you are. She was four years older than I was, but she was always so sweet and friendly to me. She had corn-yellow hair that floated along the back of her neck and the tops of her shoulders. It was always neatly trimmed, with bangs over her cerulean eyes. I envied her for her happy disposition. She walked in sunshine.

"No matter what the weather, to her it was beautiful outside. She was one of those people who see the glass half full and never half empty. I had a terrible crush on her. I was too young to think of her as anything but a sort of angel. She smelled so good, too. I don't remember what she used or if it was just her shampoo, but it was fresh and vibrant, as if she opened every morning like a beautiful flower.

"After she and her parents had left, I often came into this room and sprawled on the bed thinking about her, because I could still smell her wonderful fragrance and imagine her here. The last time she visited, she kissed me good-bye, a little peck on my cheek, but I clung to it like a life preserver. Sometimes, when I was much older and depressed about something, I would come to this room and just sit in this chair or on the bed.

"Little boys are hopeless and helpless when it comes to their crushes. Sigmund Freud wrote that we are never so vulnerable as when we love. My cousin could have easily crushed me with one reprimand, one sour look. But she didn't. Did you know," he asked, finally turning to me, "that scientists believe it takes a man only eight-point-two seconds to fall in love? I have no doubt that was all it had taken me. And when I first looked at my wife Samantha, I saw my cousin. I never told her that," he quickly added.

He smiled. He actually smiled in a warm and loving way.

"I don't think any woman wants to hear that she reminds you of someone else you loved. You all want to be the first, especially in romance, right?"

"Yes," I said, afraid to move, even to breathe, and cause him to stop talking.

"I'm a cardiac specialist, but I cannot tell you that there is anything specific about the heart that enables you to love. I think that's more in the mind perhaps."

I waited. Why was he telling me all this? Had he somehow fallen in love with someone else, someone he was going to marry and bring to live at Wyndemere? Did he think that would make me angry because of how it might affect my mother? Maybe many of those surgeries and appointments were really secret dates. After all, despite the Revelations, there was no sign of any deeper affection between him and my mother. He had always spoken to her more softly and politely than Bea had, but I saw nothing special in the way he looked at her before or even now. My mother didn't seem to mind, but after what I had learned, it bothered me. I wondered if he could tell.

Was that why he was here?

"So much has happened and consumed us all since I came to your room that day and told you I was your father," he continued, "but I don't want you to think I have forgotten you and what surely was quite shocking information. I blame so much of this on myself. When you make a mistake in life, it's often like throwing a rock into the water and watching the ripples go out and out. Everything we do, even the smallest of things, has some consequences beyond the immediate. Anyway, what I wanted to tell you is I'm very proud of how you've handled it all, how mature you've been. I know your mother is very proud of you, too.

"But I'm also very worried about those ripples," he added.

He was looking at me now the way I was told he looked at his patients, full of that intensity. He never held back on his diagnosis or prognosis, even if he was saying dark days were right around the corner. Rationalizations, sugarcoating, was simply impossible for him. He had always been that way when it came to Ryder and even me before he acknowledged who I was.

"What do you mean? Why?"

"I'm worried that you've been wounded so

deeply that your future happiness is in jeopardy. I may seem oblivious to what's happening here, what's happening with you, but I am aware of the fact that you don't do much of anything other girls your age are doing."

"I do things."

"Not very much and certainly not as much as you used to do, Fern. You cannot blame yourself for what's happened to Ryder. I appreciate how devoted you've been and how you and Samantha have helped with his therapy, but rushing home after school, not doing anything with friends on weekends . . . you're sentencing yourself to his fate. Don't say you're not," he added quickly.

I looked at my desk. Of course, I couldn't deny it, but I couldn't explain why without hurting him, making him feel even more guilty.

"After the holidays, I'd like to see you out and about more. Join some of the extracurricular activities at school. You were once in the drama club, weren't you?"

"Yes, but . . ."

"So why aren't you in it this year? I want you to enjoy these high school years. You're a good student, a very good student, but when it comes time to apply to colleges, they're going to consider how well rounded you are, too. It's why I was happy Ryder had done so much."

"Won't he ever get better?" I asked. I didn't

want to talk about myself and what my future could hold.

"He'll improve, I'm sure of it, but it will take more time, and when he does, he'll still have a long road back. As the Chinese say, a journey of a thousand miles begins with a single step. We have to be patient."

Whom was he trying to convince, I wondered, me or himself?

He rose. "I see from what your mother has told me that we're having a real old-fashioned Christmas dinner," he said, "with all the fixings, as they say. I've cleared my schedule to make sure I don't miss this one."

"Good," I said. So he wasn't planning on spending it with someone else, some new female acquaintance.

He started out.

"Dr.—Daddy," I called.

He turned around slowly. He didn't smile, but he looked pleased that I had finally dared to call him that. "Yes?"

"What happened? Did you ever see your cousin again?"

"Oh. I went to her wedding. She lives in San Francisco now and has three children, a girl and two boys. Her husband is a commercial airline pilot."

He leaned toward me.

"She's about twenty-five pounds overweight

and has lost that innocent, angelic look in her eyes." He smiled. "But I'll never see her that way. She's forever frozen in my mind as the beautiful young woman she was."

He turned and left. My emotions made me feel as twisted as a French knot. He was telling me not to think about Ryder as much, which depressed me, but he was more my father in the past ten minutes than he had been my whole life.

Could I become the daughter he wanted me to become? Ironically, to do so, I would have to be what I had tried so hard not to be: selfish. I would have to put my concerns about Ryder aside and start my new life.

I might have begun to do all that if Samantha hadn't come into my room a week after my conversation with my father to tell me what she had seen Ryder doing and how he was holding my picture at the time.

Something about our relationship was stirring inside him. Slowly, it was all returning. Why shouldn't our days right before the accident be at the top of his resurrected memories? Maybe what he saw in his mind now was just like my father's image of his beautiful young cousin, captured forever like a cameo. The vision would come and go, tormenting, teasing, but something he obviously still cherished. Ryder was struggling to grasp it. Should I help him?

Surely, someday he would seize it and realize

who I was, who we were together if only for a very short time. That was, in my mind, at least, a very intense time.

How could I ignore that possibility now? How could I continue to avoid any references, even avoid looking at him too lovingly?

Maybe worse, despite all the warnings and alarms, how could I not be happy about his possibly waking up one morning and saying to me, *Don't worry, Fern. I won't ever stop loving you now that it's all returned.*

Was that dreadful? Was I being too selfish?

Would both my father and my mother be angry?

Did I care?

4

Actually, I admired my father for not tolerating rationalization. Rationalization is really such an evil thing. It makes it possible for you to justify, at least in your own mind, something you shouldn't have done or shouldn't be doing.

I knew what I was tempted to do would not please my mother or my father, but I was telling myself I wouldn't be doing it only to please myself. I'd be doing it for Ryder, to help him recuperate faster. Once he regained most of his memory, we could work out what happened between us and how we had to behave now. Wasn't that good? Or was I lying to myself?

I couldn't shake out of my mind what Samantha had told me about the picture she had seen in Ryder's hand. A part of me wanted to believe her, but another part, perhaps what should have been the stronger part, did not. When I finally went to sleep that night, I lay there thinking about it, wondering what it really meant if she wasn't lying. What sorts of twists and turns were going on in Ryder's mind as he battled to find his memory?

Suddenly, I sat up, wondering why I hadn't thought about it before.

How and when did Ryder get a picture of me in a silver frame? I had never given him one. If he really had one, why hadn't I seen it displayed when I had been in his room all this time? Certainly, no one would have given him a picture of me since he'd returned. Didn't that prove that Samantha had made up the whole thing? What a sick thing for her to do.

There was no way I could fall asleep after thinking about this. I searched through my own memory, trying to tie in something I had forgotten. Surely, I wouldn't have forgotten giving him my picture, even when we were both much younger. I didn't recall him ever asking me for one for his room or even a smaller one for his wallet after we had begun being more like a boyfriend and girlfriend. The only framed pictures in his room that I knew of were of his real mother, him and our father together, and him in his baseball uniform during the school's championship game. Shortly after the prom and the disaster at the party, he had gotten rid of all his pictures of Alison. I didn't know what he had done with his prom picture with her. I had put mine and Paul's in the garbage.

When we were getting ready to move back into the main house, I had put all my cherished pictures and albums in a carton. That carton was still in my closet, unpacked. Even my father didn't have a framed picture of me, not yet anyway. I imagined he would place my graduation portrait in his office someday. My mother had some pictures of me in her room, of course, but never mentioned one missing. Anyway, Ryder didn't wander in and out of anyone else's room but his own. Samantha dragged him into hers occasionally, but she had no pictures of me. As far as I knew, he had never been in my room while I was at school. My mother surely would have told me.

When I considered all this, rage, rather than curiosity, got me out of bed. I felt like it had filled my veins with scalding steam. If Samantha had concocted this whole thing, created another one of her lies or fantasies to make herself more important, I vowed to myself that I'd go into her room one night and hold her down while I shaved off the rest of her hair.

I flipped on the lights and went to my closet. My carton of pictures looked untouched, but I couldn't be sure. I opened it and slowly began taking out everything. After it was all on the floor, I realized there was one picture missing, but it was one I had taken out of the carton shortly after we had moved into the main house. It was in the bottom drawer of my dresser. Mr. Stark had taken that picture of Ryder and me when Ryder, dressed for the prom, had come to bring me to our father's office so he could see me in the dress that Alison, Ryder, and I had found among Ryder's mother's things still in the attic. My mother had it tailored for me.

On our way out of the kitchen that night, Mr. Stark had stopped us to take a picture of the two of us all dressed up. I remembered thinking how much I wished I was going as Ryder's date and not his friend Paul's.

Because of all the turmoil that followed the prom, Mr. Stark's taking our picture, like so many other things surrounding it, was forgotten. The day my mother and I were gathering our things to move back into the main house, Mr. Stark arrived and gave me the framed photograph in an old paper bag. I could tell from the way he was behaving that he hadn't reminded my mother about the picture or told her he had intended to give it to me.

"It's a memory," he said, "and in and of itself, it isn't a bad thing to have. I've got my own copy in my house," he added in a whisper.

I couldn't stop the tears from coming when I looked at it. How healthy, bright, and handsome Ryder looked, and how perfect we looked together. Mr. Stark put his hand on my shoulder and hugged me. I quickly swiped the tears away and smiled.

"He'll be all right; you'll be all right," he assured me.

"Thank you."

He looked at the doorway leading into the main

house. It was like crossing over the Rio Grande or the Rubicon.

"If I was you, I would keep the picture to myself for a while," he said, "considering . . ."

He didn't have to explain. I nodded and stuffed it into the bottom of my carton of pictures. Occasionally, those first few weeks we were in the main house, I had taken it out to look at it, but I still hadn't placed it anywhere where it would be visible to others, and since Ryder had been brought home, I hadn't taken it out at all. I transferred it to a dresser drawer. I was sure that neither my mother nor my father would be pleased if I had it displayed. We looked too much like we were dates for the prom, and I was sure my father would think that the sight of it would confuse Ryder.

I opened the drawer in which I had hidden it and lifted away the sweaters folded neatly there.

The picture wasn't there!

That little bitch, I thought, shocked and angry. But when I sat back on the floor and thought about it, I was also very confused. Why would Samantha have stolen my picture and then given it to Ryder? Really, how would that make her think she was more important? There had to be some other reason. What had she been up to now?

She might have overheard my mother talking to me about my relationship with Ryder, warning me to be extra careful about what memories I mentioned. She wouldn't understand the full reason my mother cautioned me, but because I was ignoring her and her dramatic crises so much these days, Samantha was just spiteful enough to plant that picture so I'd be blamed for doing something without our father's permission or my mother's, and especially without Dr. Seymour's. That would be something that would especially anger our father. She was in what I knew would be a never-ending competition for his favor ever since he had acknowledged I was his daughter.

I glanced at the clock on the night table beside my bed and saw it was twenty after two in the morning. It was very late, but I was thinking Samantha was more apt to reveal the truth if she was surprised. Maybe there wouldn't be enough time for thinking up denials and lies, even for her.

I rose, got into my robe and my slippers, and, as quietly as I could, walked out of my room. The long hallway was always kept dimly lit by the row of small chandeliers equally spaced along the ceiling. The moment I stepped out, I thought that every shadow awoke. I knew it was my overworked imagination, but long, gray and black shady streaks along the walls seemed to come alive, straighten up, or curl like caterpillars on my right and on my left. I smothered a gasp. I was imagining the air crackling around me and sparks raining down from the ceiling. I wanted to be extra quiet, of course, and not wake up my father or my mother when I passed their rooms. Practically tiptoeing, I went past Ryder's room.

The door to his room was always kept slightly open. My mother especially slept with one ear awake in her room, closest to Ryder's. She and my father often discussed Ryder's condition, and on more than one occasion, I heard both of them express the fear that Ryder would awaken at night and be terrified because he didn't know where he was, much less who he was. I had yet to hear or learn such a thing had happened, but it was always out there, looming with every other dreadful expectation that haunted this mansion.

Consequently, my mother's door was always slightly ajar as well. When I reached Samantha's room, I paused and looked back to be sure no one had heard me and stepped into the hallway to see what was happening. The crackling I had imagined was gone, and the hallway was as quiet as it could be. But the mansion was never perfectly quiet. That was something I had gotten used to years and years ago. A house this big and this old had tiny crevices and cracks that sucked in the swirling night breezes and winds. It was easy to imagine every shadow moaning. A chandelier might tinkle; the gusts that usually came in over the lake sounded like the fingers of hands with long witchy fingernails marching up and down and across the windows.

It was especially like that tonight.

I put my hand on Samantha's door, and as silently as I could, I pushed it open enough for me to slip into her room. Samantha always slept with a small night light on. It threw enough illumination for me to clearly see her curled up on her left side, her light pink comforter pulled up and around her shoulders. In her four-poster king-size bed with its four oversize pink pillows, she looked smaller than ever and quite innocent, making me feel guilty for coming to accuse her of something so sinister.

The floor of her room was covered with a plush light pink shag rug, easily hiding the sound of any footsteps. As usual, her room was messy, with blouses draped over chairs, a pair of jeans still on the floor where she had taken them off, gum wrappers, and a bowl of ice cream. Two pairs of sneakers lay outside her closet door, and a celebrity gossip magazine was open and on her bed, just on her right.

I approached her and stood there for a few moments gazing down at her. I was hoping she would open her eyes herself. She didn't, so I finally touched her shoulder, gently at first, and then, when she didn't waken, I shook her. Her eyes popped open. Before she could scream out, I put my right hand over her mouth and the forefinger of my left hand on my lips. When she realized it was me, the terror left her eyes, which were now filled only with confusion. I lifted my hand from her mouth.

"What are you doing here, Fern? What time is it?"

"Forget about the time. Why did you take the picture of Ryder and me from my dresser drawer and give it to him?" I asked.

"What picture?"

Her eyelids fluttered. She pushed herself grudgingly into a seated position. Then she ground the sleep from her eyes and turned to me angrily.

"I didn't take any picture, and I didn't give any picture to him," she said. She pouted and folded her arms. "Daddy is going to be mad at you for accusing me and for waking me up, too."

"Not when he hears what you did with it," I said.

"I didn't do anything with it. I didn't take it."

I stepped back, scrutinizing her. Samantha was so good at lying, stretching the truth, telling half-truths, and pretending ignorance that maybe surprising her didn't matter at all. A seasoned detective would have doubts.

"Tell me again what the picture you saw in Ryder's hand was. How was I dressed? Was I the only one in the picture? Was it just of my face? Are you sure it was in a silver frame?"

"I don't remember," she said. "I'm tired. If you don't leave me alone, I'm going to get Emma."

"Don't call her Emma." I took a deep breath. "You're lying, Samantha. You're going to be really sorry this time. Believe me, I'll make sure of that. I won't talk to you again until you tell me the truth. Don't come into my room until you do. And don't ask me to help you with any of your homework. I'll find a way to get even. You'll be sorry."

I turned and started out of her room.

"You weren't alone in the picture," she said before I reached the door. I turned around. "He was with you, and you were both dressed up for the prom. I remember the dress you wore. It was Ryder's mother's dress."

I stared at her. She fell back onto her pillow. I rushed back to the bed. "Did you take that picture from my room and give it to him? Why?"

"I didn't take it from your room and give it to him. Leave me alone!" she cried, loudly enough to be heard down the hall. She pulled the comforter up and over her head.

My heart pounding, I left her room, half expecting my mother to be out in the hallway. I would have a lot of explaining to do.

But she wasn't there, and I wasn't going to press my luck. I practically ran all the way back to my room and closed the door quickly behind me. When I got into bed, I just lay there thinking. Of course she had to be lying. How else would he have that picture?

I debated telling my mother or even my father. With Samantha doing her usual good perform-ance of deception, suspicions might flow in my direction. They'd surely think I had given that picture to Ryder, and they would conclude that I had been trying to revive his romantic love for me. I could almost hear their accusations. Was I now blaming Samantha because I thought they would soon discover the picture in Ryder's room? My mother would ask Mr. Stark about the picture, and he would confess to having given it to me. Why hadn't I told her about that picture until now? Why had I hidden it under my things? It all appeared dark and sneaky.

Look at how much trouble Samantha could have caused. That was surely her motivation. My father and my mother might want to restrict my contact with Ryder, even with someone else present. I could easily imagine the conversation with me.

For now, it would be better for you both, maybe especially for you, to limit your contact with Ryder, Fern, either my father or my mother would say. *Participate only in activities he shares with us all, but do not, not ever, go into his room and be alone with him, even downstairs in the living room or the game room. At least until his memory has improved and he's about to understand everything.*

Hadn't my father laid the groundwork for this?

He wanted my attention and my energy to be attached to activities outside this house. He didn't say it exactly, but in so many words, he suggested I find a social life, maybe even a boyfriend. The busier I was with my own activities, the less I would dwell on Ryder.

Leave him in the hands of his therapist. You'll only complicate matters now and cause setbacks to his recovery, my father would surely say.

I had no arguments to offer.

Samantha would get what she wanted; she would dominate whatever attention Ryder could give to anyone other than himself.

I thought I'd feel like the daughter of the house manager again. Maybe I would spend more time in the help's quarters. Maybe I'd move back there.

A mixture of rage and sorrow kept me from falling asleep for hours. By the time I did, the sun had risen to glitter off the now frozen blanket of snow Mother Nature had cast over everything around Wyndemere. I moaned and saw it was well after nine in the morning. No one had awakened me, and it was, after all, Christmas morning.

My mother peeked in.

"Hey, sleepyhead," she said. "Your sister will have a nervous breakdown if you're not up and ready to open presents soon. Even Dr. Davenport has had his breakfast and is waiting for you."

It was on the tip of my tongue to say, *You mean my father,* but I didn't.

"Oh. Sorry," I said. I realized, of course, that Samantha had not told about my late-night visit. Was that because she was guilty after all?

"Mr. Stark and Cathy will be at our Christmas dinner," my mother added, coming into my room and immediately scooping up whatever I had left unhung or out of a drawer.

I imagined a mother, especially one like mine, never could stop looking after her children.

She paused when she saw my opened carton and all the pictures and albums on the floor beside it. "What's this?"

"I started looking through it all last night and stopped," I said. "I need to get some pictures into albums."

That was true, but my answer was still a lie. Samantha was rubbing off on me. And now, when they found the picture in his room, she would recall my going through the carton of old photographs. I felt like I was falling deeper and deeper into the trap my jealous half sister had created.

I got out of bed.

"Ryder's downstairs. Dr. Davenport gave him his first gift. It's a book about birds. He used to be interested in them, and the doctor thought for the spring, when he's out and about again, he'd have something to do. He bought him a new pair of binoculars, but he hasn't given him that yet."

"Spring's a ways off."

"Everything is a ways off these days," my mother said, pausing to look at me curiously now. "Why couldn't you sleep?"

"I don't know," I said quickly. "I never knew Ryder had an interest in birds," I added to quickly change the subject.

"No? Well, he did," she said. "Take a nice shower and wake up. I'll make you some French toast."

"Okay."

When I started for my bathroom, she left. Was she right? I wondered. Was Ryder always interested in birds? There was probably a great deal about him that I didn't know. After my mother and I had been moved into the help's quarters, I did grow up significantly apart from him, and when we were both older, he had his friends and I had mine. What had happened between us hadn't happened until his senior year, and we didn't really get to spend all that much time together, intimately together, before the tragedy on Lake Wyndemere.

Anyway, right now, to him, I was like someone new he was meeting, and it was getting to be quite a bit like that for me, too. I hurried to shower and then dressed in a pair of boot-cut jeans and a denim button-down shirt. When I went downstairs, I just peeked into the living room on my way to have my breakfast. Ryder was sitting on one of the settees, thumbing slowly through his new book. Samantha, who looked like she was pouting, saw me looking in and practically leaped out of her chair.

"Everybody's waiting for you," she said.

My father looked up from the newspaper he was reading and saw me. He looked more surprised than upset about my oversleeping.

"Don't wait for me," I said.

"Good."

"We'll wait," my father said firmly. "Christmas goes too quickly as it is."

Samantha groaned.

"Don't worry, Samantha. None of your gifts will disappear," he said.

"Can I open the one from Mommy?" she asked him. I doubted he would oppose that.

Nevertheless, I hurried to the kitchen. My mother had put out my dish on the kitchenette table. She had the French toast batter ready.

"Get your juice and coffee," she said.

"I'm sorry I overslept on this of all mornings, Mummy. I should have been helping you."

"It's all right. I'm better when I'm busy," she replied. Then she surprised me by adding, "George says the lake is frozen thicker than he's seen it for years. Good ice-skating."

"Ice-skating?"

"You're very good at it, Fern, and you've always enjoyed doing it. Don't act so surprised.

Mr. Stark said he'd clear a big area for you and Samantha. You should get some fresh air. The both of you are staying in the house too much."

"I won't go back on that lake," I said, and sat slowly. I hadn't been in the lake all summer or taken a boat ride all fall, even though I had jogged near it.

"Don't be foolish. What happened had nothing to do with the lake. A great many people would love to have the opportunity you have with what's practically your backyard."

I didn't say anything.

"Maybe Ryder's doctor will think that's good for him, too," she said, almost muttered. "Fresh air is important to anyone recuperating from anything."

"Really? But wouldn't that revive bad memories? Does his doctor think he's ready? I know he's walked down to the shore with him a number of times. Has something finally happened? Is he remembering that day?" It was impossible to contain my curiosity.

"I don't know, Fern. I haven't heard anything like that. I'm just suggesting everyone take advantage of it. It's just a possibility. Everything is just a possibility now. If you do it and Samantha does it, he might ask to do it. That's moving in the right direction, don't you think?"

"I suppose, but I'd be afraid for him the whole time. What if he was out there and it suddenly came rushing back and Dr. Seymour wasn't here? Wouldn't that be terrible?"

"He won't be there unless someone in charge is with him, of course," she said. Then she paused and looked at me. "Maybe you should ask some friends to join you. Don't just mope around all this holiday, Fern."

"But Dr. Davenport was firm about Samantha not inviting her friends here to gawk at Ryder. Wouldn't he be afraid mine would do the same?"

She served me my French toast. "Your friends will be more mature."

"Sounds like you've been talking to Dr. Davenport about me," I said. She paused. I looked up quickly. "I mean my father."

She smiled. "He did mention that he'd like to see you out and about, doing more with yourself. He's not wrong. There's no reason for you to isolate yourself like this. It worries me, too."

"I just thought . . . holidays were for families," I said. I was reaching for excuses, and my mother knew it, too.

"Families and friends, Fern." She narrowed her eyelids. She could aim her words like sharp arrows when she thought it was necessary. "Don't drive your friends away as a form of self-punishment."

I looked back sharply. "Self-punishment? You have been talking about me?"

"Yes, of course, we talk about you," she said,

correctly reading the expression on my face. "Don't be so surprised. You're just as much a topic of conversation between the doctor and myself as Ryder is these days."

Before I could respond by asking, *Did you ever discuss me when we lived in the help's quarters? Was I of any concern to him then?* Samantha came to the kitchen doorway and held up a new iPad. Our father had given in and let her open one of her mother's gifts, as I suspected he would.

"You already have one not even two years old," I said. "I imagine your mother didn't know. I imagine she doesn't even remember what grade you're in."

Her gleeful smile evaporated. "This is the thinner one, anyway."

"You could have just put the one you have on a diet," I said.

My mother laughed.

Samantha's eyes widened. "I'm giving my old one to Ryder," she said. "My father thinks that's a very nice thing to do."

"It is," my mother said. "Good for you, Samantha."

"He forgot how to use everything, especially on his computer, but I'm going to show him," she said. "He likes me helping him," she added, looking at me.

"Very good, Samantha," my mother said.

Samantha gave me her best *So there* smile.

"He didn't forget how to use his computer, Samantha. He just doesn't use email," I said softly.

"I can still show him stuff, stuff I bet even you don't know," she said, and returned to the living room.

"How long will it be before she outspites her mother?" I said.

My mother gave me her big eyes. "Patience is a virtue," she said.

"Or a few customers for a doctor, especially a psychotherapist," I replied. I started to clear off my dishes.

She laughed. "What will I do with you? Go on to the living room," she said. "I'll be right there. It's our first Christmas in the main house in a long, long time, Fern. Maybe Ryder will remember those happier days, too. You'll want to be a part of that."

I nodded. Of course I would. My mother always had a way of getting me to do whatever she wanted.

When we were all together, I began to unwrap gifts. I was surprised at how many my father had bought or had someone buy for me, probably my mother. There were new blouses and slippers and a special watch that he said kept track of how much exercise you did daily, how much you walked or jogged. *Hint, hint,* I thought. *Get out of the house. Be active.*

This wasn't the first time my father had bought me a Christmas present, but when I was much younger, when we were living in the main house because my mother was Ryder's and Samantha's nanny, I didn't really remember or appreciate that the gifts were coming from him. Afterward, when my mother and I opened our gifts in the help's quarters, there was always something for me from Dr. Davenport, usually something for school like a new book bag or, relatively recently, a new laptop computer. Those days, my mother had me write a special thank-you note as well as thank him when I did see him. It wasn't until the past year that Ryder and I had begun to exchange gifts. Before that, his stepmother frowned on it. She was surely not going to give me anything, even if Dr. Davenport was.

The first time I bought Ryder something, I spent hours and hours shopping for just the right thing, something that to me seemed special. After all, he had almost anything a boy his age could want.

Last Christmas, I had bought him a personalized pen set and had it inscribed *For a special Ryder*. He thought that was so clever and made sure that all his friends in school saw it. I wondered where the pen was now. I hadn't seen it in his room. It wouldn't surprise me to learn Samantha had taken it and thrown it out.

She was certainly more interested in my gifts

than her own, worried, I was sure, that I was getting something extra special. I had to think our father had anticipated that. He'd bought her more than he had bought me. She didn't hesitate to rush over to him and hug him her thank-you. I glanced at my mother. She nodded, reading my thoughts. My father hadn't hugged me, nor I him, since the day he had come to my bedroom in the help's quarters and told me what had happened. I rose slowly and approached him, glancing at Ryder, who watched with interest. What would he think of all this? Was this finally the way to let him know we were half brother and half sister?

"Thank you," I said. "I love my presents."

I leaned over and hugged my father. I could see his arms lifting, but hesitantly. He didn't embrace me; he touched me, and I thought he actually blushed when I kissed his cheek. Samantha looked angry and quickly turned away. I could practically see the smoke flowing out of her ears. My mother smiled. I went to her and hugged her and thanked her for the gifts she had bought me as well.

When I glanced at Ryder, I saw how confused he looked. He dropped his eyes quickly to his book on birds and then unwrapped the box and lifted out his new binoculars.

"Can I use them?" Samantha cried, and practically tore them from his hands.

"Those are Ryder's," our father said sternly.

"Give them back, Samantha. After he uses them, he'll give them to you to use when he wants. Go on."

She smirked and handed them back to Ryder. He glanced at me and saw me shake my head in disgust.

A week before Christmas, I had asked my mother if I should buy Ryder something. I knew I couldn't just do it now.

"What did you have in mind?" she had asked cautiously.

I'd shrugged and said, "A nice shirt?"

She had thought that would be fine. Even so, when Parker took me to the mall, I did look for something different, something cute. I found a hooded sweatshirt that was perfect for Christmas. On the front, it read, *Dear Santa, Define "good."* All I had told my mother was that it was a sweatshirt.

Now I plucked it out from under the tree and brought it to him. My father's, mother's, and Samantha's eyes felt like rays of cold ice on my back. I knew how closely they were watching. What sort of gift had I chosen? What memories might it resurrect, memories only he and I would appreciate, perhaps? My hands actually trembled when I presented it to him. He looked at it and then up at me with surprise.

"Merry Christmas, Ryder," I said.

He took the box and glanced at our father as if

he was seeking permission to accept it. My father nodded, and Ryder began to unwrap it. I stood back, practically holding my breath. Had I been too cute? Was it too revealing of my feelings? Would my father and mother be upset? Maybe I shouldn't have bought him anything. Maybe it was too soon.

He opened the box and slowly unfolded the sweatshirt, first holding it up with the back of it to us all. Then he smiled. It was a smile like none other since he had returned from the clinic. He turned it around to show our father and my mother and Samantha.

"That's stupid," Samantha said. "Anyone knows what 'good' means."

Ryder looked at her and then at me, and with a brightness strong enough to melt an arctic glacier, he laughed. My mother didn't laugh, but her eyes widened with delight. My father smiled, and Samantha looked shocked and confused.

"Thank you," Ryder said.

"Very funny, Fern," my father said.

"Why is that funny?" Samantha asked, visibly annoyed.

"If you're not good, Santa will leave a chunk of coal in your stocking," my mother said.

Samantha smirked. "That's even sillier," she said. "Besides, there is no Santa."

"But there is coal," I said. *Not that you'll*

ever get any, I thought, *and if you did, it would probably be gold-plated.*

Afterward, I went into the kitchen with my mother to help her prepare our Christmas dinner. Samantha gathered her gifts and went upstairs to her room. My father decided to take Ryder for a short cross-country-skiing trip around the property. It was something they often had done together whenever he was able to spend time at home in the winter.

"We're going to have quite the appetite when we return," he promised.

Ryder looked a little unsure about it but followed him upstairs to get dressed for the exercise. When he looked back from the stairway, I thought he smiled at me differently. He waited for me to respond, so I smiled back. The exchange should have made me happy. It was, after all, something a little beyond warm and friendly. But instead, it filled me with unexpected trepidation. I quickly checked to see if my mother was watching.

She wasn't.

He held his gaze on me one moment more and then continued upstairs.

The moment lingered like a bright light slowly diminishing. I so welcomed it.

But it was as if we had just shared a secret that in the end might destroy us both.

And that's just what it almost did.

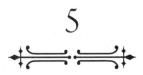

5

For the remainder of Christmas Day, whenever we were together, I watched Ryder more carefully and thought I caught him looking at me more intently. I was alert to anyone watching us exchange looks, especially my mother. Dr. Davenport didn't seem as concerned. Samantha, thankfully, was always absorbed in herself and her presents and never noticed, and whenever Ryder did look at me in what I thought was a different way, he seemed cautious, never doing so when either his father or my mother was present. As soon as either appeared, he looked away. I did nothing to encourage him to be sneaky about it. I didn't smile differently or whisper something that would be secret between us, even though I wanted to, wanted to very much.

Perhaps, I told myself, it was all my imagination anyway, my wishful thinking. I was reading more into his look than was there. I was thinking too much about this. He wasn't that attentive at our Christmas dinner, barely looking at me, actually, even when I spoke. Exercising with our father had brought a healthy crimson tint to his cheeks and brightened his eyes. He looked much more like himself before the tragedy on the lake. He was even more handsome than our father. Ryder always liked to have his dark brown hair a little longer than Dr. Davenport wanted. I didn't know whether it was something Dr. Seymour, the therapist, insisted on, but Ryder's hair was cut and shaped the way it always was, even when he was in the hospital and the clinic. My guess was that changing the way he was used to looking might endanger his recovery.

No one could change his soft blue eyes and slightly cleft chin. Even when I was very young, I realized that he smiled just the way Dr. Davenport did. It was a smile that always began in his eyes and then rippled out over his high cheekbones. Those smiles were rare now, but Ryder was more relaxed at our Christmas dinner.

He was fascinated with Mr. Stark, who related one story after another about his days as a teenager. Even though he still looked like he was listening to stories about someone else, I saw how happy my father was and grateful to Mr. Stark, who had Ryder mesmerized and probably laughing at stories he had actually heard many times. Cathy Stark and my father entertained my mother with some of the sillier things that had occurred during their work at the hospital. Samantha was the only one pouting. No one was paying much attention to her.

Mr. Stark brought up ice-skating on the lake when my father revealed that he and Ryder had cross-country-skied across a thick frozen area not far from the dock. I was quite surprised and watched Ryder's expression while our father described it. Apparently, going back to the lake hadn't stirred up any terrible memories. Was that good, or did it mean he would never remember . . . anything?

Cathy followed up by describing how she had often taken Ryder ice-skating when he was a little boy. He listened with a small smile on his lips. Was he envisioning it again, slowly folding away the darkness?

It occurred to me that maybe he would return to himself chronologically, recalling his youth and then inching along until where he was before the near drowning. It was the first time I seriously considered that I might be nothing more than a few moments along the way, an interlude violently interrupted during a spring storm.

Perhaps my father was right about my getting out of the house and doing things with my school friends. My mother's earlier concern wasn't foolish. I was on the verge of losing any sort of relationship or contact with most of them. I knew I wasn't very pleasant when any of them asked me questions about Ryder. I left no doubt in their minds that he was a subject I considered out-of-bounds.

Everyone remembered him quite vividly, of course. Some of the girls in my class had never stopped drooling over him. Their curiosity about his illness, however, was sick to me. "Can he feed himself? Can he go to the bathroom himself? Does he slobber when he eats like some mental patient?" I knew they craved the grisliest details. When I mentioned this once to my mother with Mr. Stark present, he piped up first to say, "That's why people slow down to look at traffic accidents."

"It's ghoulish," I said.

"No. It's just human nature," my mother said, "especially when it concerns someone who had been so prominent in the school community."

Nevertheless, I felt I would be betraying Ryder if I ever told any of them any details about his condition. I had nearly gotten into a bad fight with Denise Potter during our lunch hour two days before the Christmas break, when she'd described seeing him walking with Dr. Seymour on the property.

"My mother and I were riding by Wyndemere," she'd begun.

She had this annoying habit of bouncing her head from side to side when she was revealing something she thought was special information that no one but she had. It was as if she was keeping rhythm to music only she heard. Her mother let her put light blond streaks in her dark brown hair, which she had cut and styled into something she called a beach wave. Despite her "forever diet," she had a pudgy face with sinking hazel eyes and a lower lip that looked twice the size of the upper. Consequently, to me she appeared to be constantly pouting.

"And I looked over to my right and saw Ryder walking with this man."

"The man is his doctor," I said.

"I thought his father was his doctor," she replied smugly.

"His father is a cardiac specialist. Ryder's doctor's name is Dr. Seymour. He is the head of the clinic that treats patients like Ryder."

"Oh. Well, he looked normal!"

I practically pounced on her when I sat forward. "He *is* normal," I said.

She cringed, looked at everyone else at the table, as if she felt stupid for being so frightened. "If he's normal, why isn't he in college?" she fired back, nevertheless timidly. Her words seemed to rise from her like tiny bubbles in a fishbowl.

"He's still recuperating. Do you know what that means? Recuperating? Like you're still recuperating from birth."

"Huh?"

The three other girls at our table smiled gleefully. No one really liked Denise, but she was good at clinging and inserting herself into everything we did together. For me, that list had diminished to almost nothing.

"How is he really doing, Fern?" Ivy Mason asked softly after I had calmed and began to eat again.

I liked her the most of all my school acquaintances, because she, like me, had spent most of her life fatherless and, perhaps because of her mother's struggles caring for her, always seemed more mature than the others, even more mature than I was at times. She was certainly a better student than most, hovering at the top of our class.

There were a number of other students who came from one-parent families, mostly because of divorces, like Ivy did. Because my mother had me out of wedlock, I often felt very different from them as well. Up to the past year, my father's identity had been a mystery. I sensed how other girls' mothers looked at me with suspicion. Somehow, because of what my mother had done, they believed I surely would be a bad influence on their daughters. Even though Dr. Davenport was one of the most highly respected doctors in the community, his living with someone people thought of as his mistress now influenced how they thought of me. As it was, even before my father was revealed, I was often left out of parties, something that seemed more painful for my mother than for me. I knew she blamed herself.

As time went by, however, boys paid more attention to me, and little inroads were made in my social life. The barriers began to crumble more and more every year, maybe partly due to how my mother was becoming more accepted as well. After all, she worked for one of the most respected men in our community, and there wasn't anything else negative anyone could say about her. She was hardworking, always nicely dressed, and well spoken.

What didn't hurt either was that I, like Ivy, was one of the top students in our class. When I did join the drama club and performed well in some school plays in junior high, I inched a little closer to full acceptance. It was clear now that I wasn't a bad influence on anyone, despite the way Bea had viewed me and surely had discussed me with her friends. But they were all what my mother said the English called "toffee-nosed." The expression didn't come from the sugary brown sweet but from *toff,* which was the slang term the lower classes gave to stylishly dressed upper-class people who were considered snobby.

However, as time went by and I was accepted more and more, Bea became increasingly irritated and even more critical of everything I did. This was before the Revelations, when she would go beyond irritation to explosion. I remembered that once my father had come to one of the plays I was in during seventh grade. Bea didn't come with him, and he didn't sit with my mother. She sat with Cathy Stark. He had brought along a young intern, who probably came because he didn't want to displease my father. He surely would have preferred being with friends on a rare night off, but that was how revered my father was. An invitation from him, regardless of what it was for, was like gold. I had no idea how much he was respected in the medical world until I learned about his articles in medical magazines and feature stories written about him.

"He's improving a little every day," I said to Ivy now, "but it's a long process of recuperation."

"How hard it must be for Dr. Davenport," Ivy said.

She had a soft, warm smile. Her turquoise eyes would brighten with clear sincerity. Unlike almost everyone else around her, including me at times, she moved and spoke with a calmness some would easily mistake for disinterest. She was the smallest in our group, standing a little more than five foot three, with diminutive facial features, and consequently looked years younger than everyone else. Jennifer Sanders, who for reasons I never understood disliked Ivy, once whispered to me that she was "one of those girls doomed to always be cute and never beautiful." She thought that was a clever nasty thing to say.

Maybe it was true, but I didn't see it as a terrible criticism.

Denise, who was still smarting from my crushing comeback, immediately piped up with "If he's improving, he's not normal right now."

"Well, if that's the way you want us all to think of it, I guess you'll never be normal, then," I said.

Everyone laughed.

"At least I have a chance," she said. "You don't even have a real mother and father. I mean, you have a mother, but she's not married to your real father. She's like—"

"Shut up, Denise, before you say something you'll really regret," I warned.

I guessed my face was red with rage and scary enough. She looked away quickly. I wasn't fooling myself, however. I knew what was said behind my back.

When the Revelations became public knowledge, my friendships and social life were peppered with new minefields. I didn't dare mention any of the new nasty remarks to my father, or even my mother, for that matter. After all that had occurred and where we were now in the Wyndemere home world, I certainly didn't want to present myself as a victim again. I knew and believed how sorry my father was for all that had happened. My mother shared that regret. Why make them feel worse? For years, they had avoided revealing what had happened, but now, with our moving back into the main house and Bea's rage and suit for divorce, and all of it public knowledge, the skin had come off the scars.

In the beginning, the most obvious questions came at me. "Is your mother still Dr. Davenport's lover? Are they going to get married now? Should we be calling you Fern Davenport and not Fern Corey? A simple no never would satisfy any of them. "I don't know" kept it all going. Whatever I did or said, I knew there were those who were smiling behind my back gleefully.

Many of the girls in my class were still jealous of my having been chosen prom queen, despite all the trouble that had come from the wild party afterward that night. I was the first ninth-grader in our school to enjoy that honor. Envious, they were pleased by my new discomfort. When my mother and my father wanted to know why I wasn't doing more with friends and activities in school, I tried to avoid really answering and bringing in all this baggage.

I didn't want to resurrect all the trouble that occurred that prom night, but another reason for my retreat from doing many social and extra-curricular activities in school was the inevitable stain of association I had suffered from having been Paul Gabriel's prom date. My not having been directly involved with the drugs and Paul's getting himself into trouble after I had left him that night, thanks to Ryder, didn't do that much to change anything. I knew that many thought I had gotten away with it because I was associated with Dr. Davenport. The revelation that I was actually his daughter only confirmed their suspicions.

How could I tell my parents all that without causing everyone more pain?

Actually, if it wasn't for my concerns about Ryder and my devotion to him, I would have asked my mother and, of course, my father to transfer me to another school, probably a private school where my past could have been better hidden. One of the main reasons I avoided going on dates this year was my feeling that the boys who asked me probably thought I'd be easy sex. Some simply blamed it on my being snobbish now that I was a Davenport. As a result, I had yet to be invited to anything this year, and I knew there had been a few house parties and two birthdays when parents had invited their daughters' friends to dinner at one of the better restaurants.

I told myself that it didn't bother me. I had more important things to do and to care about, mainly Ryder's recuperation. Now, with both my father and my mother pressuring me to have a life outside Wyndemere and my realization that I really might not be helping Ryder, I decided to get back into the world.

The question was what would I have to give up to do so, and was it worth it?

The following day, I called Ivy, ostensibly to

talk about auditions for the new play scheduled right after the Christmas break. Mr. Madeo, the English teacher in charge of the drama program, had announced that he intended to do *Dracula*. Lucy Westenra was the lead female role, the one I thought I might audition for. No one knew at the start of the play that Dracula was slowly draining her blood, which was a little like the way I felt right now. My emotions had been subdued so long I felt like my life was dripping away. Ivy wasn't going to try out for anything until I suggested she try out for Renfield.

"Have you read the novel or the play? I have," Ivy said. "Renfield is a man."

"Yes, I read it. He's weird. He eats insects. I think you could do it with some interesting makeup and make it fun."

I didn't want to stress that she had a little boy's figure.

She thought for a moment. "Maybe I could," she said.

We laughed about it, and then I asked her what she was doing Saturday night and if she would like to go to a movie.

She was quiet again for a moment, so I quickly added, "Unless you're busy with your mother and your sister . . ."

"No. I was just thinking. You weren't invited to Mindy Harker's holiday party Saturday night, either."

"Didn't even know about it. I don't think I've said ten words to her this year."

"Yes, well, she does have a limited vocabulary," Ivy said. I laughed. "Sure. I could meet you at the mall earlier, and we could get something to eat. You want to see *Someone's Watching*? It's a little scary, but it has good reviews."

"Okay," I said. "What time?"

"Six will work for me. My mother is taking my sister somewhere close by about that time. I'll meet you in front of Tops."

"Okay."

"You know who would be perfect to play Dracula, don't you? I mean, Dracula has got to be charming to lure the female victims," she added.

"Charming? The boys in our school? Is there anyone?"

"I was thinking of Dillon Evans," she said. "He was in *Our Town* last spring, played George."

"Yes. He's kind of shy, though, isn't he? That part fit him. I mean, Dracula can't be shy."

"My mother always says, 'Beware of the shy ones.' "

I laughed. "Maybe she's right. Anyway, being as he's your neighbor, you know better than I do."

"I'll suggest it to him. I'll let you know what he says. I know what we'll do," she added. "You and I will interview him and decide whether or not to press it."

Perhaps she had a crush on him, I thought. "You and me? Interview him? Where? How? I have yet to say anything to Dillon Evans."

"Really?"

"Maybe I'm afraid of his bite," I said.

Her laughter made me feel good, hopeful, in fact. Perhaps I could escape the shadows of Wyndemere after all.

I told my mother about my plans. She couldn't have been more joyful if I had won the lottery. She was sitting in the kitchen with Mr. Stark. For years, she had tried to get him to drink brewed tea. He had finally given in only if the tea was accompanied by her homemade scones.

"I'll be happy to drive you, Fern," Mr. Stark said. "And pick you up."

"I could take a taxi back."

My mother and he looked at each other. Ever since the disaster after the prom, both were very concerned about almost anything I did.

"I mean, you'd have to pick me up, take me home, and then go home. What do you think, Mummy?"

"Well, I suppose you're right."

"Now, Emma, you know that's not a big deal to me," Mr. Stark said.

"No, but . . . we have to let Fern take more responsibility for herself. I wasn't that much older than she is when I set out across the pond for America, and the farthest away from home

I'd been at the time was Salisbury. I hadn't even been to London, and here I was headed for New York City all by myself, not knowing a soul there."

"You were eighteen," Mr. Stark reminded her.

"Just eighteen." She looked at me. "Somehow I think Fern's grown up faster nevertheless. Besides, she'll soon be driving herself everywhere. Dr. Davenport and I have been discussing that."

"Really?" I asked. Did that mean he would buy me a car?

"See?" Mr. Stark said to me. "See how fast a woman makes a man obsolete?"

"Oh, go on with you, George Stark, reaching for our pity now. Shameful."

Mr. Stark laughed. "If there's a way to win with this woman, it's a national secret," he said.

She slapped him playfully on his arm.

He laughed. "Well, I'll certainly help you with driving instructions when you're ready," he told me.

For a long time, I had suspected that he was really my father. It was impossible to believe a man could be as devoted to my mother as he was without being in love with her, and devoted to me as well without being my father. Then I had learned about my mother's one true love affair here in America. It was with the doctor who had delivered both Ryder and me, Dr. Bliskin,

119

a married man who had triplets. He had left to work somewhere else, but when he returned for a visit earlier this year, I suspected immediately that he might be my father. I learned that he had left because although he loved my mother, he loved his family and didn't want to hurt them. When I asked her, my mother assured me he was not my father, but she held back on the truth until it became necessary to reveal it.

Now, after I told my mother of my plans with Ivy and seeing her buoyant reaction, I felt like I was rising out of some dark, cold place in which I had entrapped myself. My father's key words rang so true. I had been committing myself to the same fate Ryder was suffering, and that wasn't doing him or me any good.

When my mother told my father my plans, I saw his look of not only approval and satisfaction but also some relief. It wasn't until then that I fully realized the weight of the guilt he had carried on his shoulders all these years. My mother had been clear about what had occurred between them. Dr. Davenport and his first wife, Samantha, had brought my mother to live at Wyndemere and to serve as their in vitro surrogate, but at the time, neither anticipated her being or doing anything more.

In New York, my mother had fallen behind on her rent; it was actually her landlord who had set up the meeting for her with Dr. Davenport and his first wife. They offered my mother seventy-five thousand dollars, which was a fortune for her. The money guaranteed that she could avoid retreating to England. After she gave birth, Dr. Davenport offered her an additional fifty thousand dollars to remain as Ryder's nanny for the year. She told me that she didn't believe it would last much longer.

"I was even thinking of returning to New York and taking another toss at becoming a professional singer."

However, when Dr. Davenport's wife was killed in the automobile accident, my mother was still breastfeeding Ryder. Dr. Davenport was beside himself with grief. Slowly, as she had described it to me, she became more and more like a wife and mother. He threw himself into his work, but when he returned home, he was almost immediately submerged in a darkness that nearly drove him mad. She was his respite, his comfort, and one thing led to another, until she was eventually pregnant with me.

"I was just there," she told me. "I know it's not enough of an explanation, but sometimes you really do have to be there to understand why we didn't develop into something more substantial."

Of course, I would wonder about that. My mother had been and was still a very attractive woman. She had all the characteristics that would make her a perfect doctor's wife. She was bright and sociable. When she was involved with other people, she was never at a loss for conversation. Perhaps my father's parents had instilled class distinctions in him. It was the only real reason I could think of for his marrying a woman like Bea Howell.

Once, when my mother was particularly annoyed with Bea, she muttered that it was mainly Dr. Davenport's guilt that drove him to marry a woman like her a few years after his first wife's death. Bea's father was head administrator at the hospital at the time, so it was probably a good career move as well.

"There was never any real love between them. I've seen so many marriage like that, marriages of convenience," my mother told me.

So despite how she presented it, it was bothering her, I thought. She had slept with, made love to, Dr. Davenport, cared for him, nourished him out of his grief, but even when she was pregnant, he did not offer to marry her. I couldn't believe that deep down in his heart, he didn't want to marry her. I tried to find out, but my mother thought she had said too much to me already, so she shut up about it and refused to answer any of my questions. Until now, that is.

With every passing year, we were becoming more like sisters than mother and daughter. It was easier for that to happen when your mother was young when she gave birth to you. I sensed that in years to come, if not sooner, I would understand more and more about the strange relationship my mother and my father had and still, to some extent, had today.

Maybe it was Wyndemere. Maybe this house had the power to turn everything into something dark and mysterious. Perhaps my imagination never did run wild, and the shadows I saw moving and the moans I heard coming from the uninhabited places in the mansion were as real as anything else. Sometimes I awoke in the night and thought we were all actually in some danger. Eventually, the house would claim more victims.

Who would be next? My half brother was already a victim. My half sister was as infected with jealousy and as conniving as any evil ghost trapped in the shadows could be.

When Samantha found out that I was going to the mall for dinner and a movie on Saturday, she whined at breakfast that she should be permitted to go, too. Ryder hadn't come downstairs yet. A new medication he was taking caused him to sleep more.

"It's not fair," she moaned, quickly bringing on her crocodile tears. "Why should Fern be able to go and not me?"

I expected my father to acquiesce to her demands as usual, but he shook his head. "Fern is going with her friend, someone her own age," he said. "You have to do things with your own friends, and we have to be sure there is proper supervision. When you're her age, you'll have more privileges, too. I'll see about my schedule. Maybe I can take you to Jolly Joe's. You like those submarine sandwiches," he offered as a consolation.

"I don't want to go to Jolly Joe's. That's for kids."

"You're not exactly an old lady," my mother said.

Samantha looked up at her so hatefully that I thought I might just reach across the table to slap her silly.

"We might bring Ryder along," my father said.

Samantha's eyes widened with surprise and delight. "Really?" she said.

"Dr. Seymour thinks it's time he was exposed to more people and places."

"I'll take care of him," Samantha said quickly. "I'll tell him what's good to eat, too." She smiled at me triumphantly.

It took all my self-control to keep from heaving my glass of water at her elated, reddened face, a mirror image of her mother's spiteful joy.

My father looked at me and saw it, I'm sure. "We'll see later if he's up to it," he said. "He's adjusting to some new drug therapy."

"He'll be up to it. He'll be up to it," Samantha insisted. "He wants to get out, too. He's told me so many times."

Of course, she was lying.

My father said nothing. He finished his coffee and rose, looking to my mother as if he anticipated her doing or saying something to rescue him.

"I'll bring Ryder his breakfast this morning," she said.

He nodded. "I should be home by four. Behave yourself," he told Samantha, who grimaced and stabbed her egg yolk so it would bleed over her plate. He glanced at me, a smile in his eyes to show me how pleased he was with my decision, and then left.

"I'm going to tell Ryder that we're taking him out to Jolly Joe's," Samantha said when my mother went into the kitchen.

"You'd better wait for Daddy to decide," I warned her. "He might decide against it, and Ryder could be disappointed."

Her eyelids narrowed, and her eyes grew steely cold with her inner rage, just the way her mother's would. "You want me to call your mother Ms. Corey all the time. You should call my father Dr. Davenport like you used to have to," she said. "He's probably not really your father. He probably made all that up to make you feel better about what you did to Ryder."

"I didn't do anything to Ryder. How dare you say that?"

She shrugged. "If you didn't make him take you

in the boat just before a storm, he'd be fine," she said, making it sound like an obvious fact. Was it possible she'd overheard two of the maids saying that, or one of the grounds workers? Perhaps it was a topic of conversation she had with her equally spoiled-rotten school friends?

I was about to blast her with threats and expletives, but she got up quickly, flashed a spiteful smile, and practically ran out of the room.

My mother appeared with Ryder's breakfast tray. She looked at Samantha's plate. "She's hardly eaten a thing. Where is she?"

"Making a witch's brew in her room," I said. "You want any help with that?" I asked, nodding at Ryder's tray.

"No, it's fine. But that child's beginning to worry me," she said, nodding at Samantha's empty seat as if her nasty presence always lingered for a few moments. She left to go upstairs to Ryder.

There was an understatement, I thought.

I began to clear the table. During the holidays, my mother had less help. I knew she was looking forward to Mrs. Marlene's return and, along with her, the part-time maids. Helping to clean up and tidying the living room took up the morning. I spent most of the afternoon organizing my room and reading, doing my best not to think about Ryder. Despite everything my father and mother had said, there was still this guilt gnawing at my conscience, a guilt my father had specifically warned me against.

It wasn't what Samantha had said about my causing the accident. No, what was on my mind now was that I was going out, to socialize and enjoy myself, while Ryder remained confused and lost. The best to hope for was my father taking him out to a fast-food place, probably inundated with children Samantha's age and younger. Some Saturday night out for the boy who was the most popular in our school. If anyone there recognized him, he wouldn't know it, and he wouldn't understand why they were looking at him with pity.

Samantha's hateful words had stung me, though.

In a way, she was right. I should not have been so eager to go for that boat ride. I was so excited about our being alone that I had let that overwhelm my caution. I had seen what was coming in the ominous clouds. When the storm hit, Ryder had struggled so hard to try to get me safe. I couldn't help wondering if my father ever considered it that way, too. It was at least somewhat my fault.

On the other hand, his regret had to be that he had never insisted on the truth about being my father being known long before Ryder and I had become secret lovers. If that had happened, nothing intimate would have occurred between

Ryder and me, and we would surely not have gone for a romantic boat ride.

And then I wondered, wouldn't we? Would we have backed away from each other? We might just as easily have become even more defiant, frustrated, and angry about a secret kept hidden for so many years.

Still, it had to be something my father wondered about often, and in that sense, he bore more responsibility than I could for what had happened to Ryder. It didn't make me feel much better, though.

Everyone in this house, in one way or another, lived with some guilt, I thought. Why should I be spared?

To keep myself from thinking all these heavy thoughts, I spent more time on my clothes, makeup, and hair than I had for the past six months. I'd been barely concerned about my appearance these days, forgetting to put on lipstick, running my brush quickly through my hair, and only vaguely thinking about what I would wear to school.

I laid out some pants, shirt, and sweater combinations on my bed and then matched up a pair of leather ankle shoe boots. In the end, I chose a pair of black stretch pants and a turquoise sweater with a sweetheart collar, with one of my Christmas gifts, a black cashmere poncho. After I showered, I decided to wear my hair up, with a pair of yellow gold hoop earrings my mother had bought me for my last birthday.

I was at my vanity table, still wrapped in my bath towel and doing my eyes, when I felt someone's presence. I turned very slowly. My door was opened slightly. I knew I had closed it when I entered my bedroom. I set down my eyeliner pencil and rose slowly. For a moment, I stood there, listening and watching the door. I walked to it, listened sharply again, and then opened the door quickly.

My heart stopped and started. Ryder was walking back to his room. I stepped into the hallway.

"Ryder," I called.

He paused and looked back at me.

"Did you want something?" I asked.

He started back toward me and then stopped. We could both hear Samantha running up the stairs. He turned away and quickly continued to his room.

Samantha stopped and looked in my direction and then at Ryder's room.

"Was Ryder just in your room?" she cried, as if not including her was a cardinal sin. "Why are you walking around like that? What did you do?"

"Nothing," I said. "He wasn't in my room."

Before she could say anything else, I returned to my bedroom and closed the door. I remained there, my heart thumping. I expected she would come knocking, demanding to know what had happened, nagging me, but she didn't. I still didn't move. The look on Ryder's face remained on the surface of my eyes. Maybe it was all in my imagination, in that part of me that wished none of this had occurred and we were still secret lovers. He looked full of the sort of pain that comes from a desperate longing to be loved.

Or was it just more confusion? How much did I see, and how much did I want to see? Later, would Ryder even remember he had come to my room? Perhaps he was simply trying to find his way through the maze of twisted memories. Best to make nothing more of it, I thought, best to make the turn my father was urging—no, demanding—that I make.

I turned back to preparing myself to go out with Ivy and start something of a social life again. I couldn't snap down on the feeling that I was battling to rise to the surface of some dark pool, a place to which I had retreated both in disappointment and in fear.

After I had dressed, I paused to look at myself in the full-length mirror next to my dresser. Was I pretty again? Had I ever really been? There was no doubt in my mind that my mother had been pretty and still was. I looked mostly like her, didn't I?

What did I inherit from Dr. Davenport? It was a little more difficult to see the resemblances, because I had never looked for any. A part of me wanted to deny that I looked at all like Ryder. No one had ever said so, and in fact, no one said so now.

This house had so many secrets and lies embedded in its walls and in every shadow.

My mother's and Dr. Davenport's confession could be another secret embedded in this house for reasons I had yet to discover.

Couldn't it?

If you wanted something so much, with so much of your every breathing self and soul, could you make it true?

No one had asked me who I wanted to be. Did I want to be a Davenport? Or did I want to remain a Corey? Was I comfortable in my new skin? It was a question impossible for anyone to imagine, I guessed.

But the girl in the mirror was asking.

I fled my bedroom as if I feared the answer she demanded, an answer dancing on my lips.

6

Despite how we had fooled around about him on the telephone, I didn't expect to see Dillon Evans waiting alongside Ivy in front of Tops. She had a silly grin on her face, anticipating my reaction. He was standing there with his hands in his pants pockets and staring at the ground. He wore a black hoodie, black jeans, and a pair of western-style boots.

When I had described Dillon as shy, I really wasn't giving him much thought. A better word for him was *loner,* which was why I wasn't astonished that Mindy Harker didn't invite him to her party or, if she had, why he didn't attend it. He wasn't very social at school. As far as I knew, he had no close friends. However, I wouldn't deny that he often drew my curiosity.

Most of the time, he either had his face in a book or was scribbling something in his note-book that absorbed all his attention, even at lunch, whether he was alone at a table or even when he was not. Whenever someone spoke to him, he looked startled that he or she even had noticed he was there, but from what I could see, he usually showed little interest in what anyone was saying. Sometimes he didn't respond at all; most of the time, he had a monosyllabic reply and returned to what he was reading or writing.

Dillon was a senior, so I didn't have any classes with him. His excellent performance as the character of George in Mr. Madeo's production of *Our Town* astounded his teachers as much as it did the students who were aware of him as someone who looked like he was gone but whose body kept moving through the school. One of the girls in the cast, Sari Cook, said he came to rehearsal, did his part, and stayed off to himself. She said whenever any of them tried to talk to him, he claimed he had to remain in character.

Nevertheless, I always perked up when someone mentioned his name. According to the girls in his classes, he was a good student but not like some who enjoyed answering questions as if they were on *Jeopardy!* I gathered that he wasn't competitive and acted as if he really didn't care what anyone's opinion of him was, teacher or student. He'd wait to be called on and always looked like he wasn't paying attention, yet he always had the right answer. Some sounded annoyed about it.

I knew a little about Dillon from scattered conversations. He was an only child. His father was some sort of salesman, and his mother worked on and off as a dental hygienist. He and his parents lived in a modest ranch-style home two houses south of Ivy's house, which was why I thought she probably knew him better than anyone else in our school.

I sensed that his aloofness actually frightened some of the students. They misinterpreted his disinterest in them and their school activities as aggressiveness, belligerence, a *don't bother me with your personal information, I couldn't be less interested* sort of attitude. There were rumors that he was friends with some of the boys at the community college and went to wild parties, which was a popular reason for some of the girls at school to explain his indifference to them.

After he had done so well in the play, I watched a few girls flirt with him, but he didn't show interest in any of them. They concluded that he was either hanging out with older college boys or perhaps was gay and closeted. No one would admit she was simply unattractive to him. Most couldn't imagine being unattractive to anyone. Some of them took enough selfies to cover all the walls in the Pentagon.

I always thought there was something interesting about Dillon, even though I never said so. He was certainly good-looking, with his rich dark brown hair just a little unruly, the bangs slightly uneven and swept to one side, which was kind of sexy. Not quite six feet tall and slim, he sauntered along the hallway with his eyes down, his shoulders back. He looked like he was navigating through a maze and was worried about stepping on a land mine, but I couldn't help thinking he was intriguing. It was as if he had a secret, something we all should know. I understood how many of the other girls felt about him, why some avoided him. It was easy to imagine there was also something dangerous about him.

"Hi," Ivy said. "Guess who wanted to see this movie, too?"

"Let's see," I said, looking around and pretending to think about it. "Dillon Evans?"

Anyone else would have laughed. He looked at me and shrugged. "I don't have to sit with you if you'd rather be alone."

"What? Yes, you do," I said forcefully.

"Oh, yeah? Why?"

"You're buying the popcorn."

He didn't smile as much as he relaxed his lips and brightened his eyes, which I now realized were a strange bluish-green. Whenever I had looked at him, I hadn't looked long enough directly at him to read the true color of his eyes.

"Let's eat," Ivy said. "The movie starts in forty-five minutes."

Tops was one of those fast-food restaurants where you ordered your food and then moved down a counter and picked up your glass for a drink, your silverware, and your napkins and then paid for what you ordered and sat where you wanted. They had individual-size pizzas, sandwiches, burgers, and fries, a real grab bag of foods that seemed perfect before or just after a movie.

Dillon entered behind us, far enough behind for me to lean over and whisper to Ivy without him hearing, "Did you say anything about *Dracula*?"

"Yes. He wasn't interested. Until I mentioned you were trying out for Lucy," she added, and ordered a pizza.

"What?" I glanced at Dillon quickly and moved forward. "What do you mean?"

"Just what I said. When I told him about the play, he shrugged and looked disinterested, but when I mentioned you were trying out, he asked me when the auditions were."

She didn't sound bitter, jealous, or disappointed about it. Instead, she sounded amused. Now I was sure of the reason she had invited him to see the movie with us. Suddenly, she had become a little matchmaker. I wasn't convinced I liked the idea, but whatever, this was turning out to be a much different night out from the one I had anticipated.

Dillon followed us with his tray to a table toward the rear. Until tonight, even though I admitted at least to myself that he was intriguing, I hadn't said two words to him, actually, not even one. A few times, when he was passing me in the hallway, going in the opposite direction, I almost said "Hi" but didn't, maybe because he didn't give me as much as a passing glance. Why was my going out for *Dracula* suddenly important enough to him to drive his auditioning for it as well? I always had assumed that I was as invisible to him as he was to almost everyone else.

"How's your brother?" he asked when we were all settled at the table.

It wasn't something I had anticipated he would ask immediately, despite the sensational aspects of the boat accident and the revelation of my real father being Ryder's. At the start of the school year, it was on the lips of everyone in the high school almost daily, but other things began to take almost everyone's attention away; that and my refusal to talk much about any of it drove it off the headlines. Hardly anyone asked about Ryder anymore. Andy Warhol was credited with saying that in the future everyone's fame would be fifteen minutes long. In my school, at least, it was five. A deep, long conversation was Snapchat.

"He's better, but he has a long way to go."

"Who doesn't?" he said, and began to eat his hamburger. "What?" he asked when he saw my clear expression of dissatisfaction. He continued to eat, not waiting anxiously for my response.

"I don't think it's the same thing, whatever it is you mean. We haven't lost part of our memory." I couldn't help sounding defensive, even angry.

"Forgetting things isn't always bad," he said, unaffected by my sharp tone.

I looked at Ivy, who had this amused little smile on her face. It was as if her bringing Dillon and me together was some sort of behavioral experiment.

"Things you might want to forget, yes," I said. "But Ryder didn't have that choice."

"Here's a question," Dillon said, nodding. "If you were struggling to regain your memory, would your mind censor those memories you always wished you'd forget? It could be like starting with a clean slate. You know, like an Etch A Sketch."

He wasn't smiling, so I wasn't sure if he was kidding or not, but I assumed he was. "You really think it's funny?" I asked.

He didn't look embarrassed or frightened by the directness of my question. He looked thoughtful. "Not funny, exactly. More like ironic. You know, like that expression 'Every cloud has a silver lining.'"

"Well, I haven't seen that silver lining yet. Ryder was a top student, an athlete, and very popular both with students and with our teachers. He had a wonderful future ahead of him."

He shrugged as if my pointed comebacks were like flies on an elephant. "Maybe he still will," he said. "Don't be so quick to be pessimistic."

Despite how quickly I had been annoyed, I

felt myself relax. His calm manner made me feel a little foolish getting angry and annoyed. I guess I did have a hair trigger when it came to talking about Ryder. "Hopefully, you're right," I said.

"Of course he is," Ivy said.

"What do his doctors say about it?" Dillon asked.

"His doctor, a therapist, is optimistic. Actually, you weren't far off with what you said. The theory is that he does fight the memory of unpleasant things, and we were advised not to make reference to any that could upset him."

"Logical. Sometimes the experts get it right," he said.

I laughed. "Well, they'll be glad to hear you approve."

We all ate. I felt Dillon's eyes on me, but when I looked at him, he looked away.

"You ever think about how much food we eat in our life, how much liquid we consume?" he asked. "Twenty-one meals a week, eighty-four a month, one thousand eight a year. Say you live to be eighty. That's eighty thousand six hundred and forty."

"Not counting popcorn," I said.

"Exactly. Or cookies and candy."

"Is this what you're doing when I see you scribbling in your notebook? Figuring out how much we do things?" I asked.

"Dillon writes poems," Ivy said before he could attempt an answer.

"You do? About what?"

"Nothing," he said. "Everything. And don't say you'd like to read one."

"Okay. I wasn't going to say it. Lately, I have more than enough to read."

Anyone else would have probably been annoyed, even insulted, but he looked pleased. We were nearly finished eating.

"Do you want to be a writer?" I asked.

"I'm thinking of it. I was accepted to Michigan State and might pursue journalism. Our guidance counselor recommends it. He said it would be a perfect fit, as if a career was the same as a pair of shoes."

"Well, good luck," I said.

"Yeah, luck, that ever-present ghoul of fate. Speaking of which, Ivy says you're thinking of going out for a part in *Dracula*," Dillon said, sitting back and drinking his soda.

"Maybe. Why?"

"I've always been intrigued by Dracula. I don't think he's as happy being who he is as most readers think. The part should be played with a little sadness, a sense of tragedy. It's bad enough that we normal human beings have to eat nutritiously and sleep seven or eight hours as it is, as I explained. Tons of food and drink. I guess I could compare his lust for blood to our need for water, but I don't think vampires enjoy food the way we do. The experts on horror characters tell us they have a heightened sense of pleasure, but an emotion like love makes no sense to them, unless the one you love will live as long and share what you have. So he pursues Lucy. She's in great danger, but you have to feel sorry for him, too. I mean, what's the point in living forever if you're living only for yourself and everything you do is redundant?"

I realized I was sitting there with my mouth wide open, looking stupid, and quickly regained my composure. "Do you always think so deeply about everything?"

"Don't you?"

"Is that why you write poems?"

"Why would that be a reason?"

"I imagine it's a form of release," I said. It was like we were playing ping-pong with ideas and words.

I looked at Ivy, who was still sitting there with that silly smile on her face.

"How so?" Dillon asked.

"Feelings can build until you want to explode. It's good to have a safety valve." I shrugged. "Poetry might be yours. Music was Mozart's."

He nodded. "Talk about being deep. So? What about you? What's your release?" he asked.

"Maybe I don't need one," I said, "as much as other people do."

"Yes, you do," he countered.

"How do you know?"

"What's that expression? It takes one to know one."

"You don't know me. We've never even spoken in school."

"I know you," he said confidently. "And I don't mean through Ivy or hearing gossip."

"Then you should go out for Dracula. You have superpowers," I said.

I wasn't sure if I was irritated or flattered again, but not being sure made me uncomfortable, left me feeling disadvantaged.

He smiled. "I always thought I had super-powers."

"Goody. Shouldn't we leave for the movie?" I asked Ivy.

She checked the time and nodded.

"You're not going to write a deep analysis of the film, are you?" I asked Dillon as we rose to go.

He didn't smile, but I didn't think he was annoyed. I thought he was really considering it. "Maybe," he said. "Let's see whether it's worth it first."

I walked ahead with Ivy.

"He's interesting, isn't he?" she asked.

"Now that I've spoken to him, he's more like infuriating," I said.

"So? That's interesting, too, isn't it? He's worth investing more time in to see, right?"

I looked at her and smiled. "Who would have thought you could be so wicked, Ivy Mason?"

"I have no idea why you would say that," she said, smiling.

I bumped her shoulder with mine. "Sure you don't."

Dillon rushed to buy popcorn as soon as we entered the movie theater, smiling like an impish raccoon. When it came to choosing seats, he waited for us to sit and then sat beside me.

"I figured I'd better not get between two girls," he said, and offered popcorn.

"I really don't know what this movie is about," I said. "Ivy said it got good reviews."

"I think it's better if you don't know too much. That way, you form your own independent opinion."

"I just said I don't know anything at all. Forget too much," I said.

"It's about a stepbrother and stepsister who run away from his horrible father and hide out in an old, run-down hotel, not knowing someone or something lives there. That enough?"

"Just," I said. He sat back but placed the popcorn on the arm of the chair.

I leaned over to Ivy. "Have you ever been anywhere or done anything with him before tonight?" I whispered.

"Not really," she said. "But now that he's been

with you a little, I can tell he really likes you."

"And exactly how can you tell that?"

"He's already said more to you than anyone else I know."

"I'm overwhelmed with gratitude," I replied, glanced at him, and sat back as the screen lit up.

The movie was so good that none of us said a word until it ended. I felt like I had been on a real emotional roller coaster, grasping the arm of the chair and then sinking in my seat. Once I grabbed Dillon's arm. He turned, surprised, and I apologized. He simply shrugged.

The moment it was over and we got up from our seats, both Ivy and I began chatting about the movie, how tense we had been and how surprised at the outcome. We started up the aisle toward the lobby. Dillon walked behind us, listening but not saying anything, his hands in his pockets, his head down, looking just the way he did when he walked through the halls at school. I paused when we stepped out in front of the theater.

"So?" I said. "What did you think of it?"

"You'll have to wait for my review," he said.

It was nearly impossible to tell when he was serious and when he was not. Nothing changed in his eyes, and there was barely a movement in his lips. He stared at me, too, almost daring me to complain.

"You're really writing a review? So you decided it was worth it?"

"I'll do it for the school paper. I give the editor something now and then."

"I don't remember seeing your name on anything."

"It's not. I'd rather be anonymous."

"You are that," I said.

He smiled much more warmly than he had previously. "I'll take that as a compliment. Thanks." He turned to Ivy. "Thanks for inviting me to join you."

"We can have a soda or something," she said. "It's not that late."

"I've got to write while my ideas are fresh. See you." He started to leave and then turned back. "Oh. I'm going out for *Dracula*."

"Good," I said.

"Good? What if I really was a vampire?"

"Then you'd know better than anyone how to act like one," I said.

He gave me that outline of a smile again, nodded, and walked off.

I turned to Ivy. "Let's go somewhere to have something so you can tell me everything you know about him," I said.

She widened her smile, hooked her arm in mine, and led me on. We found a booth in a Marie Callender's and ordered some apple pie and coffee. I couldn't help looking at my watch and thinking about Ryder. Had he gone with our father and Samantha to Jolly Joe's, and if he had, how did it go?

"So?" I said. "Is he really a vampire?"

"We're neighbors, but I don't know all that much about him," Ivy began. "No one introduced us or anything. One day, I just started to talk to him, and after a while, I think he grew more comfortable talking to me. Before he could drive, we'd walk to the bus stop together. Usually, I'd do most of the talking."

"You said he wrote poems. Have you read any of them?"

"No. He doesn't show them to many people, as far as I know."

"Really? What's his family like?"

"He never talks much about his parents. I get the feeling sometimes that they don't have all that much to do with him. I don't think he's that much different at home from how he is at school. I've met his parents. They seem nice. I mean, I don't think there's trouble. There's just . . ."

"Silence?"

"Yes, maybe," she said, nodding. "I guess parents can have trouble understanding or knowing their own child. He's a challenge to them."

"To everyone, I imagine."

I thought about my relationship with Dr. Davenport, the man I was told only recently was my father. All the previous years, we were a little more than strangers. I was always afraid of him. He rarely smiled at me or spoke to me. Maybe I was a challenge to him. It occurred to me that perhaps he was afraid that somehow he would reveal the big secret without my mother's permission. So, yes, I knew what it was like to live in a world where there were long, deep silences. It got so I longed for echoes.

"I know. But maybe that's what makes him interesting," Ivy said.

"His parents would rather be bored, I imagine. They can be challenging. Is he friends with anyone at school, or does he have friends who don't go to our school? There is that rumor about him hanging out with older boys."

"I never saw him with anyone from our school or elsewhere, but I don't watch him night and day. I know he's hard to like, maybe, but I like him," Ivy said. "If anything, there's something sad about him at times. Join the club, huh?"

"Yes. I won't rave about him, but yes, I'll agree that he's interesting, more interesting than most other boys at school. Although maybe that isn't saying much."

Ivy laughed and then told me she'd decided to try out for *Dracula*, too. She had been thinking of the part of Renfield like I had suggested.

"I'll practice talking in a deeper voice."

We talked more about the play and Dillon's

interpretation of Dracula himself, and then we left the mall. I was heading to call a taxi. Ivy's mother was waiting for her. She had texted her a little while ago. We hugged, and she got into her mother's car. Her mother waved to me, too, maybe as happy as my mother was that I had a friend.

Despite some of the earlier tension between myself and Dillon, I thought the night was quite successful. It had been a long time since I had felt so content. It was as though I had decided to return to the living. My mind was sizzling with possibilities, the lead sizzle being built around the question of who was this Dillon Evans. What had made him like he was? Was he habitually angry or sad?

I surprised myself.

I really wanted to know. It wasn't just mere curiosity, either.

Before I reached the taxi parked at the curb, a familiar pickup truck pulled up. Mr. Stark looked out at me, a smile as big as any splattered like an egg across his face. I stood there with my hands on my hips, looking indignant.

"I just happened to be passing by," he said, hoisting his shoulders.

"Sure. And fall just happens to follow summer."

I went around and got into his truck.

"Before you say anything," he said, putting up his right hand, "your mother did not send me to get you. She was quite willing to let you do your own thing."

"And you're not?"

"I've always been a worrywart," he said, then shifted and started away. "Have a good time?"

"Yes."

"I'm glad you went out with friends. I was beginning to worry that you were becoming one of the antiques in Wyndemere."

"Very funny. Do you know if Dr. Davenport took Ryder with Samantha to Jolly Joe's?"

"He didn't," Mr. Stark said. "Your mother told me they're cutting back on his medication. He wasn't up to going out. He could barely stay awake."

"I'm sure Samantha made the doctor's night out with her miserable, then."

He nodded. And smiled. "I'm sure she did. She's a pip."

"A pip? My mother's already gotten you to drink warm beer," I said. "Soon you'll be singing about the queen."

He laughed. "So what did you do? Who were you with?" he asked, the way a parent might.

I described Ivy and the movie. When I mentioned Dillon, he nodded.

"Possibilities?" he asked. I guessed I was a little more than exuberant.

"No. Well, maybe."

He laughed. All my life, Mr. Stark really was

149

the father I never had. Even now, even though I knew Dr. Davenport was my actual father, Mr. Stark remained in that place in a young girl's heart reserved for her dad. I still couldn't imagine being as warm and casual with my father as I was with Mr. Stark. The one time just recently when my father described the crush he'd had on his cousin came the closest to something warm, but he didn't carry that change into our daily lives. My mind still went to calling him Dr. Davenport. Even though I had done it, I still felt a little uncomfortable calling him Daddy.

I did sense how hard he was trying to be different from the man he was before the Revelations. I believed he wanted to be closer to me, although not at the point where I would say loving. He certainly wasn't loving with Samantha. I suspected her resemblances to her mother prevented him from being so. He seemed to be constantly reprimanding her whenever he was with her in Wyndemere. Maybe he saw that he wouldn't be able to change her. His smiles about anything were tempered considerably since Ryder's near drowning and the aftermath, but I thought I could count on the fingers of one hand how many times I witnessed him smiling at Samantha or at something she had said, even before the accident.

However, it wasn't all that different for me, at least not yet. When he heard about my plans to go to a movie and meet a friend, he didn't volunteer to drive me. To be fair, he had to deal with Samantha, but still, couldn't he have arranged it so he took care of both of us? People as rich and as busy as my father did depend on help, drivers, and secretaries. My mother filled so much of that role for him, but she always had. The Revelations hadn't changed any of that very much. I wondered if things really ever would change.

When we arrived at the mansion, I kissed and thanked Mr. Stark. My mother was in the living room reading a new novel, which I knew she was doing mostly to pass the time while she waited for me. My father was nowhere around, and neither was Samantha or Ryder.

"Mr. Stark was there waiting for me the moment I stepped out of the mall," I said immediately.

She lowered her book and shook her head. "That man doesn't know the meaning of 'No, thank you.' When he sets his mind on something, he is the most bullheaded man you'll ever meet. But his heart is in the right place. Remember, he's been watching over you since your first cry."

"I know."

"And your evening?"

"The movie was exciting." I hesitated, and then I thought to say it. "Ivy invited a boy to join us, Dillon Evans. She's practically the only friend he has at school. He's a senior, but he doesn't hang out with anyone in his class."

"Oh. Only one friend? Something wrong with him?"

"He thinks too much," I said.

She smiled. "Such men are dangerous."

I laughed, too. She was referring to Shakespeare's line in *Julius Caesar*, a play I had read last year. She had seen it performed in a theater in Guildford when she was fifteen.

"I do feel there is something dangerous about him. But not in a bad way," I quickly added. "I think he's a Sagittarius. You know, unemotional, someone who says what he means and doesn't hold back."

"I see. So do you like him or not?"

I hesitated, and she raised her eyebrows, a gesture that pushed me to think about my feelings. It was always easy for me to reveal them, to talk about them, with my mother.

"I'm not sure. He's going out for the play, too."

"Okay." She smiled. "You're auditioning for a part, then?"

"The female lead."

"Why not?" She closed the book she was reading and reached for my hands. "It's good to see you enthusiastic about something outside of this house, Fern." She pressed her fingers to my palms and then let go. The stamp of approval, I thought, but I'd always want hers. Nevertheless, deciding to do something that could take me from Wyndemere after school for months shook my conscience.

"How is Ryder? Mr. Stark told me he was unable to go out with his father and sister."

She nodded. "The medicine has to be adjusted, but he's fine. I made sure he ate well."

"And my father?"

"Getting some desperately needed sleep, I imagine. I think he would have rather performed a bypass than take Samantha to Jolly Joe's."

"I bet. Going up to bed," I said.

"I want to read a while. Tomorrow's the end of your holiday, isn't it?"

"Yes. I have some reading I was supposed to do and a paper I was supposed to write, so I'll have my face in books most of the day."

She nodded. I kissed her good night and hurried up the stairs.

When I reached the top, I glanced toward Ryder's room. I debated looking in on him. How would that be interpreted if my father saw me do it? Why did it need to be interpreted as anything more than healthy concern? It irked me that everything I did with Ryder from now on, anything I said to him, even how I looked at him, was always going to be scrutinized. I had felt it in my heart since the day he returned from the clinic. The truth was that my father really didn't trust me. Perhaps he sensed the underlying stream of anger that still flowed inside me. Maybe he expected me to defy the forbidden as an act of rage as much as an act of love. Wouldn't anyone, any other girl, feel this injustice, this quiet betrayal and deception that had been going on inside Wyndemere for all her life?

I think it was a different sort of suspicion for my mother. She knew better than my father could how much I longed to be loved. She knew how vulnerable I was, perhaps how desperate. The passion Ryder and I once enjoyed was not easy to reject or even put aside. It would hover in every look, every soft smile, and yes, every touch, no matter how insignificant that might be. He could brush against me, and my heart would still flutter.

When would that end? Maybe it wouldn't. Was that a curse? This mansion could be as much of a home to curses as it was to secrets. In fact, curses and secrets were my true inheritance, my true parents, I thought.

I was about to turn toward my bedroom when I saw Ryder standing there in his doorway. He was wearing only his pajama bottoms. I glanced quickly down the stairs. How long before my mother would come up? I looked down the hallway toward my father's bedroom. It was quiet.

"How are you?" I asked.

He didn't answer. He stood there looking out at me.

"Ryder?" I stepped toward him.

He stepped back and closed the door.

It gave me a chill.

It was as if he was angry I had gone out.

Of course, that was foolish, my own wild imagination at work again. I stood there for a few moments, and then I heard my mother starting to come up and I turned quickly and hurried to my bedroom. When I had closed my door behind me, I stood there thinking and coming to the realization I had been avoiding.

I had to find a way to get over this, this passion that lingered. If I didn't, I would only hurt myself and Ryder even more.

7

I couldn't have been more surprised when my phone rang late Sunday morning and the voice on the other end said, "I wrote a new poem last night, one that I'd like you to read."

I was stunned. Ivy had told me that Dillon didn't let many people read his poems. She, in fact, hadn't read one.

When I didn't answer instantly, he added, "In case you're wondering, I'm not stalking you. Ivy gave me your phone number. Are you going to be mad at her now?"

"Of course not. Is this poem about the movie?"

"No. That's a review, not a touch of poetry in it. It's done and emailed to the editor of the school paper. Before you ask, I don't like emailing my poems. I think it's important to be there when someone reads them."

"Who have you shown them to?"

"Why?"

"Teachers?"

"Teachers don't count," he said, "but I've never shown any to any teacher I thought would just say nice things and pat me on the head."

"So no one, then?"

"Very few. The point is, I can tell when some-one is being honest or not."

"Doesn't that put more pressure on the reader?"

"Sure," he said without hesitation.

I had to laugh at how honest he was. "Okay. I guess tomorrow when—"

"How about I pick you up in an hour and we go to lunch?" he asked quickly. "I know this cool restaurant called Nature's Ways."

"In an hour? Today?"

"In an hour would have to be today unless I called you at midnight. Too soon? You need more than an hour? What, did you just get up or something?"

"No, I . . ."

Every time during the past few months when-ever I looked at a boy in school with an inkling of romantic interest, I immediately thought of Ryder. Just taking a second glance at another boy flooded me with waves of guilt. There he was at home, incapacitated, and here I was thinking of how to get back into the swing of things and with a different boy. Of course, everything I had learned about myself and everything my mother had wanted for me now urged me not to feel this way, that, in fact, feeling this way was morally wrong for both Ryder and myself. The guilt and especially the deeper romantic feelings had to end.

Nevertheless, I sat back, thinking about Ryder

before I could respond to Dillon's invitation to lunch. I hadn't seen Ryder all morning. He wasn't down for breakfast, and when I had come upstairs, his door was closed. My mother had told me everything was fine. My father had gone off to the hospital, and Samantha was planning to go to a friend's house for lunch and probably the remainder of the day, the last day of the vacation, which she treated as if it was the last day of freedom, gasping about how short the holiday had been.

For the first week or so of a new school year, there was always the excitement of new classes, new teachers, and often new students. Opportunities for socializing arose. There were sporting events, school events, and parties friends would have, as well as plans to do things together on weekends. This year, until now, really, none of that had seized my attention enough for me to do anything. I was absorbed in two things: my schoolwork, yes, but also Ryder and his recuperation. The possibilities of dating seemed nonexistent for me, which was the real reason I had rejected the few invitations I had received, but now, suddenly, I was attracted by the idea. I felt like I was rising out of some darkness. Maybe that was because Dillon Evans was definitely different; it all seemed different.

"No, an hour's fine," I said. "Do you know how to get to my house?"

"Are you kidding? It's practically a historic landmark. And not just because you live there, although I'm sure that adds to it."

"Very funny."

"See you soon. Oh, and you don't have to wear anything fancy. It's sort of a bohemian hangout, stuck in the sixties. They play a lot of Bob Dylan. You know who he is?"

"I know who he is. I don't live in a bubble."

"Don't knock living in bubbles. You can float above everything. Ciao," he said.

Ciao? I thought, and smiled. Cathy Stark was always saying "Ciao for now" ever since she had returned from a vacation in Rome.

As soon as I hung up, I was filled with a sense of dread. Had I made a terrible mistake? This would be the first time I'd be alone with a boy since I was alone with Ryder. What if I had nothing to say? What if I looked too nervous? Maybe I wasn't ready for this.

I called Ivy to tell her. She picked up so quickly I imagined she had been waiting by her phone, anticipating my call. Dillon must have just asked her for my number.

"I had a suspicion that was going to happen," she said when I described his call and invitation.

"Well, you would. You gave him my number."

She laughed. "I didn't want to scare you off, but I didn't tell you everything last night," she said after a pause.

159

"Meaning?"

"He asked me about you before I mentioned auditioning for *Dracula*," she said.

"When did he ask?"

"A while ago."

"What did he ask?"

"What were you really like. Were you seeing anyone, maybe from another school? Was your brother's accident the only thing that depressed you and made you put on your funeral face?"

"He said I had a funeral face?"

"You haven't exactly been the life of the party these days," Ivy said. "Not that I blame you. You've been through so much."

Had I confided too much in her? She was practically the only one I had told anything about my family.

"I never realized he was watching me so closely. He never said a word to me before last night, and suddenly he calls to take me to lunch and to read his poem. It's a little freaky."

"Maybe that's what you need."

"What?"

"A little freaky," she said, and laughed. "You'd better call me later and give me a full report about your date. I'm responsible for this. I invited him to join us last night."

"And you gave him my phone number. I'll either blame you or—"

"Thank me? I'm actually a little jealous. He's

never asked me to read one of his poems. You connected with something in him. I suppose the question is, will you connect with something in him?"

"Don't turn it into a soap opera," I warned.

She laughed.

"I'll call you," I promised, and hung up, running to find the right thing to wear.

After hearing what Ivy had said, my nervousness changed to excitement. It really shouldn't have surprised me. This was my first real date since the prom disaster. Ryder and I never had a chance to go out on a date, and now we certainly wouldn't. We had planned on doing it as soon as things calmed.

"The first chance I get, I'm taking you to dinner in a fancy restaurant," he had said. "We'll get very dressed up. Everyone will be looking at us, wondering who that beautiful couple is."

"The plans of mice and men," I thought. Who knew that the roof would come crashing down on our short romance and condemn it forever and ever?

And yet when I paused to look at myself, I thought I saw some self-deception. Deep in my heart, I still harbored the belief that I could not feel as close to any boy as I still did to Ryder. Going out to lunch with Dillon was safe. How could I get involved with someone so different? This was just an amusement, I told my image in the mirror. Nothing would come of it.

After I fixed my hair, did my makeup, and dressed in simple jeans and a light blue sweater, I hurried down to tell my mother my plans. Mrs. Marlene had just arrived, returning from her holiday vacation, looking happy and rested. She and my mother were catching up in the kitchen.

"Well, just look how this sneaky one goes and grows more mature as soon as I leave the house," Mrs. Marlene said.

We hugged.

"Was Santa good to you?"

"Very," I said.

My mother saw that I was carrying my coat. "Where are you going?"

"I've been asked to lunch," I said.

"By Prince Harry? You look dolled up enough." She turned to Mrs. Marlene. "My father wouldn't let me wear lipstick until I was seventeen and never in the house. I had to stand outside and look in a window to put it on. He insisted it made me look cheap. So?" she asked me. "What's this about?"

"No, he's not your Prince Harry. Prince Dillon Evans," I replied.

"Oh, the boy you mentioned from the movies."

"Yes."

She smiled. "I thought you had a ton of left-over work to do." She turned to Mrs. Marlene.

"They're all the same, leaving everything until the last minute."

"I'm sure she'll do what she has to do. Who's this Dillon Evans?" Mrs. Marlene asked, crossing her arms over her bosom and putting on her scrutinizing face. I really had two mothers in Wyndemere as I was growing up.

"As my mother said, just a boy I met at the movies last night." Essentially, I thought, that was true. I couldn't say I had met him previous to that. "He goes to our school. He's a senior," I said. "He had a big part in the last school play, and he writes poetry."

"Does he, now?" Mrs. Marlene said.

I looked at my mother. She was caught between a smile and a worry.

"Okay?"

"You know, now that I think about it, I didn't go on my first date until I was seventeen, and that was for fish and chips," my mother said as a way of saying yes. "He was a shy boy, Michael Cook, but he took off his mitten to hold hands with me to and from the pub. I thought that was a nice gesture."

"I won't talk about my first date," Mrs. Marlene said. "I almost swore off men."

They both laughed. Sometimes life, not birth, turned two women into sisters.

"Where is this prince taking you for lunch?" my mother asked.

"A place called Nature's Ways."

"I swear, the names they come up with for restaurants these days," Mrs. Marlene said. "The most popular restaurant in my hometown was Joe's."

"Nothing compares to the names of pubs in England," my mother said, fondly recalling. "The Bull's Head, Crocker's Folly, the Blind Beggar, just to name a few."

Mrs. Marlene smiled, but my mother suddenly looked sad, homesick. It was interesting how rarely I saw that expression on her face. I thought the older I got, the more it began to show, the more she thought about herself and what she had left behind.

We heard the doorbell. I looked at the clock above the refrigerator. He was right on time.

"Shouldn't I meet this Dillon Evans? He could be Jack the Ripper," my mother said. "Even though he writes poetry."

"I guess," I said, but I knew I would hold my breath the whole time. Who knew what Dillon would say or how he would look? She might shut the door in his face.

When I opened the door, Dillon was standing there in a dark blue wool peacoat, a pair of jeans torn at the knee, pretty scuffed-up black shoe boots, and a New York Yankees cap with the letters almost completely faded. He wasn't kidding when he told me we weren't going to a fancy place.

He was looking down as if he was very shy.

"Hi," I said. He looked up and saw my mother beside me.

"Hey."

"This is Dillon Evans," I said. "Dillon, this is my mother, Emma Corey."

"Hi," he said. He kept his hands in his pockets, something I knew my mother noticed.

"Hello," my mother said. "Do you live far from here?" she asked. Maybe she wanted him to go home and change into more acceptable clothes.

He looked at me for some hint and then shrugged. "Far? About thirty minutes."

"And how long does it take to get to the restaurant?" she followed.

" 'Bout twenty, I guess."

"If you travel slowly, especially on these roads right now?" It was a question, but it really was an order.

"Oh. Yes. If I were driving fast, I could get here in twenty and to the restaurant in ten. I don't drive fast on dry roads or wet," he added. "Accidents hurt."

I looked at my mother. She had that glint in her eye that told me she was a little amused.

"Are you a Yankees fan?" my mother asked.

"What? Oh. This is my father's hat. He's an insane Yankees fan."

"Not you?"

"Let me put it this way, Ms. Corey. If I were a baseball fan, it would be the Yankees just so I could coexist at home."

I looked at my mother.

She smiled and nodded. "Peaceful coexistence is fine," she said, and took on a stern expression. "If you want to have that with me, be careful."

"Yes, ma'am."

"Very careful. And of course, have a good time."

"Will do both," he said, winking a smile. At least, that was the way it looked to me.

I stepped outside. When he took his hands out of his pockets, I thought he wanted to take my hand but then quickly changed his mind as if he was afraid to do so in front of my mother and turned. I looked back at my mother, who watched us walk away before closing the door. She nodded. I knew she was worried just as any mother would be when her daughter was leaving on a date, but I was positive now that she was happy I was going out, too. In fact, her reaction to Dillon caused me to give him a second look.

"Your mother's very pretty," he said, reaching for the passenger's door. He had a late-model Ford Taurus.

"Thank you." I got in. "Is this your car or your family's?" I asked when he'd gotten in.

"My mother and I share it. My father has a new

BMW." He started the engine and then paused a moment before shifting into drive. He leaned forward and looked up. "Who's watching us?" he asked.

"What?" I leaned forward and looked. The curtain in my room was open, and Ryder was looking down at us. He was still in his dark blue pajamas. The sight of him there took my breath away.

"Is that your brother?"

Despite how much time had passed since my father had been revealed, it was still difficult to get used to someone referring to Ryder as my brother. I was sure that when it was first known and someone called Ryder my brother, I had a confused expression on my face. Of course, I didn't want to think of him that way; I still didn't.

"Yes."

"I wondered if I'd meet him," he said, and drove to the road. "I remember him well. He hasn't gone anywhere since he's been home, has he? I mean, he doesn't see any of his old friends?"

"No."

"None came by during the holiday? He was pretty popular."

"No."

"Maybe they're just afraid."

"Afraid? Why?"

"It takes courage to see someone you admire diminished like that. Does he get out of the house at all?"

Usually, I didn't like talking about Ryder's problems, but Dillon had a sincerity about him, even a little surprising compassion. Getting to know someone new was always difficult. You held back a lot. Most people were naturally distrustful, but my mother always taught me and believed that people had auras about them. Despite how they looked or even sounded, their true nature was right before your eyes. Something inside you sensed the positive about them if it was there. There was good energy. Right now, I thought I saw that in Dillon. I was fearful, however. I was simply too out of practice when it came to caring about friendships and relationships. It all required a level of trust I hadn't given anyone besides my mother and Mr. Stark for some time.

"He goes out with my father occasionally. For walks and some cross-country skiing on the grounds," I said. I was still determined not to get too specific.

"So he's otherwise pretty healthy?"

"Yes."

"I guess amnesia is like being in a sort of prison. He's at quite a disadvantage, too, not knowing whom he can trust and whom he can't."

Oh, how true that was, I thought. I looked away, my heart still racing from seeing that Ryder had gone into my room. His room didn't have a view of the front of the mansion. How did he know I was leaving? Or had he gone into my room looking for me and just looked out the window, perhaps hearing us speak below? What would have brought him to my room?

Either because of my mother's warning or because of his own caution, Dillon drove very slowly over the recently plowed street. It was a partly cloudy day, vacillating from dark and gloomy to bright, which was how I felt, too, bouncing from one emotion to another.

He looked very thoughtful. "I guess you were surprised I called," he said. "Didn't expect it, right?"

"Dillon, I hardly know you, but somehow I doubt anyone can predict what you'll do from one moment to another, even your parents," I said.

He laughed. "My mother says the same thing, only she says 'even your father.' "

"Why is that? Why are you so unpredictable?"

"Maybe because I rely on how I feel rather than what I know is expected," he said. "Hemingway wrote that you should rely on your intuition. I always thought he was right."

"So if I feel something is right, I should do it no matter what anyone else says?"

"I think so. In the end, if you're not happy doing something or not doing something, what have you accomplished?"

"But that puts your own happiness over everyone else's," I said. Nothing could have hit the bull's-eye in my troubled thoughts more sharply.

"I don't know about you, but being around someone who is unhappy, deeply unhappy, makes me miserable."

"You don't think I'm deeply unhappy?" I asked, really curious.

He paused and looked at me. "Hey, you're the one getting deep and heavy now, not me. Don't blame me. I mean, I'm just taking you to lunch to read my poem. Sometimes things are not much more than they seem."

What was he saying? Did he mean I shouldn't think he had any other interest in me?

"Yes, but you started it. You're the one who said I was probably surprised you called."

"Well, I'm not afraid to admit I was surprised you accepted my invitation."

"You don't act like someone with any lack of self-confidence," I said. "You didn't sound very doubtful when you asked me."

"You already know how good an actor I am." When he looked at me this time, he raised his eyebrows in anticipation.

I smiled. I did go home wondering about him last night, despite how irritating he was at times.

170

Right now, I was enjoying him, although I wasn't going to let him know that so fast.

"I'll hold my judgment on that. We'll see how good you are at the audition."

"You know, if we get the parts, we'll have to learn how to stay up all night and sleep all day. Just to stay in character, of course."

"Very funny. So tell me about your new poem."

"No."

"No?"

"You'll read it, and you'll tell me about it," he said.

"I take back what I said. You don't cover up your lack of self-confidence well. You don't have a lack of self-confidence."

He smiled. "I look at it this way," he said, quickly turning serious again. "You'll never lack for people putting you down in your life, so why do it to yourself? And before you say it, yes, I'm a bit arrogant, but let me also say that the line between arrogance and self-confidence is shady anyway. Those who wish they had self-confidence always accuse you of arrogance. It makes them feel better about their weakness."

"So you really do think you're better than everybody?"

He shrugged and smiled at me. "Just people I've met. Until now," he quickly added.

I sat back. I didn't want him to see my face. I was sure I was looking pleased, maybe too pleased. What I really feared was investing my feelings in anyone else as fast as someone who was starving for attention might.

And that was surely me when it came to any sort of romantic relationship: someone starving for attention.

"Tell me about this restaurant, Nature's Ways. I've never heard about it."

"They're into all this organic food, great salads, basically vegetarian. I've never seen anyone from our school there, so I'm not surprised you've never heard of it."

"You're into all that?"

"Yes. I'm arrogant about my food, too. I expect it to improve my health, not challenge it. Needless to say," he continued, turning to me, "I drive my mother and father nuts when it comes to dinner and eating out."

"I bet."

"What was it like being prom queen last year?" he asked, pivoting quickly back to me.

"Fun." After a pause, I added, "For five minutes."

He nodded. "Of course, like everyone else, I heard all about what happened. I watched how you handled yourself during all that commotion at school. I thought you were pretty cool for a ninth-grader."

"I didn't feel cool. I felt terrified. And I didn't know you were watching me. In fact, I can't recall you saying a word to me, much less looking my way."

He made a few more turns, reached a side street in town, and slowed to turn into it.

"There it is," he said, indicating the restaurant and ignoring what I had said. It was on the corner, with a very simple sign above the entrance in large black Gothic letters. "I recommend the pesto salad, but I always favor the peanut butter, honey, and banana sandwich if you want a sandwich," he said as he pulled up to the curb. "They have great salads and soups, too, and other entrees."

We got out of the car, and he walked ahead to open the restaurant's door for me. Some customers paused in their eating and talking to glance at us. He was right about the music. It was vintage Bob Dylan. The hostess, a woman who looked to be in her fifties, with her graying dark brown hair falling wildly about her neck and shoulders, smiled and approached. She wore an abbreviated apron over a pair of jeans and a dark blue blouse. She didn't wear any makeup or jewelry.

"Hi, Dillon," she said. "Your favorite booth just opened up."

"Serendipity," he said. "Thanks, Maya."

She smiled at me and led us to a booth in the far right corner. The restaurant itself was as simple as the sign above the entrance: about a dozen tables and four booths on the right side. The cork-panel walls had scattered framed prints of nature scenes, ranging from rivers running through valleys to mountain vistas and wildly overgrown fields. There were no portraits or scenes with people or animals. The kitchen was in the rear and open. I saw the chef and two assistants, who were quite busy.

The waiter who approached us also looked well into his fifties. He wore dark blue jeans and a flannel shirt with the sleeves rolled up to his elbows.

"Welcome," he said, handing us the menus. "Cranberry juice?" he asked Dillon.

"Sure. They have interesting fruit teas," he told me.

"I'll have the same, cranberry juice," I said.

"It's pure cranberry," Dillon warned. "Not sugary sweet."

"I'll dip my finger in it," I replied.

His bluish-green eyes brightened more than I had seen. "Two then, please, Breck," he told the waiter.

"Right," he said, and walked off.

"I guess you do come here often. Favorite booth? Maya? Breck?"

"They like to know their customers and for me vice versa. This is no fast-food joint."

I looked at the menu. "Shepherd's pie?"

"It's made with tofu," he said. "Soy."

"I'll have to try it and tell my mother."

"Well, then, maybe I'll have the spinach lasagna. So," he said, folding the menu and sitting back, "how did your mother get to Wyndemere?"

"I think a limousine, but it might have been a bus."

He bit down on his lower lip but kept his smile. "And I thought I was going to be the wise-ass in this couple."

"Are we a couple?"

"Two people are usually referred to as a couple," he said, not skipping a beat or having even a tint of a blush.

The waiter returned with our drinks, and Dillon gave him our order.

"Okay," Dillon said. "No small talk." He reached into his top pocket and took out a folded piece of paper. "I've shown my poetry only to Mr. Feldman, my English teacher," he said. "I haven't even shown them to my parents. Parents are probably the worst critics because they'll always tell you something like 'nice' or 'terrific,' just to get rid of you." He held the paper firmly between his thumb and forefinger and looked like he was still debating whether to give it to me.

"Why did you want me to read it, then? I mean, why me?"

"Somehow I thought you might appreciate it, and I think you'll be honest. You didn't hesitate to give me your opinions last night."

175

"Neither did you."

"Birds of a feather." He handed me the paper. I unfolded it slowly and sat back.

> *There is a suddenness of birds this morning, a blast of premature spring.*
> *Nature is stirred by me and not vice versa.*
> *I rose with expectations because the sunlight was inside me washing away the clouds of sleep, which has always been an escape.*
> *But not today.*
> *Today I want to be, to enjoy every one of my senses.*
> *Today I am like Lazarus.*
> *My mind dares to imagine. I am stirred, touched, reborn.*
> *I will not give what's happening to me a name; I will not reduce it to a word.*
> *Like a newborn baby, I will reach out to see if it is truly there.*
> *And then, only then, will I risk a whisper.*

Even though I had finished reading, I kept my eyes on the paper. I could feel Dillon's intense look, his expectations. I deliberately reread it. I wasn't simply making him wait; I wanted to sound intelligent.

"It's deeply moving," I said. "What makes it effective is how simple it seems, but it's far from that. It's . . . full of surprise. If you really had this feeling, I envy you."

A tiny smile formed around his lips. "Go on. Be a little more specific."

I looked around. "Am I in a spotlight?"

He laughed.

I looked at the poem again. "I especially like the line 'Nature is stirred by me.' "

"Why?"

"The narrator is feeling a unique sense of power, control. I like that. He's not a victim. Usually we react to nature, not nature to us. Rainy days put us in a certain mood, just like sunny days. The narrator feels . . . strong, perhaps hopeful. The poem is full of hope, but there is also a sense of fear. At least to me," I added.

"How can you tell that?"

"He's cautious . . . 'only then will I risk a whisper.' Even a whisper is a risk."

"That's pretty good," he said, reaching to take the paper back. "Would you say you liked it?"

"Very much. I like things that make me think more deeply. What are you going to title it?"

"I don't know, but nothing as trite as 'Resurrection' or something like that." He folded it up and put it back into his pocket.

I looked away. Although I wasn't a poet, his poem could easily be my poem, I thought. I wondered if he knew that and had wanted me to read it because he thought it would find a welcome home in my heart.

"What are you going to do with it?"

"Do with it?"

"Send it to the newspaper or a magazine?"

"No. I'm not ready to do that. Sometimes I write simply to get what's inside me out. Just as you suggested last night."

Breck brought our food.

"Smells delicious," I said.

"Careful, it's hot."

"So really, what made you choose me to read your poem?" I asked, and blew on a forkful of my shepherd's pie.

"Hemingway. Intuition," he said. "We all have a third eye. Not all of us use it, of course, but when I looked at you with my third eye, I thought, there's someone who knows, someone who's been there."

"Been where?"

"The land of disappointment, despair."

"And you've been there?"

"Yes. How's the shepherd's pie?" he asked, obviously to avoid getting into any detail.

"It's different, of course, but it's very tasty. I'll have to tell Mrs. Marlene."

"Mrs. Marlene? Who's that?"

"The cook at Wyndemere. My mother can cook, but it's not her forte."

"Your mother was a singer, right?"

"She tried to be a professional singer many years ago. Ivy tell you that?"

"Yes."

We ate quietly for a while. I was thinking how he was inquiring after me all this time and I had no idea. He was good at keeping that secret. I truly couldn't recall him giving me so much as a passing glance in school, yet I sensed I shouldn't press him on it. Talking with him now, as it was before, was like walking slowly and carefully over thinning ice.

And I was afraid to think it, afraid I was the one being too arrogant, but I had the impression I was in his poem in another way. I was that mysterious feeling he was afraid to assign a word to; I was the risk.

"So how is your brother really?" he asked.

"He's struggling with the gaps."

"I imagine that when he realizes things, when something specific about his accident returns to him, it's going to be quite traumatic. It's almost like a secret that's been kept from him."

"Yes, I suppose it is."

Of course, it was, but I wasn't about to tell Dillon why.

He looked away and then back at me. I could see in the expression on his face that he was battling with himself to tell me something. *We all have secrets,* I thought, *and hate to have them pried out.*

Secrets needed trust, and trust was not easy to find or believe. Apparently, he had found some in me. Another reason he wrote the poem, I thought.

"I woke up one day and found out I wasn't who I was," he said.

"Excuse me?" I smiled, confused.

"My parents are not my parents," he said. "They kept that little detail from me until I was sixteen."

"Oh." I nodded. "You were adopted."

Ivy had never told me that. Did she know? Had he chosen me for his biggest secret?

"Plucked like a piece of fruit," he said.

Now some of this made sense to me. "And you know that my father's identity was kept from me until recently, too," I said.

"Yeah, everyone knows that."

"So that's what you meant when you said I had been in the land of disappointment, too?"

"Yes, but at least you now know lots about your family background. I'm sort of just me," he said, forcing a smile. "I'm like out there in space with no gravity pulling me anywhere." He paused. "You're the first person I ever told that."

"I'm sorry."

"Yeah, well, the worst thing is to say that. You should know. We don't want people feeling sorry for us. And you know what? I bet your brother, when he realizes it all, won't want anyone feeling sorry for him, either. Pity can be like poison, no matter who spoons it to you."

I sat back. He was right, of course, but he had a condescending way about him, which still irked me. Whether he was bitter or not, he had to learn not to behave as if he had all the answers. Would I tell him? Would I care enough to tell him?

Maybe he saw the disapproval in my face. His expression quickly softened. "They have interesting desserts here," he said.

"That shepherd's pie was quite filling. Thank you," I said, my voice sharper.

He signaled for the waiter abruptly. Did he now think I wanted to get away as quickly as I could, that I didn't want to hear about his troubles?

"I enjoyed it," I said. "Thank you for taking me here."

He looked at me oddly. "I'm not that sensitive," he said. "I don't have to be placated."

"I wasn't saying it to make you feel better, Dillon. I was saying it because I believed it. I know you suspect everything and everyone because of how your parents handled the truth about you. I could be the same way, but not everyone lies. And if someone was placating you, he or she obviously cared about you enough to avoid upsetting you. Everything is not so black and white."

My stern response took him aback for a moment, but only a moment. "Everyone lies sometimes, whether it's placating or not."

"Not all the time," I countered. "You can't treat

people like they all do, always. If you believe that, you'll never be anything but alone, whether it's floating in space or walking through our school hallways as if you're walking on Mars."

He took out money for the bill and placed it on the table. "Ready?" he said. He wasn't one to take any criticism. That was for sure, but I could be just as stubborn.

"No."

"What?"

"I changed my mind. I need something to sweeten me. I've been eyeing that apple pie. I'd like to see how it matches up to Mrs. Marlene's."

He looked stunned for a moment and then, finally, with no inhibitions, laughed harder and louder than I thought he could. It made me smile.

"I think I've just met my match," he said.

"I wonder if you would know."

"Okay. Okay." He signaled for the waiter. "Truce," he begged.

Afterward, he was even far more talkative on the way home than he had been on the way to the restaurant. In fact, it was as if a dam had broken. I had the feeling he had been waiting a long time for someone he could speak to without worry and hesitation, someone interested in him enough to stand up to him.

"I'm conflicted about pursuing my genealogy," he said. "On one hand, I suppose it's only natural to want to know what you hatched from. Are you Russian, English, French? Was your father a serial killer? But on the other hand, I think, why would I want to know about people who were willing to give me away? They should be on the bottom of my list, not the top."

"Maybe your mother had no choice."

"You mean, maybe she was fourteen or something? Yeah, I thought about that. She had kept it secret that she was pregnant, and when her parents found out, they made all the arrangements. But don't you see? If I don't find out the truth, I can create all these different stories for myself and discard one to take another when I'm bored with it.

"Maybe my mother was someone famous and had to keep her pregnancy a secret. Maybe she had an affair with a powerful man or a famous politician, and she didn't want to have an abortion even though he volunteered to take care of everything. Someday I could walk into an office and tell my father, 'I'm here. I'm the baby you helped give away.' There's a look I'd love to see in person, huh? Was I there to blackmail him? Just make him feel terrible? Get a job? Find my mother? It's a novel. What do you think? Which makes me more interesting, being the lonely adopted guy or the guy who pursues his parentage and stumbles on one of these stories?"

I thought about my own situation, the years I had spent not knowing who my father was. And of course, I thought about now, about getting the knowledge that would end my relationship with Ryder before it had a chance to develop into anything.

"Maybe you're better off being your own person, completely," I said. It came out far more cynically than I had intended.

I knew that took him by surprise. Of course, he had no knowledge of what Ryder and I were becoming before my father's and my mother's confessions. All people knew was that we had gone boating when we shouldn't have. No one knew what really had gone on at Wyndemere, no one but our parents and Mr. Stark and Mrs. Marlene.

He looked at me curiously.

"What?"

"Funny to hear you say that now. Look at what you're inheriting."

"Yes," I said, and under my breath added, "look at what I'm inheriting."

I left that hanging. He glanced at me but didn't pursue it. How well he knew me already, I thought.

When we pulled up to Wyndemere, I saw Dr. Seymour's car. My father's limousine was there as well.

"My brother's doctor is here, and so is my father."

"Oh. I hope nothing bad is happening."

He sat back, thought a moment, and then

reached into his pocket and took out his poem.

"I'd like you to have it," he said.

"Really, but . . ."

"I wouldn't have written it if I hadn't spent time with you. You're the muse."

I took it. "Thank you."

"Maybe you'll come up with a title for it."

I nodded. Then he got out and came around to open my car door. Instinctively, I looked up at my bedroom window, but Ryder wasn't there. Of course, I was worried about him, but I was also happy he wasn't watching us.

"Thank you for a lovely time," I said.

"Would you like to go to another movie with me? There's something playing at the art theater I think you'd enjoy. Friday night?" he blurted as if he couldn't say it any other way.

"Yes," I said, this time without a moment's hesitation.

His whole demeanor changed, with a warmer, brighter smile. He walked me to the door.

"See you in school," I said.

"Yes. 'Bye," he added, then started away, stopped, and rushed back to kiss me before I had a chance to prepare for it. He hurried to his car.

It gave new meaning to "stole a kiss," I thought, smiled to myself, and entered Wyndemere, feeling as if I had just stepped off a wild merry-go-round.

But I was about to get on another.

8

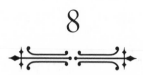

The house was so quiet that my footsteps echoed from the foyer to the top of the stairway. I heard a door close above and saw my mother starting down the steps, her left hand sliding along the mahogany banister. She walked with her head bowed, something she often did when she was whispering a frantic prayer.

"Mummy?"

She paused when she saw me. "Oh, Fern. I'm glad you're home." She had one of her lace handkerchiefs clutched in her right hand and quickly dabbed under both eyes.

"What's wrong?" I asked quickly. I could feel the static in the air.

She continued to descend. "Ryder had a setback of sorts," she said, approaching me, her eyes red with worry. "Dr. Seymour and Dr. Davenport are still with him."

"What? What happened? What's a setback mean?"

She stood there, looking like she was struggling to find the right words. Whatever had happened had clearly overwhelmed her, and it took a great deal to overwhelm my mother.

"I'm not sure how to describe it, really. We'll have to wait for Dr. Seymour's diagnosis. Ryder had something of a tantrum is the best way I can put it."

"Tantrum?"

She nodded toward the living room, and I followed her. She sat on the settee and lowered her head to take a deep breath. I quickly sat across from her, anxious.

"What do you mean by 'tantrum,' Mummy?"

"He tore up his room, smashed some things, broke a mirror, and threw some of his clothes about, among other things. Mrs. Marlene and I were reviewing what we needed from the supermarket when we heard this horrible commotion coming from above. Fortunately, Mr. Stark was repairing a light fixture in Dr. Davenport's office and joined us. He was able to subdue Ryder, and I called Dr. Davenport, who called Dr. Seymour. He rushed over and gave him an injection of something to calm him. He's dozing now on the settee in his room. His bed is . . . wrecked."

"Wrecked?"

She shook her head and took a deep breath. "You'd think a tornado had gone through the room. They're discussing whether he should be brought back to the clinic."

"Oh, no." Tears rushed into my eyes from every direction. "What happened to him? He was doing so well, looking healthy, exercising with his father, enjoying his things, and eating well, too. You even said he was making progress with his memory, Mummy."

"I don't know, Fern. You have to remember that losing your memory, short-term or not, is very traumatic for anyone, especially for someone as young as Ryder. I know he's terribly frustrated. Sometimes when he's sitting with me in the living room while you're at school, I see the struggling going on in his face, in his eyes. From time to time, he recalls certain things, yes, but it's difficult for him, because he remembers only this and that. It's not a complete memory, complete recognition."

"I know." Of course, I had seen that, too.

"Dr. Seymour said on more than one occasion that his recalling a detail here and there is a good thing, even though not recalling it all leaves him angry and exasperated. Frankly, I don't see how that's true. To me, it's tantalizingly cruel, but I'm no psychiatrist. All I know is when I remember little details in my life, usually that leads to something bigger, something significant, whether happy or unhappy. For Ryder, it's like following a hallway that runs into a wall. All you can do is turn around and follow the same path back so you can start again. Torture, I'm sure."

I stared at the floor. I knew in my heart that whenever Ryder saw me, he was battling with his memory of us. His eyes were bursting with the torment of the struggle, and it was on the tip of my tongue to end it by saying, *Yes, I'm your half sister, but when we didn't know that, we were becoming lovers.*

Right now, I was feeling terrible about feeling so good a few moments ago outside the front door of Wyndemere. It was the same way I felt on Christmas and every time we all laughed and Ryder looked lost. He might force a smile, mimicking the rest of us, but I knew he was crying on the inside and suffering more because he didn't know why. He didn't even know what had happened to him, exactly. Did he actually ask? Did they say you had to remember it all yourself? What a giant tease.

"Dr. Seymour says he's struggling not only to remember facts but to have emotional reactions to things as well as people. He still stares at the trophies he won, stares as if they were won by someone else. He's very unsure of himself, how he should behave, what he should dislike and like and . . ." She paused, deciding whether to go on.

"And what, Mummy?"

"Ryder said an odd thing this morning."

"Why was it odd?" I held my breath. Did he admit to having deeper feelings toward me?

"He was eating some peach jam on toast, when he stopped chewing and looked at me and said, 'I have the feeling I never liked peach jam.' I assured him he had and I wouldn't give him anything he didn't like, but he was still skeptical." She leaned forward. "And to tell you the truth, I wasn't sure he had said it because he truly wondered or if he had said it to shock me. Ryder could be quite impish, even as a child."

She paused, and from the way she was looking at me, I could tell that she had something to add, something I might find personally unpleasant. I could read my mother's face as well as she could read mine.

"What is it, Mummy? There's more."

"Your father is going to ask you as well, Fern, so please be forthcoming."

"Ask me what?"

She sat up straight, firm, what I playfully called "English firm." "Have you . . . talked to Ryder about your little love affair?"

My face lit hot like I had just stepped into a sauna. "I wouldn't call it a little love affair, Mummy. It didn't go that far. We were just getting to know each other in deeper ways."

"Whatever, Fern. This isn't the time to play semantics. Did you talk about it recently with him, even suggest it?"

"No, not a word. If you accumulate all the times he and I have been together, I've barely spent a full hour alone with him since his return."

"It's not a matter of how long you have spent

with him; it's what was said when you were. And I wasn't hovering over either of you night and day."

"It doesn't matter. It wasn't said!"

There was never this much distrust between us when we lived in the help's quarters at the rear of the mansion, I thought. Crossing over to the main house was like losing all your innocence and all the faith you had. This was a different world within the same mansion.

Despite my denial and how vehemently I had said it, my mother still looked quite troubled. A thought both exciting and frightening burst like a Fourth of July rocket in my mind. There was more. He wasn't only talking to her about peach jam or anything else that was minor.

"Has he said something about it to you, something you had to ignore, Mummy?"

Her hesitation widened her eyes. "No, not in so many words, but I was mother enough to that boy to know what's turning inside him, even in the condition he's currently enduring."

My brain felt like it was twirling like a top. Was he finally understanding his feelings for me? Was the confusion now disturbing, resulting from my apparent indifference? Was that the reason for his tantrum? Should I have disobeyed my parents and spoken to him about it?

I was about to tell her that I had seen Ryder in my room just before Dillon and I had left for lunch, but before I could, we heard Samantha scream as she burst into the house.

"I'm home!"

My mother rose quickly and went to the doorway.

"Stop your bloody yelling and get in here," she ordered.

Practically on tiptoes, Samantha entered the living room. She recognized that my mother rarely took as stern a tone with her. It was a reluctance on my mother's part that always annoyed me. For as long as I could remember, she leaned more toward feeling sorry for Samantha than chastising her properly. Samantha was not one to appreciate the way my mother sympathized with her. She was one to exploit that kindness.

"I didn't do anything," she said before either my mother or I could speak. Of course, that immediately stirred my suspicions.

Samantha had gone to Raegan Kelly's house for the day, and I knew that Raegan, as hard as it was to believe, was even more spoiled than Samantha. She was one of the three girls who had gotten the hairdo Samantha talked our father into letting her get. Raegan lived in a fifty-five-hundred-square-foot Victorian-style house that was quite historical. Of course, her parents had restored and upgraded it. Her father owned and operated one of the biggest plumbing-supply companies in the county. He drove a Bentley.

Raegan's mother, heading many charities, had been Bea Davenport's closest friend. They gave each other "snob transfusions." It was how Samantha became so friendly with Raegan, whom posh Bea had thought was one of the few to be worthy of Samantha's time.

Some of my classmates, mostly the girls, loved to tell me about Raegan Kelly's clique, of which Samantha was a member. A story always began with "Since she's your half sister . . ." I could see the glee in the informant's face and the faces of those around us listening. Now that I was Samantha's half sister, I had to share in her sins and indiscretions. Supposedly, Raegan's little house parties usually involved some pot, alcohol, and quite a bit of sexual talk. I had warned Samantha about what I heard, and of course, she denied it. Right now, she was glaring at me, suspecting I had told my mother something.

"This has nothing to do with you, Samantha," my mother said. "Unless you have something to tell us about things you've said to Ryder that might have upset him."

"I didn't say anything to him," she said reflexively. She looked at me and then at my mother. "About what? What do you mean, 'upset him'?"

"Ryder had a bad episode. Your father and Dr. Seymour are still with him discussing whether he needs to be in the clinic again. You were told what things you should not speak about. Did you talk about any of those things?"

"No," she said. "Maybe Fern did," she quickly added.

"No one is blaming anyone right now," my mother said, the frustration draining color from her face. "All right. Go up to your room. If you have any schoolwork left that you were supposed to do, be sure to do it. We'll have dinner at the usual time."

Samantha still looked at me with suspicion, crossed her arms over her chest, and pressed her lips together. Defiance was the flag under which she marched. Why wouldn't she hoist it now when she thought she had an advantage?

"What's 'a bad episode' mean?" she demanded. "If Fern knows, I should know."

"Let's wait for your father and Dr. Seymour to explain it all," my mother said.

Samantha turned her glare on me like a policeman's flashlight. "You told her, didn't you?" she said.

My mother's eyelids narrowed as the first signs of anger began to show themselves. Samantha's growing insolence and cheekiness had really begun to sprout during the past few weeks and months. She was ready to challenge any order and was even taking less care with her room and her things, practically for spite. I was confident my mother had discussed this with my father and with his permission was now ready to be firmer about it.

"Told me about what?" my mother asked. She realized Samantha was concerned about something completely different.

"Nothing," Samantha said, realizing I might not have told my mother about her spying on Ryder and what she had seen after all. She had almost trapped herself.

"Then do what I say!" my mother screamed at her, and took a step toward her. To be truthful, I had never seen her as irate as this. Whatever calmness she possessed had been strained like a rubber band and broken.

Samantha's eyes nearly popped. The shock took all the steam of disobedience out of her. Tears came to her eyes. She looked like she couldn't swallow. No one but me ever spoke to her as hard and directly as my mother was now, not even her own mother.

"I'm going to tell my father!" she cried, turned, and ran out and up the stairs.

My mother took a deep breath. Then she muttered something that shocked me to the bone. "I do wish that man would find another wife who can be a full-time mother to that child. It's exhausting."

I knew what many people were thinking "under their breath," as my mother would say. After the truth was revealed about who my father was, everyone assumed my mother was his mistress. I thought no one who worked here believed that, despite seeing her at the dinner table with us, and none of them spread stories. They had too much respect for her. Whatever social event my father attended after Bea had gone, mostly out of obligation to his position at the hospital, he attended alone. He had not taken my mother out to a restaurant, even with either Samantha or me. He didn't even go shopping with her to help buy us things we needed like many fathers and husbands did.

However, I'd be the first to admit that it was an especially awkward situation at Wyndemere, especially for anyone who visited. There was my mother in her established role as house manager, seeing to this or that but never socializing alongside my father. When he had a dinner guest, she usually didn't sit at the table, either.

Although they were quite polite to each other and he was continually thanking my mother for things, mainly anything to do with Samantha or Ryder, I had never seen them show any sort of loving affection toward each other. I had never seen him kiss her, even on the cheek and even on her birthday. If anything, he moved around her like there was an invisible circle that could not be penetrated. She supervised the care and maintenance of his bedroom and his office but never spent any significant time alone with him in either.

Watching the two of them behave like this, I slipped back into thinking I was truly someone who had just happened miraculously. No sex involved. She would never go into any detail about how it really had happened, how her sympathy and comfort had turned into something more intense, something passionate and sexual. There was only this mysterious, almost supernatural possession my father had experienced whenever he returned to Wyndemere after his wife's death. Somehow he had projected her onto my mother, and when he couldn't stand the loneliness and sorrow any longer, he rose from his bed like a sleepwalker and went to her bed. If she had resisted, I wouldn't be here.

Sometimes I wished she had.

"Go on and change if you want, or do the schoolwork you have left to do, Fern. I'll let you know what Dr. Seymour and Dr. Davenport decide to do."

Before I could respond, she left the room. I sat for a few moments, wondering if I should have told her more, and then rose and went upstairs, looking toward Ryder's room. The door was closed. I went to my room and changed into a dark gray sweat suit. I had some reading to finish and a report to do, but concentrating on anything was almost impossible. Every time I heard a sound, even if it was just a loud creak, I rose and went to my door to listen.

Finally, nearly an hour later, I did hear distinct footsteps and stepped out of my room. I saw a nurse I had never seen before come up the stairs. She was short and stout, with gray hair that ballooned in puffs from under her cap. She went directly to Ryder's room. Moments later, Dr. Seymour and my father stepped out and stood out in the hallway talking. My father paused when he saw me but then continued talking to Dr. Seymour. Minutes later, the nurse appeared, with Ryder holding her arm and looking dazed. I hadn't heard my mother come up earlier and go to Ryder's room, but she followed with a small suitcase. The nurse and Dr. Seymour carefully led Ryder down the stairs, my mother right behind them. I felt my throat tighten with an ache that built up quickly in my chest. My father didn't speak to me or even look my way again. He followed everyone downstairs. A small sob felt like a bubble stuck in my throat.

Samantha emerged from her room and looked my way. "What's happening now?" she asked.

I didn't answer. I returned to my room and rushed to the window that looked out onto the front. Parker was waiting at the limo with the rear door open. He took the suitcase from my mother, and then the nurse helped Ryder into the rear of the limo and followed. Dr. Seymour and my father talked for a few moments, and then

Dr. Seymour got into his vehicle. My father and my mother reentered the house. I watched the limousine drive off slowly and disappear down the road.

I felt sick to my stomach. Surely, there was something more I could have done. What did this mean? Was Ryder going to be institutionalized? Would he never come home again? Would I be able to visit him?

I was in such deep thought that I didn't hear my phone ring before I saw the buttons light up. It was Ivy.

"I've been sitting on pins and needles. When you didn't call for so long, I thought you might hate me now or something."

"It's not that, Ivy. My brother has had a bad episode and was just taken back to the clinic. I don't feel like talking to anyone right now, especially about a lunch date," I said, emphasizing "date."

"Oh. So sorry. Anything I can do?"

"If I can't, how could you?" I snapped back, which I immediately recognized as unnecessary and mean. "I'm sorry. I'll call you when I get my wits."

"Okay," she said. "I'm here for you."

"Thanks."

I hung up and sprawled back on my bed, staring up at the ceiling. I was so deep in thought that I didn't hear my father enter my room. Suddenly, I realized that he was standing there staring at me. I sat up quickly.

"What's happening to Ryder?"

"Dr. Seymour is afraid he might be suicidal," he said without hesitation.

I knew my father's reputation as a doctor. Once he had made his diagnosis, he never used euphemisms or softened the blow just to make someone's relatives feel better or hopeful. His concentration was solely focused on his patient. Relatives and friends were tolerated but not his high priority. He was the same way now, even though his own son was the patient and I was his family.

"Oh," I said. My face was trembling in an earthquake of sorrow.

He brought his right hand up and showed me the picture of Ryder and myself in the silver frame. "Why did you give him this after I had asked you not to stress what went on between the two of you?" he asked. When my father was angry, his consonants were sharp and his vowels were precise, but other than the cold, steely look in his eyes, there was no other warning or indication. "Guilt was absolutely the last thing we wanted him to feel right now."

"I didn't give that to him," I said.

"Where did it come from?"

"That was a picture Mr. Stark took of us just before we went to see you in your office to show you how your first wife's dress was tailored to fit me. He gave the picture to me before we moved into the main house. It was a memory, a good memory at the time. He was just doing something to cheer me up after the lake tragedy."

"It was found under Ryder's bed," my father said.

"I had it hidden here. I swear. It was in a drawer and never put on display. Ask my mother. Ask anyone except Samantha."

He stared at me, deciding whether to believe me. "Why not Samantha?"

"I think Samantha might have found it and given it to him," I said.

His forehead creased. "Samantha? Why?"

"She can be spiteful." I took a deep breath. "She told me he had it."

"She did?" He thought a moment and then pounced. "Why didn't you come right to me to tell me? It was very important I knew something like that. It mattered."

I looked away. This was horrible. I felt like I was betraying Ryder even more. Damn Samantha. "I was embarrassed," I said. "Embarrassed by what she told me. She was spying on him."

"Spying?"

"It amused her, I guess. She'd go to his door and open it a little so she could watch him in his room."

"What's that have to do with this picture?"

201

I looked up at the ceiling. What was my father going to think of me now?

"Fern?"

Okay, I thought. If his MO was to speak directly and frankly, that was what he would get from me.

"He was naked," I said quickly. "He had the picture in one hand and, according to Samantha, he was doing something sexual with the other. Samantha said she saw it and came running to tell me. I warned her not to tell anyone, especially any of her friends."

He stared dumbfounded and then shook his head. "I should have been told," he said. "I'm very disappointed in you. Did you tell your mother?"

"No."

"Why not? Why didn't you at least tell your mother? You knew how we were all watching him closely, looking for signs of improvement or setback."

He waited, but I didn't answer. I had no other answer except a deep hope in my heart that Ryder was realizing his feelings for me. I had kept it to myself because I didn't want that to end. How could I confess such a thing to my father now?

Instead, I started to cry. He looked at the picture and then tossed it onto my bed before he turned and walked out.

I curled up and sobbed. I felt as if everything inside me, especially my heart, had been turned inside out. I ached so. Probably more as an escape than anything, I fell asleep. When I awoke, it was very late in the afternoon. These days, the sun went down a little after five. My room was dark. I reached over and turned on the lamp on my side table. The light revealed my mother sitting in the Churchill nailhead leather chair. She was asleep. For a moment, I didn't move. She looked like she had aged decades.

"Mummy?" I said in a little over a whisper. "Mummy?"

She opened her eyes and just stared at me a moment as if she was trying to remember who I was. Then she sat up, pressing her lips together. "Your father told me everything," she said. "I couldn't explain why you hadn't told me."

"I'm sorry," I said. "I had heard it all from Samantha, so I didn't know whether to believe it or not."

She didn't change expression. "That's not a good reason, Fern, but even if you believed that, you still should have told me, at least about the picture. Dr. Davenport had words with Mr. Stark, who now feels terrible about giving it to you."

I felt like I couldn't breathe. Who was left to hurt in this house? "That's not fair. He didn't fire him or something, did he?"

"No, but Mr. Stark feels terrible. It's the first time he and Dr. Davenport have had bad words between them, as far as I know."

"He shouldn't have been angry at him," I insisted. "I'll tell him so and tell him he should apologize to Mr. Stark."

"You'll do nothing of the kind, Fern Corey. I didn't bring you up to be disrespectful."

"It's not disrespectful to stand up for people who love you and whom you love," I said forcefully. Defiant I was, and defiant I would be.

She took a deep breath and shook her head. "When he was angry at me, my father used to wish I would have a daughter just like me tormenting me like I was tormenting him. Looks like he's gotten what he wanted."

"I'm not deliberately trying to torment you." I looked away.

"I know, but I want you to tell me the truth, Fern. Did you give Ryder that picture?"

"No, and I never showed it to him after the accident. I told Dr. Davenport the truth. It was buried in my bottom drawer. I'm sure Samantha found it and gave it to Ryder."

"For what purpose?"

"She only wants to make trouble. She's a vicious, spiteful little Bea, and the next time I see her—"

"Stop," my mother said, standing. "There's enough thunder and lightning in this house. We'll have to let time pass. Don't start fighting with Samantha. If she did it, it will come out. Rot has a way of rising to the surface. Mind yourself.

We're having dinner in an hour. The doctor has gone to the clinic to see about Ryder." She started to turn and stopped. "Is there anything else, Fern? Anything more to tell me?"

"Yes." I would keep nothing locked inside myself, not now.

She brought both her hands to the base of her throat in anticipation. "What?"

"When I got into Dillon's car to go to lunch, we saw Ryder in my room looking down at us."

"Here? Your room?"

"Yes. I never saw him in my room before, and he never came in here while I was here. As far as I know, he's never come into my room when I was in school or downstairs."

She thought a moment and then nodded. "Okay. Dinner in an hour."

"I'm not very hungry."

"Dinner in an hour," she repeated with emphasis. "We're all quite upset downstairs. Mrs. Marlene has prepared her special meat loaf. My mother always told me, 'Good food gives you strength to deal with sorrow.' You always raved about Mrs. Marlene's meat loaf. She cried the whole time she was preparing it. Start considering everyone else's feelings."

I watched her leave and then fell back against my pillow and looked up at the ceiling. The lamplight created creepy, crawly shadows that seemed to flow up from the walls. I thought they would rain down over me, burying me with the darkness I felt in my heart.

I didn't know why my parents were so surprised about my not telling them what Samantha had described. This was the house of secrets. Keeping your own was practically a requirement for living here. Who didn't have them? My parents certainly couldn't claim not to have any. Their past together, regardless of how much they had revealed, mostly remained sealed in both their minds and hearts. The only witnesses were the walls. When most people thought of haunted houses, they thought of ghosts, but the whispers in the corners of Wyndemere came from the nightmares that escaped from its inhabitants whenever they put their heads on a pillow and closed their eyes.

The same, I guessed, would be true for me. It was only a matter of time. The walls in my room were waiting to be fed, and I was sure I had the nightmares coming.

I rose to take a shower and get dressed for dinner. I wondered if my father would return in time and if he would say anything more to me. I had never seen him so angry. Less than a year ago, I would be trembling so inside that I couldn't dare look at his face, but I was my mother's daughter. Defiance when it came to doing and saying what I thought was right was stronger than fear. When I calmed, however, I realized that the person I should be worrying most about wasn't myself; it was Ryder. My mother was right. I had to consider other people's feelings.

After I dressed, and brushed back my hair and pinned it, I started out, pausing for a moment at the closed door of Ryder's room. What had he done in there? How bad was his tantrum? Since there was no one around, I opened the door and looked. No one yet had gone back in here for sure, I thought.

His computer and computer monitor were on the floor, the screen shattered. His desk chair had been beaten into pieces, the legs torn off. Everything on top of his dresser had been shoved off, with anything breakable in pieces. Something had been thrown against one of his windows, and although it hadn't entirely broken, there were large cracks crisscrossing it. His bed linen had been torn off, and he had stabbed one of his pillows with something, probably scissors, so that its filling was scattered about. He had gone into his closet, too, and torn most of his clothes off hangers. I saw a jacket hanging, but he had stabbed it as well so that there were large rips on one side. The sitting area was untouched. I imagined Mr. Stark had gotten up here before Ryder could start on that.

The sight sickened me. There was no doubt. Anyone who had done all this needed intense professional care, most likely around the clock.

Considering him potentially suicidal was no stretch of the imagination.

I closed the door softly and started down the stairs, pausing when I heard a door close in the hallway above. Samantha appeared. She looked like she had been crying.

"You told on me," she said. "I don't care what my father says. You're not my sister, not even my half sister, and you'll never be."

"From your mouth to God's ears," I replied. It was one of Mr. Stark's favorite expressions.

"What?"

"I hope you're right, Samantha. I hope they finally discover that you were hatched from some egg left by the devil at the front door and we're really not even half related."

"Ha, ha," she said, but she looked a little shaken. She was afraid to get too close to me on the stairway.

"You gave Ryder that picture. You came into my room, searched my things, and found it. Someday, when he is well again, he'll tell, and then what will you say?"

As if she had been worried about that exact thing and had been working on a defense for weeks, she smiled and said, "I didn't do it, but if my father believes you, I'll just say Ryder's only protecting you because you made him promise he would. Then he'll believe me instead."

Bea Davenport never left this house, I thought.

All her cruel, self-centered, and arrogant ways simply shifted from her to her daughter. It was like a disease passed down genetically.

I'd probably start locking my door at night.

I said nothing else. Extracting any remorse out of Samantha was like trying to squeeze juice out of a peach pit. I continued down the stairs, and when I was close to the bottom, she started to descend, accompanied by the deepest, darkest shadows of Wyndemere.

They had found a real friend.

9

Dr. Davenport didn't return in time for dinner. He didn't call to say he was having dinner with Dr. Seymour until we were almost finished. I was twisted with contradictory emotions, relieved that I wouldn't have to face him so soon but unhappy that I would learn nothing new about Ryder. In fact, I realized that he might never trust me again with any information concerning Ryder. I had little appetite, but I ate because my mother was watching me and Mrs. Marlene was coming in and out to be sure we were all enjoying her food.

Samantha certainly was. She behaved as if nothing terrible had occurred. She was ravenous, looking forward to dessert, Mrs. Marlene's home-made pecan pie. This was how I remembered her mother. If something unpleasant had happened, especially something caused by her, she would ignore it. It was as if she thought she could erase anything terrible she had done with a simple wave of her hand. It didn't exist; it never existed. The world would be shaped the way she saw it, or it wouldn't be shaped at all.

Maybe she never had an iota of conscience, only a stack of disappointments to be tossed into a garbage bin. When I looked at Samantha now, I saw the spitting image of Bea and then thought that was why Bea had given her up so easily. She didn't want to be attached to anyone as selfish as she was. There wasn't enough room in her world for two of her.

As soon as she had finished eating, Samantha practically flew out of her seat and the dining room. Besides avoiding helping clear the table, she was eager to get up to her room and her phone to call her friends and suck up as much sympathy as she could.

"You can go up to do whatever you have left for school, Fern," my mother said.

She sounded so tired and defeated. There was never any doubt in my mind that she felt as close to Ryder as his natural mother would. The effect the surrogacy had on her went deep into her very soul. What had happened to him today tore her apart inside, and what she saw as my small betrayals only compounded her grief.

"I'm sorry, Mummy. I really didn't mean to keep secrets."

She nodded. "We'll get through it all," she said.

She was digging way down in her store of hope and optimism to come up with some cheerful words. When I thought about what I knew about her life, her struggles, I realized this little woman had more grit in her than ten men. If I could be only half as strong, I'd be fine, I thought.

I didn't have much left to do for school. Organizing and looking forward to returning didn't excite me or depress me. I was strangely indifferent to the future. I finished up what I had, but before I prepared for bed, my phone rang. It was Dillon.

"Hey," he said. "Ivy told me about your troubles at home. I'm sorry."

"It was horrible," I said. I really still knew little about Dillon, but having someone to whom I could pour out my sorrow was quite welcomed.

"Can you talk about it? Sometimes that helps, not that I'm any sort of expert on other people's problems. I'm certainly no expert on my own, and I've got enough for two of me, maybe three."

Whether he knew the right things to say or not, he did. I actually smiled at his confession. Someone else who didn't know him would think little of it.

"I don't know any of the medical, technical terms. My mother called it a tantrum. He destroyed much in his room, went wild. He had to be taken back to the clinic."

Dillon was silent a moment. Then he said, "You have no idea why?"

"No."

"People who get very angry or frustrated often are self-destructive," he said. "At times, I've thrown something against the wall and then regretted it. I did that once with my cell

phone. Maybe because I didn't use it much,"
he added. "My parents wanted me to have one
for emergencies. I felt like some elderly person
being given one of those devices to press if they
fall down or something."

I laughed through my tears.

"He must be all twisted up and frustrated," he
added. "They'll work him out of it."

"Thanks."

"Maybe we could have lunch together in
school. Won't be as good as what we had at the
restaurant, but . . ."

"Sure," I said.

"Call me anytime you want. That way, I won't
throw my phone against the wall again." He gave
me his cell-phone number.

After we ended the conversation, I fell into that
emotional dilemma again. I enjoyed talking to
Dillon, enjoyed being with him earlier, but then
there was that guilt accompanying my feelings.
With every smile, every laugh, everything that
drew me closer to him, I felt myself drifting
away from Ryder, deserting him just when he
needed me the most. But how could I help him
now? What could I do? And from my father's
perspective, I was literally dangerous. At least,
that was the way he had caused me to feel.

In my wild imaginings, my father was growling
like an attack dog, just waiting for me to ask
something, say something, anything that proved

my feelings for Ryder were as romantic as ever. Right now, he was convinced that when I should have been discouraging any resurgence of those sorts of feelings in him for me, I was doing the exact opposite. Why couldn't he see it? Most of the time, especially when he was present, I acted as if I didn't care about Ryder's memory issues. The least my father should have seen and believed was that it wasn't on my mind continually. Ironically, the one thing that might seal that for him was my developing a relationship with Dillon.

Now I wondered if that was more my motivation than anything. What if Dillon realized it, somehow understood what had occurred between Ryder and me just before the boat accident in the storm? What if one day, he looked at me and said, *You're only with me to avoid being with your brother?* How would I respond? Would he believe me, believe anything I said? Even knowing him for so short a time, I was confident such a suspicion would drive him away forever.

But could that accusation be true? If I kissed him, would I be kissing him to service the memory of a kiss between Ryder and myself? Would he sense that and say, *You seem so distant, even when we kiss, Fern?* That was what other boys accused me of being, indifferent and distant, wasn't it?

Maybe I needed a therapist as much as Ryder

did. Why didn't my father and my mother realize that learning that the boy I had developed a crush on was my half brother would have a traumatic effect on me, so traumatic that it could change my life? I didn't think I was overstating it. I did feel like it had changed my life.

Before I turned off my lights and got into bed, I heard voices and then footsteps on the stairs. I had left my door slightly open just for that purpose. I went to it and peered out. My father had come up. I watched him pause outside Ryder's bedroom door. Then he opened it and stood there contemplating the mess. I wanted to run to him, to embrace him, to comfort him and reassure him that I had nothing to do with this, but I couldn't move. My mother appeared, and he quickly closed the door.

"I'll see to it tomorrow," she said, nodding at Ryder's room.

"No," he said. "Don't touch it."

"Are you sure?"

"Yes."

"But what if he's released in the near future, Harrison?" she asked. It was so rare to hear her refer to him by his given name.

I held my breath. They were close and looking at each other in a way I had never seen.

"He won't be back in the near future," he said.

She shook her head and whispered something I could not hear. Even a man as controlled and professional as my father, the cardiac specialist who had to keep his emotions firmly in hand, could not keep them chained forever to some deep, dark place inside himself. He made one small gesture, one step toward her, but that was enough. She embraced him. He raised his arms, held them frozen like that for a moment, and then embraced her.

Without any further words between them, they parted and went to their respective bedrooms. When they closed their doors, I closed mine.

How could one house, even one as large as Wyndemere, contain so much sorrow? Maybe it should be burned to the ground in a fire like a funeral pyre so that every dark shadow would be cremated and go up in smoke, to be washed away in the winds coming in over the lake.

Maybe then and only then would we all be free.

He won't be back in the near future?

What did that mean? How long would he remain at the clinic? I went to sleep thinking of little else. In the morning at breakfast, all my mother would tell me was that Ryder was in treatment. Dr. Davenport had left very early. Samantha was her usual energetic self, babbling about her friends whose descriptions of their Christmas gifts fell far short of hers. She would parade her new purse, wear her new shoes, exhibit her new cell phone, and flash her new watch.

"I'll have to move through a sea of jealousy,"

she announced without a hint of humility or gratitude.

"Yes, like Moses," I said. "You'll part the sea, and then your friends following you will all be drowned."

Mrs. Marlene practically bellowed. My mother smiled. Samantha looked shocked and even a little frightened, even though she didn't understand or maybe because she didn't understand.

"She's not funny!" she cried. "I wish my mother would come back. Then you'd all see."

No one responded. My mother gave me a warning look. I finished my breakfast in silence. What had become of my new family? I thought. My half brother was in therapy, my father was so disappointed in me that he might not speak to me much ever again, and my half sister was as distasteful as any spoiled teenager possibly could be and especially resentful of me.

I looked toward the rear of the house, toward the help's quarters and the simple yet quiet and happy world in which I had spent most of my youth. What would my mother say if I packed up my things and returned to it? I'd even keep to entering Wyndemere only through the rear door. The very idea brought a smile to my face. My mother saw it and tilted her head in confusion. I shook the feeling off quickly. *Say nothing. Add nothing to her troubles now,* I told myself.

When we stepped out of the house to go to the

limo, with Parker standing by the open rear door, Samantha charged ahead of me and practically dove into it. She was that anxious to get to school to parade herself and her gifts. Parker and I looked at each other, both expressing our sorrow about Ryder without saying a word. I got in slowly. As soon as Parker closed the door, Samantha turned to me.

"Are you going to be mean to me every day now?" she asked, all sorts of threats building behind her words.

"Truthfully, I'm not going to give you a thought," I said, "until you confess to what you have done."

"I didn't do anything," she said, folded her arms, and looked out the window all the way to school.

Parker gazed at me in the rearview mirror. I saw the wry smile on his face. Considering all the times he had driven Bea Davenport and had overheard her conversations, I was sure he was prepared for any déjà vu. I wasn't. Instead, I sat back and prepared for Dillon Evans.

I was looking forward to seeing him as soon as I entered the building, but he wasn't in the lobby waiting to walk me to my homeroom. Disappointment had sunk whatever little optimism I had this morning. He was simply too unpredictable. How could I invest my feelings in someone like that? Ivy was there, as she often was, and hurried to my side.

"How are you? I was hoping you'd call me last night. I was so worried for you."

"I went to sleep early," I said. "It was all emotionally exhausting."

"I'm sorry. Did you learn anything more about him?"

"Just that he won't be coming back very soon," I said as we walked to our hallway lockers. I kept looking for Dillon. Would it seem selfish of me if I asked after him? I didn't have to. She saw the way I was looking about.

"Dillon usually comes to school just in time," she said. "He compares it to going to the dentist." She looked around, too. "I was wondering if he would be different now. You know, you're the only one in school he's ever taken anywhere. I haven't told anyone," she quickly added. "So can you tell me now? How was your lunch date?"

"It was the highlight of my day," I said. I said it as merely a statement of fact.

"Really? That's exciting. I hope you'll tell me all about it."

I looked at her. Was this going to be one of those friendships in which one girl lived vicariously through the experiences of the other?

"You told him about my brother last night."

"Oh, I hope you're not upset about that. I thought he should know, just in case he was expecting you to call him. He's really very sensitive, almost paranoid, you know."

219

"Really?"

"He's always complaining about how other guys look at him in school, even some of his teachers. That's why he compares going to school with going to a dentist."

"Great. That's all I need right now, another person with a psychological issue."

We both paused when we had turned the corner to start toward our homeroom. There was Dillon by the door, leaning against the wall as if he was on some street corner. He was looking down but seemed to sense I was nearing. He stood up as I approached him.

"Hey," he said. "I wanted to give you this right away." He handed me an envelope.

"What's in it?"

"I thought of an appropriate title for my poem and printed it out in a nice script font."

Ivy stood beside me as I opened the envelope and took out the paper. The poem was titled "Fern's Hope."

"No one will understand," I said.

"The one person I care about understanding it understands," he said. "See you later." He sauntered off.

"Can I read that?" Ivy asked immediately.

"I'll have to ask him first," I said.

She grimaced. "I'm the one who brought you two together," she moaned.

"Somehow I think we might have met

eventually anyway, but thanks. It's his personal thing. Let me ask him. I'm sure he'll say yes."

For now, that was enough to wipe the disappointment off her face, but I would surely have to share a lot more with her if I lived up to her expectations. At the moment, I didn't feel like sharing anything with anyone, even the air we were breathing. I put the envelope into my book bag and entered our homeroom. One of the announcements for the day involved auditions for the school play starting tomorrow. I wasn't sure I was up to it now.

Later, however, when Dillon and I met to sit together at lunch, it was the first thing he brought up for discussion. Ivy sat with us.

"Oh, don't blow off the play," he said. "If anything, you need to do this more, Fern. You've got to get your mind off the problems at home. Actually, that was why I went out for *Our Town* last year."

"He's right," Ivy said.

I glanced at her and then turned back to Dillon. "You're assuming I'll get the part," I said.

"I'm not assuming anything, but why don't we practice today after school? I have the play. I downloaded it," he said, and then showed us the pages in his book bag. "I've already underlined all your lines and mine."

"Where would we do that?"

He shrugged. "You could come to my house, or I'll come to yours."

"I'll help," Ivy said. "You'll need an audience, and I can read Renfield and practice, too."

I thought about it. Could I really get my mind off what was happening at home?

"Wyndemere doesn't exactly have the best atmosphere right now," I said.

"We can use my house if you want," Ivy said. The way she was clinging to us was beginning to annoy me, but I didn't like feeling that way. It seemed selfish, uncharitable.

"Neutral ground," Dillon said, smiling. "I'm fine with it. Fern?"

"I'll have to ask my mother, see if she needs me for anything, especially today."

"Okay." He put the pages back. "Let me know what happens. I have my car. I'll take you both to Ivy's after school."

"Good," Ivy said quickly, as if she had the right to speak for us both.

I wondered how much Dillon would reveal in front of her.

"What if you get Dracula and I don't get Lucy?" I asked.

"I won't accept the part," he said. He didn't smile. He wasn't kidding. He was going to do this only because he and I would be doing it together. "I'm sure that won't be true if you get Lucy and I don't get Dracula, but that's fine."

"I might not get Renfield," Ivy said. "The part is for a male. I don't know if I can convince Madeo that I can do it, even with lots of practice."

Neither of us replied. We were looking at each other, and neither of us really heard her. When I looked into Dillon's eyes, I could see the interest he had in me. He was searching, probably to be sure I was really interested in him. The distrust he practically radiated in everyone around him, even from the way he spoke, in his parents as well, seemed to cast out a challenge: *Make me believe you.*

I imagined that most girls, despite how sexy and good-looking he was, would decide not to bother; it took way too much effort. I could hear their thoughts, which easily could be mine.

Why do I have to prove myself to you constantly? Frankly, out of fear of displeasing you, I have to guard and evaluate every word I say before I say it. This is too hard; it's too much work. It's what I have to do with most of the adults in my life. When I'm involved with someone romantically, out to have a good time, I don't need to bring all the baggage I have with my parents, my teachers, and some burdensome friends. I want to be carefree. You're too intense.

"I don't know," I said. "You're the one talking me into auditioning, and then you aren't in the play? I don't know. I would feel bad about it."

He nodded. "Okay. Let's wait to see what

happens. That way, we don't make promises we can't keep."

"Well, I can tell you both now," Ivy said. "If I got the part of Renfield and neither of you got a part, I would still do it."

Dillon seemed to check my expression first, and then we both laughed. I didn't think I would laugh at all today. It amazed me how a good laugh could push back on the dark feelings inside you. Until now, I was like a zombie in my classes. I wondered if news about Ryder had reached someone in school who had then passed it along so that it had arrived in every one of my classes before I had. Good news traveled by boat; bad news was always on a jet.

Turning on your cell phone after lunch hour was prohibited. If you were caught, you could lose your phone and even be suspended for a day. Texting was practically a federal offense, especially during any class. The safest thing to do was go to the general office during a study hall and ask permission to call home.

"What's wrong?" my mother asked instead of saying hello. She had read my cell number on the phone screen.

"Nothing's wrong. I wanted to know if it would be all right if I went to Ivy's house after school to practice for the play audition tomorrow. Dillon Evans has a copy of the script."

"Oh. Yes. That would be a good idea, the play."

"I have to win the part, Mummy. Just because I want to do it now doesn't mean anything."

"It means a lot, Fern. If you really want to do it, you'll be motivated to really try. Dinner will be at six as usual."

"Will my . . . will Dr. Davenport be there?" I was having much more trouble calling him my father now.

"As far as I know right now, yes," she said. "I've heard nothing," she added before I could ask.

"Okay, Mummy. 'Bye," I said. My voice sounded far off, even to me. It was as if I was drifting away from myself. I wondered if that would be so bad.

I caught sight of Dillon between sixth and seventh periods. He was lumbering along, standing a little taller, I thought. He spotted me and paused.

"We're on," I said.

He nodded and moved on quickly, as if he didn't want anyone to know. He certainly didn't show any excitement or happiness about it.

"You're a queer duck, Dillon Evans," I whispered to myself.

Ivy and I didn't share the last period. Our schedules varied from each other's in the afternoon because she had moved so successfully through Introduction to French that she was in the advanced class with juniors and seniors. I was taking Spanish and doing well but not so exceptionally.

When the end-of-the-day bell rang, I left slowly. Jennifer Sanders and Denise Potter caught up with me. Jennifer actually seized my arm to stop me.

"We just heard about your brother," Jennifer said. "Raegan Kelly's brother Ian told us your sister told her. Sounds very bad."

"How bad is it?" Denise asked. "On a scale of one to ten," she added.

"No one's weighed it yet," I said, "but thanks for your concern and sympathy. I'm so lucky to have friends like you hovering about, waiting for an opportunity to pounce on bad news." I flashed a smile and left them dumbstruck.

Ivy was already at Dillon's car, waiting.

"You know," she said, "he's never offered to take me home after school. Even when I hinted about it." She stepped closer. "Actually, my mother forbade me from going to school with him or coming home with him."

"Why?"

"My mother thinks he's too weird. But don't worry about it. She's not home today. She went to New York with some friends to see a show."

"Maybe you shouldn't have volunteered your house, though."

"I said don't worry about it," she quickly added. Dillon was heading toward us.

"I gave Mr. Feldman my poem to read earlier today," he said as he approached. He looked energized. "He asked me to stop by to talk about it."

"Did he like it?"

"He told me it was good enough to submit to some magazines and suggested a few."

"Oh, wow. Will you let me read it now?" Ivy asked.

"Fern?"

"It's your poem, Dillon."

"I gave it to you," he said.

"Okay, Ivy. Read it on our way to your house," I said, and gave the envelope to her. You'd think I'd given her an envelope full of diamonds.

Maybe I had.

"Did you get the idea for this poem before you met Fern or afterward?" she asked after we had started away. She was in the rear.

"Why?" he asked quickly.

"Just wondered. It's very good."

"Why?" he asked, and winked at me.

"You captured a universal feeling, need," Ivy said. She was a top student. She was up to his challenge. I smiled to myself.

"And what is that, pray tell?" Dillon asked.

"The need to trust someone and the joy we feel when we find that someone," she said, and handed the poem back to me.

Dillon was silent. I looked back at Ivy. She was smiling impishly.

Dillon turned to me. "We're surrounded by all sorts of vampires," he said. He was smiling differently, smiling with relief. For a moment or two, at least, he was happy to be vulnerable. And Ivy was right . . . that took trust.

We drove on in silence. That wasn't good for me. I couldn't help envisioning Ryder lost and alone in the clinic. Was he medicated into a stupor? Was he gazing out a window and desperately trying to remember his own name? Was he thinking at all of me?

"Hey," Dillon suddenly said. I thought he had been looking at me on and off and realized I was lost in thought. I turned to him. "It's going to be all right, Fern. He'll come back."

I nodded, smiling.

But will I? I wondered.

10

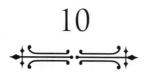

I had been to Ivy's house a half dozen times over the past few years. We had often studied for tests together. Parker or Mr. Stark would drive me there and pick me up when it was time to go home. Only once did Ivy's mother drive me home and only because she had a business meeting close to Wyndemere. There were moments when I feared that she didn't want Ivy and me to be friends. It might hurt her business if her daughter associated too closely with the daughter of a "fallen woman." And yet she was also political enough to realize like most people that it didn't pay to alienate one of the most prestigious families in the area, the Davenports. Now that I was "out of the closet" as a Davenport, I was tolerated more, but in subtle ways I was reminded that it was toleration. Of course, that was soaked in hypocrisy, especially for someone like Mrs. Mason.

Since Ivy's mother's divorce, she had become a busier real estate agent, working for one of the bigger companies. From what I understood, Ivy's father wasn't living up to his financial obligations. He had gone off to California with the young woman he had committed adultery with. Ivy had very little contact with him and rarely mentioned him. There were no pictures of her father anywhere in the house, even in her room. She said if she put one out, it would upset her mother.

"Orphans are luckier that way. They aren't forced to choose between their mother and father," she told me. She laughed afterward. That was Ivy's way after she had said something penetratingly painful. She would laugh rather than cry, but I couldn't laugh. I felt her disappointment. The most difficult thing involved with having friends was sharing in their pain and trouble.

I looked forward to knowing Dillon more, but what I already knew about him suggested this was the reason he wasn't looking for best buddies the way most of the boys in school always were. He didn't want to hear about anyone else's troubles. If I asked him why, I was sure he would tell me he had enough of his own. I certainly did as well, but I couldn't ignore Ivy. She was too sweet, too reluctant to trade nasties with the girls who bullied her, which made her too vulnerable. Half the time when we were with other girls in school, I felt like her bodyguard.

She and her mother lived in a three-bedroom, two-story Wedgwood-blue house with a front porch, family room, and formal dining room built on what I heard some people call a "postage-stamp lot." The small den had been turned into her mother's home office. Sizewise, the whole house would probably fit in Wyndemere's living room, but I thought it was cozy and warm. Ivy's bedroom was not much bigger than the bedroom I had when my mother and I lived in the help's quarters, but it was beautifully decorated, with light pink curtains, fuchsia wallpaper, a four-poster bed with a swirling mauve headboard and matching dresser and armoire, an ivory-white shag rug, and a small light oak desk for her computer.

Her mother didn't want her to "clog" the walls with posters and pictures like other girls our age did in their rooms. There was no en suite bathroom. Only her mother's bedroom had that. Two bedrooms shared the bathroom in the hall, but since, according to Ivy, they rarely had guests, the bathroom was basically hers.

In my mind, when I thought about Ivy's house, I thought of a dollhouse, not because I was arrogant about living in a mansion but because everything in her house was so neatly organized and coordinated. As a real estate agent, her mother believed it was important for her own home to be a showcase. She had even taken courses in interior design and decoration so that if she showed a property, she could give the prospective buyers some ideas for redecorating to their taste.

It hadn't occurred to me until we arrived, but Ivy's explaining why her mother wouldn't normally permit her to ride with Dillon suggested that he had never been in her house. I had no doubt she wasn't happy about them being friends. I didn't come right out and ask him or her, but from the way he looked at everything and because she had to ask him to take off his shoes, I gathered he hadn't ever been invited. We had already taken off ours. Her mother had made that point when I first visited. She wasn't afraid of the germs, she said. She believed floors and carpets would last longer and continue looking new longer if people walked barefoot or in slippers. I asked Ivy if her mother made customers who came to her home office do that, too.

"She takes off her shoes, and some do and some don't, but she'll never criticize a customer," she told me.

"Does anyone really live here, or is this a model home for sale?" Dillon asked Ivy as he took off his shoes.

She laughed, of course. "My mother's a bit of a kook when it comes to keeping everything orderly and in its proper place. She's terrified some visitor will question her ability to choose the perfect home for her customers. She thinks we're on a stage all the time. I told her we should have a curtain right here in the entryway that would open like the curtain in a theater when she brought someone into the house and maybe with some background music. Anyone want a soda or something?"

"I'm fine," I said.

"Where could we practice?" Dillon asked. "That rug in the living room looks like no one's ever walked on it. I don't want my fingerprints on anything. It looks like a bunch of sailors polished the furniture like they would their ship."

"Let's go up to my room," Ivy said, laughing.

We went up the short carpeted stairway with its glistening mahogany banister and turned right to the first door.

"I guess girls are a lot neater than boys," Dillon said as soon as we had entered.

"You wouldn't say that if you saw my sister's room at Wyndemere."

"She's right. I've seen it," Ivy said. "Sit anywhere, even on the bed," she suggested. "I'll get us some lemonade just in case we need it after we start."

She left. Dillon looked at me, shrugged, and sat on the bed. He took out the pages of the play.

"Take these," he said, handing them to me. "Dracula isn't in these scenes with Lucy. You'll do those first."

I took the pages, sat beside him on the bed, and started to read them.

"This is the first girl's bedroom I've been in, not counting my mother's," he said, gazing around. "It smells nice, and I like the way she's neatly placed all her stuffed toys and dolls on those shelves."

"I have some, too, but maybe not displayed as nicely," I said. For a long moment, we simply stared at each other. I spoke first, because he was looking at me so intently. "What?"

"I was remembering the first time I saw you in the school hallway. You resembled a doll in that green dress with a bow tied in the front. Your hair was pinned up so neatly, and you looked like you had just vaguely brushed on lipstick. The thing I remember clearly is your eyes, the way the violet was captured in the light streaming through the hall window. They were two small streaks of lavender. I thought to myself, this girl has no idea how beautiful she is going to be, not yet, anyway."

He stopped. The silence was so deep between us that you could dip a spoon in it. Actually, I was speechless. What he had said was so surprisingly sincere. There was no irony, no sarcasm. I was waiting for some punch line.

"I'm sorry," he said, now uncomfortable with my silence. "I'm talking too much and embarrassing you." He smiled. "Actually, you look a little stunned."

The truth was I couldn't swallow. I was holding my breath, but my heart had begun to race. It was as if he had been trapping his thoughts for so long that they had to explode. The idea that someone had observed me so closely and admired me so deeply for all this time without my ever knowing made me feel . . . naked.

"I am stunned. Why didn't you ever say hello or something?" I asked in nothing more than a loud whisper.

"You looked occupied," he said. "Anyway, sorry I broke your concentration. If you look at those pages, you have Lucy's first entrance on the stage. My guess is Mr. Madeo will use these monologues of hers, because she's already suffering without knowing she has been Dracula's victim. He's been feeding on her, weakening her at night after she falls asleep, to turn her into one of his own. Madeo would want to see what each candidate will do to show it."

I smiled.

"What?" he asked.

"Nothing."

"C'mon."

"Well, I was just thinking that maybe that was what you were trying to do just now."

He shook his head, confused.

"Weakening me with your pretty words."

He looked like he was insulted, angry, and then he laughed. "Now you're into it," he said.

"What's so funny?" Ivy asked, entering with a tray on which there was a pitcher of lemonade and three glasses.

"Fern just realized I really am a vampire," Dillon said. "But I'll make an exception right now and drink some of your lemonade instead of your blood."

He plucked a glass off the tray. She set it on the night table beside her bed, and he poured a glass, which he offered to me first.

I took it. My throat had tightened with excitement and felt dry. After a sip, I put it down and looked at the pages.

"Lucy's frail from the loss of blood," Dillon said. "So try to sound a little faint, but don't speak too softly or too low. You have to realize you're going to be on a stage."

That was exactly how I was feeling at the moment. I read the lines as if every word was exhausting.

"Good," he said. "Get to the part where she is describing her bad dream." He leaned over my shoulder to point it out. Just a half inch closer, and we'd be cheek to cheek. "Read it slowly, as if you're remembering the experience with some difficulty. It has to be mysterious, frightening, but you can't forget it even though you want to. Try it," he said. "Wait, imagine an organ playing under your lines. It sets a tone."

I looked at Ivy. She had an expression of amazement on her face.

"How does he know all this? Maybe he really is a vampire," she said.

"Don't make me laugh. It will put me out of character."

I sucked in my breath, closed my eyes, opened them, read the lines to myself, and then closed my eyes again for a moment. When I opened them, Dillon and Ivy were both looking at me with such expectation I was afraid to recite the lines. But I did.

When I was finished, neither Dillon nor Ivy said anything.

"I think I'm going to have a nightmare tonight," Ivy finally said. "Maybe we should have used another room in the house."

Dillon laughed and drank some lemonade. "Let's keep going," he said. "We'll do a scene between Dracula and Lucy. Madeo likes to put two possible choices against each other as soon as possible to see how they do, how they fit."

"How do you know all this?" I asked.

"It's how he ran the audition for *Our Town*," he said.

We went on. He handed me different pages. First I read them, and then we did them. It felt like we had been doing them for hours. I was happy for the rest when Ivy did lines as Renfield. Dillon suggested she speak with a nasal tone, just to sound weird.

"You have one of those eyeliner pencils?" he asked her.

She didn't, but she got one from her mother's

room, and he drew a mustache on her. We laughed at how nutty she looked. Dillon pointed out that Renfield should look and sound nutty, and she read the lines again.

"You might have a good shot at this part," Dillon told her. "The cast list is too heavily male. If you pull it off, he'll really consider you."

"You think?" She looked at me, excited.

"I think he's right," I said. Every minute with Dillon was like wiping fog off a picture. What I was seeing now was someone who was not only bright and creative but self-confident, too.

We continued with more enthusiasm. We were all really into it now, with Dillon providing suggestions and direction. No one paid attention to time. When I finally did think about it, I realized it was nearly five forty-five. I'd never be home by six.

"Oh, no. My mother's going to be upset," I said.

"Avoid it," Dillon said.

"Avoid it? How?"

"Call her and tell her the truth, that we ran over and we've decided to go for pizza. I'll be bringing you home."

"Are we?" Ivy asked quickly, making sure she was included.

"Fern?" he asked. "If she puts up a stink, you could always say you're presently in the clutches of a vampire and have no choice."

"With my mother, you never have no choice if you're doing something she doesn't want or like. But I'll try," I said.

I took out my cell phone and stepped into the hallway. I called and spoke quickly, explaining how I had lost track of time.

"It'll just be easier if we grab a pizza."

She was quiet. This was my mother's way when she was more annoyed than she wanted to reveal. "How do you lose track of time, Fern? You have a watch."

"We were really enjoying the play, Mummy. It's fun. I wasn't thinking of anything else. Please."

"I want you home right after, Fern," she said. "It's supposed to snow hard tonight. Mr. Stark says sometime after nine, possibly, and he thinks it will begin with rain."

"Oh, I'll be home well before that, Mummy. I have some serious homework. Did Dr. Davenport say anything about Ryder?"

"We'll talk when you're home," she said. "Be sure that boy drives very carefully. Cars and winter will never be a comfortable thought in this house."

"I'll make sure, Mummy. Thank you," I said.

I took a deep breath. I never liked being a manipulator when it came to my mother. She was too good at seeing through my excuses and rationalizations, but what I had said was true. I was enjoying myself.

"It's okay," I told Dillon and Ivy.

"Let's go," Ivy said before we could change our minds.

We followed her downstairs, Dillon carrying the pitcher with what remained of the lemonade. We talked about where to go for pizza while Ivy washed the glasses and put the pitcher in the refrigerator. Just like every other room in her house, the kitchen was showcase immaculate. She made sure there wasn't a drop of water on the counter.

We all put on our shoes. When we turned to get our coats and leave, however, the front door opened, and Ivy's mother stepped in, a look of astonishment on her face.

"What's this?" she asked immediately. "Why do you have a fake mustache?"

I was amazed myself at how we could have left with Ivy looking like that.

"Oh. I forgot it was there. We were practicing for a play audition tomorrow," Ivy said quickly. "I'm trying out for a part that's usually a man. But why are you home so soon?"

"There's a storm coming in tonight. We saw our matinee and decided not to have dinner in the city. Where do you think you're going at this hour?"

"We were going to get pizza," Ivy said.

"I just said there's a storm coming in." She looked at Dillon. "Is your mother letting you drive tonight?"

Before he could answer, I stepped forward.

"The storm's not due until after nine," I said. "Mr. Stark, the manager of Wyndemere, keeps track of those things. We'll be home long before that."

"Just turn yourself around, Ivy Mason. We're having dinner here now," her mother said. She kept the door open, not so subtly saying Dillon and I weren't invited.

"Thank you, Mrs. Mason," I said.

"Yes, thank you," Dillon added. He paused. "You have an . . . immaculate house." He flashed a smile and followed me out.

When we got into his car, we looked at each other and both started to laugh.

"I hope I didn't leave any blood on Ivy's carpet," he said. He started his car. "I know a place not far from Wyndemere. That way, I'll get you home way before the storm hits. Hey," he realized, "that might mean no school tomorrow, and that means no audition until the day after. Maybe later in the day tomorrow, when the roads are cleared, we could practice some more."

"Let's take it a pint at a time," I said.

He smiled. I sat back.

I hadn't thought seriously about Ryder once for nearly three hours and had only mentioned him when I spoke to my mother. It was almost an afterthought. Was that good or bad? I suspected my father might say it was good.

With Ivy in the room with us and working on the play lines, Dillon and I hadn't said anything more about his first impressions of me when I entered high school last fall. Now that we were alone, his words rolled around like marbles in my head.

How was it that I had never noticed him or even heard anyone talk about him until now? Maybe I had but didn't think much about it. I was so fixed on Ryder in those days. I wondered if Dillon sensed that and if that was what he was implying when he said I was occupied. I wasn't that obvious, was I?

"I can't imagine what would have happened if Ivy's mother had come home after we had left for pizza and Ivy wasn't there. She probably would have called the police. She wouldn't get much out of my parents, that's for sure," Dillon said.

"Come to think of it, don't you have to tell your parents where you are and what you're doing?" I asked. "Isn't your mother expecting you to be at dinner?"

"Lately, the three of us tiptoe around each other," he said. He looked at me. "I get the feeling they're suffering from buyer's remorse these days. I suspect they considered bringing me back to the adoption agency, claiming defective parts or something. Is there a warranty on an adopted baby?"

He smiled, but I didn't laugh. My memories of

being a persona non grata when Bea was living at Wyndemere were still too vivid.

"Haven't you ever spoken to them about it?"

He looked at me with his chin down, implying that was a ridiculous question.

"Did you at least try, Dillon? Ever?"

"When you meet them, you'll see what a waste of time that would be. My mother makes a nervous chicken look like a cool cucumber, and my father thinks there are two worlds: his in his business and hers in the house and bringing up baby. He's never changed a diaper or made anything to eat besides a peanut butter sandwich when my mother was in the hospital for a hysterectomy. At a very early age, I might add. Oh, he will make a cup of tea but teabag only."

"What does your father do?"

"He sells drugs."

"What?"

"Legally. He works for Novartis. Twice a year, he goes to Switzerland for meetings. Before you ask, he keeps his samples in a safe in the house. Not even my mother knows the combination."

"Why do you think they adopted you?"

He thought a moment and smiled. "My mother wasn't biologically capable of having a baby. My father isn't fond of pets. My mother wasn't satisfied with her part-time dental hygienist work. She always wanted to be more needed. In the end, I think it was either adopt a baby to keep my mother busier and happier or buy a puppy."

"Buy a puppy? That was the choice?"

He smiled.

"I don't know whether to believe anything you say," I said.

"That makes two of us."

I had to laugh. When it came to dissing himself, Dillon didn't hesitate. He might not respect most of the others in our school, but not all loners were arrogant, I thought. Now that I had grown to know him more, I would never characterize him that way.

We pulled up in front of a small pizza restaurant I had never been to. A big sign in green, white, and red announced it as Nick's Pizza Kitchen. It was squeezed between a hardware store and a pharmacy, in a red-brick building that had what looked like an apartment above it.

"How did you find this place? I never heard anyone mention it."

"My mother's maid—she needs a maid but complains about the maid's work and redoes almost everything after the maid leaves—her husband owns the restaurant. She's from Chile. Before you ask how a guy from Chile knows how to make great pizza, I'll tell you she's married to a man from Naples, where supposedly the best pizza in Italy is. As you can see, his name is Nick, and he claims it all has to do with the stone in the pizza ovens. He had their stone shipped from Italy."

We got out of the car. The sky was increasingly overcast. Some of the clouds looked like they were rolling over one another. I wondered if Mr. Stark had miscalculated the arrival time of the storm.

Dillon looked up, too. "We should be all right," he said, but he seemed concerned. "If it starts, we'll leave and take the pizza with us."

The wind seemed to have gotten stronger as well. It whipped around the corner of the street in a gust that made me cover my face. Everything not tied down on the sidewalk and in the street did a flip-flop.

"Maybe Mr. Stark underestimated the start of the storm," I said.

As if she could hear our conversation from miles away, my mother called my cell phone. Dillon had just opened the restaurant's front door to rush us in.

"Hi," I said, stepping into the entryway.

"Mr. Stark says the storm's coming in much faster than anyone predicted. He thinks you should start for home now. The temperature is dropping to freezing, and it will begin with rain, Fern."

"We're just at the restaurant," I said. She was silent. "Okay," I said, my voice dipped in dis-appointment. I hung up and told Dillon what my mother had said.

"I don't want to get on your mother's bad side," he said, opening the door again.

"I'm sorry."

"Nature can be a pain in the ass," he said.

We got back into his car.

"My father's first wife was killed in a car accident in winter. She drove off the road. I never knew her, of course, but in a way, she's never left Wyndemere."

"Ghosts?" he asked as he turned the car around and started for my house.

"Maybe. Whatever, it always looms in everyone's mind when we have our first snow or icy rain. A great deal of sadness clings to the Wyndemere mansion. I mean, it's grand and all, but . . ."

"If you still live in someone's memory, you are still alive," he said. "Doesn't have to always be a bad thing, either. My problem is I don't have anyone in my memory. I don't consider my father's brother and sister or my mother's brother as my relatives, really, so I don't remember all that much about things we did with them. Don't care to. Despite the faces they put on when they visit occasionally, very occasionally, I've always felt a distance, felt I wasn't really one of them."

"Which is why I still think you should try to find your real mother, at least."

"Did it make a difference in your life when

your father finally stepped up to the plate, besides what you will inherit, I mean?"

How could I tell him without crying? "A little," I said. "It takes time, in my case. My father's got to get used to being my father. He's avoided and ignored it for most of my life." I paused. I was already revealing more than I had intended.

"He shouldn't have to work too hard at that. Anyone should be happy to acknowledge you and get you to love him."

I smiled just as the first fat, nearly frozen drop hit the windshield. A bad patch of clouds had begun to unload a wave of rain ahead of us. My body trembled. Although it had still been spring, this was how the storm on the lake had begun. Dillon slowed. The windshield wipers started.

"We're just a few miles away," he said. "It's the winds over the lake. They twist and turn in surprising ways." He looked at me. I was sure I looked terrified. "It's okay," he said. "I'm practically down to the speed of a walk. I'm sure you didn't notice, but I have snow tires. I took driver's education, and I passed my driver's test the first time I took it. My mother once revealed that my father didn't pass his until the third time. I think he went through a stop sign the first time and forgot to signal a turn the second."

I sat back, and then he hit the brakes. Someone had panicked and driven into the back of another vehicle. A patrolman was directing traffic around the crash. Both drivers, one an elderly lady, were outside their vehicles, gazing at the damage. The rain began to come down harder.

"It's not freezing yet," Dillon said, more to himself than to me.

"Mr. Stark says most people don't know how to drive in the rain, much less freezing rain and snow."

Dillon waited for the patrolman to wave us on, and we continued, but neither of us felt like talking. The rain had gotten more intense. By the time we reached Wyndemere, it was coming down in a steady downpour. The moment we drove into the driveway, the front door opened, and my mother, snapping an umbrella open, walked to the edge of the portico. Drops striking the front of Dillon's car now were bouncing off with the texture of ice.

"I'll get as close as I can," Dillon said, moving along the driveway. "Don't slip and fall. I need you at the audition."

"Thanks," I said, and opened the door. My mother started toward us. I rushed to her side.

Dillon raised his hand to wave good-bye.

"He shouldn't be on these roads," my mother said. She didn't move. "Tell him to come in," she added after a moment's thought.

"But it will only be getting worse."

"Tell him to come in," she repeated with more authority.

I beckoned to him. He looked confused until my mother did it, too. Then he shrugged, shut off his car, and got out. We turned to the house. He ran to reach us, his head, pants, and shoes soaked by the time he stepped up to the door my mother was holding open.

"What's up?" he asked.

"You can't drive on these roads yet," she said. "You can call your parents and tell them you're staying here."

"I am?"

"Inside," she ordered. She closed the umbrella and then closed the door when we stepped into the house. "Take off your shoes. Your socks are probably soaked as well."

"I'm getting so used to this I'll probably start doing it before I enter my own house," Dillon said as he slipped off his shoes, which were really not the right ones to be wearing in this weather. They were low-riding loafers.

"Take him to the powder room so he can dry his hair. Leave your coat hanging here," she told him. "You'll take off your pants, and I'll put them in the dryer. Fern will get you a robe."

"Yes, ma'am," he said.

He looked at me and widened his eyes, obviously impressed with my mother's authoritative demeanor, but she had been running this mansion and the staff for years. She took his wet socks.

"Do you have a cell phone?"

"Yes," he said.

"Call your mother immediately and tell her what you're doing. I'm sure she's worried."

He nodded. I was afraid he might say she wasn't.

I led him down the hall. Of course, he had never been inside Wyndemere. Despite dripping with cold rain, he walked slowly, taking it all in.

"Your mother's pretty take-charge," he said when I had brought him to the downstairs bathroom.

"As Mr. Stark will eagerly tell you," I said, smiling. I urged him into the bathroom and closed the door behind him. My mother was waiting in the lobby near the sitting room.

"Go up to one of the guest rooms and get a robe," she told me.

Every bedroom in Wyndemere was always kept as though someone was about to stay in it. The cabinets in the bathrooms were stocked with sundries, including new toothbrushes and new hairbrushes.

"After I throw his pants into the dryer, I'll find him a clean, dry pair of socks. Go on, Fern. Bring him some slippers, too. The dinner is still hot. Mrs. Marlene made her version of Irish stew, which is perfect for this weather."

"Is my father here?"

"No. He's remaining at the hospital. He has an early call to do a triple bypass. Your sister is in the dining room complaining about your not being there and being permitted to go for pizza in a storm."

I hurried up the stairs to the bedroom a door down from mine. Inside the en suite bathroom were two fresh robes with slippers beneath them. Everything seemed to be happening so quickly. Within forty-eight hours, Ryder was swept off and returned to the clinic. I was clearly more involved with Dillon Evans, and as if nature had made a serious decision for us, Dillon was not only the first boy ever to be invited to dinner with me and my family, but he was also going to sleep just down the hall from me.

A part of me was excited about it all, very excited, but there was another part of me that was afraid, afraid of Wyndemere, the mansion that could snap Dillon up and into its mysteries and dark history through the portal of his dreams and easily turn his whole life into one of its cherished secrets.

Hadn't it done that to me?

11

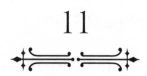

Samantha was speechless at the sight of Dillon. That alone was enough to bring a smile to my face. Even my mother looked a little impish, her violet eyes sparkling when Dillon entered the dining room with me. He was wearing the robe and slippers and had blow-dried his hair.

"I don't know if you've ever met my sister, Dillon. This is Samantha. This is Dillon Evans, Samantha."

"No," he said. "How ya doin'?"

I indicated that he should take the seat on my right so I could sit between Samantha and him. She was still staring at him with her mouth open.

"Why did you come here in a robe?" she asked.

Even my mother had to laugh aloud.

"He didn't come here like that, Samantha," I said.

"It's storming out there, and I got soaked. Ms. Corey is drying my pants and socks. I think I stepped in a puddle," Dillon told her.

"Whose robe is that?" Samantha asked my mother, ignoring him. "It's not Ryder's, is it?" she demanded.

Despite how motherly my mother had always

been to her, Samantha couldn't drop that master-to-servant attitude, quite condescending. It annoyed me that my mother let her get away with it most of the time.

"It's a guest robe, Samantha. You should know that we have robes and slippers in every one of our guest rooms. Even if they are not used, they are periodically washed. Ryder's robe has his initials embroidered on it. But Ryder has never been selfish about his things," she added pointedly.

Samantha smirked and then leered at me. "Did you have pizza? Where did you go?" she fired at me as if I was on the stand giving testimony.

"I doubt I could eat pizza and then Mrs. Marlene's Irish stew, Samantha. We had to rush back. We just told you that a serious storm has arrived. Didn't you notice?"

"No," she said. "I was watching *Moment to Moment*. Are you in Fern's class?" she asked Dillon.

"He's a senior, Samantha," I said calmly. What I wanted to do was slap her because of her attitude.

"I'm not allowed to have friends sleep over," she said with the corners of her lips drooping. "But you can just because your mother is in charge of the house and stuff? It's not fair."

"Actually, Mother Nature invited me," Dillon said.

"What? That's stupid. There is no Mother Nature."

"But I can be your friend, too," Dillon said before either my mother or I could respond to the sharp way she had spoken to him. "That would be fair, wouldn't it?"

"No. You are not going to spend any time with me," she retorted.

"Well, I don't know. What do you suggest we do since we're all stuck in the house because of the storm?" he asked.

She looked at me to see if I was going to object.

"Good question," I said. "Can you think of anything fun, Samantha?"

Her nasty attitude dissolved. "That's easy," Samantha said. "There's pool, ping-pong, cards, board games," she rattled off. "But I'm not very good at either ping-pong or pool."

"You're getting better at checkers," I said.

"I'm not good at checkers," Dillon said. "My father doesn't play, and my mother hates board games. I don't think I've played checkers with anyone since I was ten."

"Okay, we'll play checkers," Samantha said. "You and me first."

She sat back, obviously not sure she shouldn't continue whining and complaining about not having her own friends for a sleepover. Mrs. Marlene entered with her pot of Irish stew and put it on the rack at the center of the table.

"This is Dillon Evans, Mrs. Marlene," I said. "Dillon, this is Mrs. Marlene."

"Hi. That smells delicious."

Mrs. Marlene smiled. "Dillon?" She looked at my mother. "Am I right to think that's an Irish name?"

"Irish it is," my mother said. "Means loyal and true."

"Then you've come for the perfect dinner, I hope," Mrs. Marlene said. "I put a little variation in the basic recipe, so you might find it a little different from what you're used to in Irish stew. Don't ask what it is," she warned with a scowl. "It's my secret."

"My mother's Irish," Dillon said. "That's why they named me Dillon, but she's never made this. Thank you."

He looked at me. Only I knew why he was smiling. It didn't matter that his mother was Irish. He had no idea what he was, having been adopted. A name didn't make you Irish. I was sure we were both thinking the same thing.

Mrs. Marlene nodded and left. My mother served the stew.

Samantha grimaced at the sight of it on her plate. "This looks blah. I'd rather have pizza," she said.

"I'd rather be in Hawaii today," Dillon said. "Especially today."

I laughed the loudest.

Samantha pursed her lips and then started to eat. Maybe, I thought, my half sister had met her match.

After dinner, we went to the game room, and while Dillon and Samantha played checkers, I fiddled around with pool balls. Ryder and I used to play pool occasionally when Bea was gone for the day or out for a night and wasn't around to complain about my crossing her precious border into the main house. Usually, Ryder would have one or more of his friends over as well.

It was obvious to me that Dillon was deliberately losing to keep Samantha happy. Cleverly, he complained about being distracted so he could convince Samantha she was really winning. After she won two games in a row, she was okay with Dillon and me playing some pool. He knew how to play eight ball. When I did well, he said it was because he was wearing the heavy terry-cloth bathrobe and slippers and couldn't maneuver well.

"The boy with all the excuses," I said, directing myself to Samantha. To my surprise and Dillon's obvious amusement, she agreed with him. He let her take the next shot for him and praised her.

"If I practiced, I could be better than Fern," she said.

My mother appeared with his dried pants and socks. "There's a brand-new pair of pajamas in your room," she said. She looked at me. I knew they had been given to Ryder on Christmas, one of his many gifts unused, untouched. "Everything else you'll need is in the bathroom cabinet. The storm is in full swing," she added. "Mr. Stark has told me that the county highway department has not yet been able to go after the roads. It's blowing a gale out there. It looks like it will continue into the morning."

"Thank you very much," Dillon said, taking his pants and socks.

"You're welcome. You called your mother, I assume?"

"I did. She's fine with it all and asked me to thank you."

My mother smiled and nodded.

I looked at Dillon. I didn't think he was telling the whole truth. He had a bit of a mischievous look in his eyes. He was successfully playing everyone so far: Samantha, Mrs. Marlene, and now my mother.

She turned to me. "Dr. Davenport will be staying at the hospital, of course. I'll be retiring for the evening soon. Samantha, do not stay up past ten."

"Why not? There won't be any school because of the storm," she whined.

"Your father does not like you moping about because you've stayed up too late. He's asked me to tell you that if you don't go to bed when you should, you will not be permitted to go out with

257

your friends to the movies on the weekend. There will be no arguing about it."

"Ten sounds just about right to me," Dillon said. "I'm sure I'll be shoveling out my car tomorrow, so I'll need a good night's rest."

"Exactly," my mother said, gave Samantha a look of warning, and left.

"This is stupid," Samantha said. "If we're not going to school, why do we have to go to sleep the same time as usual? I don't go to sleep that early on weekends. On weekends, I can stay up to midnight sometimes, and twice I was up until one in the morning," she added to impress him.

"I'll play you checkers for it," Dillon said. "If you win, we'll keep your staying up past ten a secret; if you lose, we all go to bed at ten."

"Okay," she said.

He was smart enough not to beat her too quickly. For a moment, I actually thought she might win. So did she.

"You're pretty good. That took a lot of thinking," he told her after he won. She was already pouting. "It was fun," he added. "I like checkers now. Don't mind if we play again next time I'm here."

She brightened. "We'll play again tomorrow if you have to stay," she told him.

"Deal," he said. He held up his hand for her to slap five. She did and then gave me one of her *See? I'm better than you* looks.

"Care to consider a full-time nanny job here?" I whispered as we started out together with her moping along behind us.

"If it means I'll see you every day, yes," he replied.

I felt my ears get warm before anything else.

We looked at each other. I knew he wanted to take my hand as we went up the stairs, but with Samantha on our tail, I thought it best to be discreet. However, that was not Samantha's way.

"Are you going to be Fern's boyfriend now?" she asked him when we were all at the top of the stairway.

"I haven't decided yet. What do you recommend?" he asked her, folding his arms and looking like her opinion really mattered to him.

She studied me a moment to see if I would laugh. The gleam of jealousy built the familiar cold, green light in her eyes. I was smiling at the way Dillon was handling her, and I was sure she interpreted that as being happy about Dillon.

"Ryder will be upset," she said, then turned and hurried off to her bedroom, just like someone who had dropped a time bomb on an unsuspecting person.

I stood there looking after her. Dillon was silent.

"I'm sorry about that," I said. "That was a dumb thing to say. She's just spiteful, spoiled."

"She's a piece of work. Now, there goes

someone who's a good potential victim of a vampire," he said, nodding in her direction. "On the other hand, I don't know if he'd want her blood. It could end his immortality."

"Exactly."

We started toward the bedrooms. No matter how he joked about it, I thought, he had to be wondering why she would say what she had said about Ryder. It took me by surprise, because she knew nothing about the budding romance developing between Ryder and me before the accident. What had she sensed between us now? Or did she sense something only in him because of what she claimed she had witnessed him do with the photo? Had he said something to her when I wasn't there, something she was keeping secret? Lately, Samantha could be like a hot coal rolling around under my heart.

Dillon walked with his head down. I could feel how hard he was trying to avoid any questions or comments about what Samantha had said, but it lingered in the air.

"Don't pay any attention to what Samantha says about Ryder. My brother is obviously quite confused," I said, pausing at the door to the guest room. "He doesn't know whom to trust. Samantha hasn't been making things easier. Sometimes she deliberately says things that will add to that confusion. If anyone needed therapy . . ."

"Sure. Forget it. Your mother is quite a lady,"

he said, moving to change the subject. "Can you imagine Ivy's mother inviting me to stay because of a storm if I didn't live so close by to them? My mother would have had a breakdown if she was faced with such a decision involving you. You're a lucky girl, Fern."

"When it comes to my mother, I never thought otherwise." I turned to the bedroom doorway. "This is where you sleep. I'm a door down behind us."

He looked up and down the hallway. "It seems endless. Anyone use the hall as a bowling alley?"

I snapped on his light, and he whistled at the sight of the room, the king-size bed and its matching furniture, as well as the lamps and the oil paintings of rural settings. My mother had obviously been in here and had turned down the bedding. The pair of new pajamas still in clear plastic wrap was on the bed.

"A guest might not leave. How many bedrooms in this house again?"

"Seventeen," I said. "The bathroom is on the right. You'll find a new toothbrush and tooth-paste, even shaving cream and new razors if you want to shave."

"It's like a first-class hotel."

"Haunted hotel," I said.

We could hear what sounded like hail striking the windows now. This bedroom, like mine, looked out on the front of the mansion.

"Quite a storm," he said. "Rain to snow to ice. The roads are probably like glass."

"The wind can find cracks and crannies. If you need another blanket, it's on the shelf in the closet."

He smiled and nodded. We were alone now; the house was quite still. Mrs. Marlene would be staying over in one of the other guest rooms, and Mr. Stark would probably stay in what had been my mother's room in the help's quarters. He often did, even when there was no storm.

"Well, I guess, good night," I said.

He nodded, smiled, and leaned in to kiss me softly. When our lips touched, static electricity snapped around us, and we both laughed.

"Something tells me your mother had something to do with that," he said. "Did she really go to sleep?"

"Yes."

"Then let's try again," he said, and kissed me, this time without any static, except for the electricity that lit a spark in my heart. A sweet peace stole over me, quivering my breasts with a tingling sensation.

" 'Night," I whispered, turned quickly, and walked away, afraid that if I didn't, I might not.

"Watch out for Dracula, even in a storm," he called after me in a loud whisper.

I smiled to myself but kept walking.

When I had crawled under my blanket, I lay

back on my pillow with my eyes wide open. I was afraid that when I closed them, I would see Dillon's eyes looking deeply into my very soul, uncovering the secrets snuggled in what were supposed to be safe places, passionate secrets all wrapped and knotted with streaks of deep, sexual fantasies. Sometimes they came to me in waves, and sometimes they flashed before my eyes and were gone like shooting stars. Shame, fear, and guilt lost their grip on the ever stronger emerging woman within me.

Gradually, sleep crawled up my bed and put weight on my eyelids. I closed them and drifted off to the sound of the wind and the freezing rain splashing against my windows. I wrapped my blanket tighter around me, weaving the warmth into a cocoon, a nest in which to hatch my dreams. Hours later, I opened my eyes with a start because I sensed someone was in my room.

I sat up quickly and gasped. For a moment, I thought it was Ryder standing there in a dark silhouette. His name was on my lips.

"Hey," Dillon said, drawing closer. He was standing with a lit candle in a holder, the light casting a fine, yellowish glow over his face. "I thought you might have woken. Apparently, the electricity has gone off. I saw this on the bedside table. There were matches in the drawer. I guess this happens a lot out here, especially with a storm like this, huh?"

"Not that often, no. Anyone else up?"

"I didn't hear anyone. The hall is a sea of black ink. The lights outside are off, of course, and it's still coming down hard out there. I opened the window to check."

"What time is it?"

He brought the candle to his wrist. "Two twenty. You have a candle in case you need to get up?"

"Yes. Every room in this house has candles, some probably fifty years old."

"Yeah, sure. I thought so. Sorry I woke you," he said. He turned to leave.

"Wait. You forgot to help me light one."

"Oh, yeah. Dumb."

I sat up and opened the night-table drawer. He brought the light closer so I could find the matches and then light my own candle in its holder.

Candlelight had always been soft and mysterious to me. The glow it cast around us at this moment gave me the sense of our being cut away from the world and left in our own private place where we were free to be ourselves. I sat back. I was wearing a sheer nightgown. He stood there staring at me so intently that it brought a warmth into my face. I felt naked; I practically was, but I didn't move to cover myself. There was no need for words. The way we were touching each other with our eyes said enough. I knew what he was asking, and I knew what I wanted to say.

I shifted over to my right, creating enough room for him.

He put his candle on the table beside mine, and then he slipped in beside me gracefully. It was silent enough to be a dream. For the first few moments, we both lay there, equally hesitant, almost stunned by how events had brought us so quickly to this place, him beside me in my bed, the warmth from our bodies drawing us even closer, and the passion within us slipping out of its shackles.

Slowly, he turned to me. My hands were at my sides. He drew the blanket back and braced himself over me, hesitating. My breath quickened as he gradually lowered himself, bringing his lips to mine. The light from our candles brightened his eyes.

His lips lifted off mine only slightly before he kissed me again. Before the accident on the lake, Ryder and I had gone this far until we had turned back, both of us afraid of how demanding our bodies were being. A little further, and we would not have stopped, but that memory did not distract me or make me more cautious now.

Dillon slipped my nightgown over my shoulders. He kissed me at the curve of my neck and then kissed my shoulder. I lifted my arms and sat up a little so that he could bring my nightgown up and over my head. He took off the robe he was wearing and kissed me again, fondling my breasts, bringing his lips to my nipples, and then kissing me around my neck before grazing my lips with his. He was so quiet, so gentle, it did seem more like a fantasy.

A fleeting thought reminded me that he was wearing Ryder's Christmas present, his pajamas. Was I kissing Dillon or the memory of Ryder? I was thinking so much of our intimate times together. Was this unusual? Was it common for a woman to have flashbacks of earlier romantic moments with men she had been with while she was being intimate with someone new?

I didn't stop him when he brought his lips below my breasts and to my stomach. Then, before going farther, he returned to my lips and brought his body against me. I was holding him tighter, kissing him as hard and as demandingly as he was kissing me, raining down those kisses over every part of my body. I heard my own moaning as if I was listening to someone else.

Suddenly, he paused, lifted himself away from me, and took a very deep breath. "We're going to go too far," he whispered. "I won't be able to stop."

Ryder had once said that to me. The words were branded in that place in my memory. Should I be ashamed that I wasn't the one saying them now? Why was it always the girl's responsibility to stop before it was too late?

Would I have stopped if neither Ryder nor Dillon had spoken?

Dillon turned over onto his back beside me. I put my hand on his chest. This was unfair to him. I had invited him in beside me. I had wanted what had almost happened inside me to happen. I still did. I had read enough and I knew enough about the ache when you brought your sexual pleasure to this point of explosion and then stopped abruptly. The frustration crashing down beside us was maddening. We were both crying inside.

I reached over for some tissues and then moved my hand to his pulsating hardness as I pressed my body against his leg and began a slow gyration. If he was shocked, he didn't say, nor did he pull farther away. Instead, he turned to kiss me and then repeated my name as if he had to memorize it.

We exploded at the same time and then stopped like two thieves caught in police spotlights. Neither of us spoke. I rose and went into the bathroom. When I returned, he was out of my bed and had his robe on. Still naked, I approached him, and he embraced me, opening his robe to include me. He kissed me and smiled.

"I guess I have to take back what I said about nature," he said. "It's a bit ungrateful to complain about being caught in a storm now."

I was still reeling, floating with the realization of just how intimate we had been. How long would it have taken for us to be as loving if there hadn't been a storm? I was confident that sooner or later, it would have happened.

He released me, closed his robe, picked up his candle, kissed me again, and went to the door, pausing to be sure no one was out in the hall, that no one being especially my mother.

" 'Night," he whispered, and walked out.

I put on my nightgown and got back into bed. For a while, I just lay there luxuriating in the sensuous memory of what we had done. Tired again, I leaned over to blow out my candle but stopped when light entered my bedroom. Of course, my first thought was that he was returning. I was going to tell him it would be better if he woke up in his own bed.

But it wasn't Dillon.

It was my mother. She stood there looking at me just the way she often did in my dreams involving Ryder.

I didn't know what to say. Had she seen Dillon's candle in the hallway? My answer came quickly.

"I hope you are being careful, Fern," she said. "Trouble has found a home in Wyndemere. It won't give it up easily, and it will more than welcome a new opportunity."

She wasn't waiting for my response, not that I had one. She turned and left, the light rushing away behind her as if it had been forgotten and leaving me in the weak light of my own flickering candle, flickering like my heart. I didn't think I would fall asleep again quickly, but maybe it was a combination of one emotional crescendo after another, or maybe it was simply a way to escape.

The electricity was still not on when I awoke. Samantha could be heard complaining to my mother in the hallway as if it was my mother's fault. She was hoping to watch television all morning since school was closed. She was demanding that Mr. Stark do something.

"He's supposed to!" she cried. "My father's going to be very upset."

"Get dressed, Samantha," I heard my mother say. "We'll deal with it."

Samantha slammed her door. I waited to see if my mother would yell at her, but from the sound of it, she simply turned and went down the stairs.

At least the clouds had begun to break and some sunlight was slipping through and giving us enough light from windows to move about easily.

I washed and dressed in a sweater and jeans and then hurried to Dillon's room. I was surprised to see he wasn't there. He couldn't have cleaned off his car and driven off this soon. I saw Samantha had opened her door again, but she was sulking now in her room, sitting up in her bed, her arms folded. When she looked at me, I turned away.

I hurried downstairs. Halfway down, I heard laughter coming from the dining room. When I entered, there was Dillon at the table and Mrs. Marlene sitting across from him with Mr. Stark. There was a large candelabra on the table, all lit, even though there was a lot of light coming through the large picture window. They turned as I stepped in.

"What's going on?" I asked.

"Lucky we have a gas stove," Mrs. Marlene said. "Or your guest and Mr. Stark would be starving."

"I lived plenty of days without electricity, thank you. Rather eat by a fire anyway," Mr. Stark said.

"With the Native Americans you claim to have known? Listening to him, you'd think he was over two hundred and twenty and helped the pioneers."

Dillon laughed. Mr. Stark smiled.

"Turns out your friend Dillon here has worked with an old friend of mine," Mr. Stark said. "Rube Gibson. Has that farm over in Billsbury. Best sweet corn in the state. As Mrs. Marlene was just saying when she was giving me credit for bringing her the corn."

"Farm?" I said.

"Only part-time," Dillon said.

I stared at him. What other surprises were in store for me?

"Doing what?"

"Harvest season. When I was younger. My Woody Guthrie days," he added.

"I like a young man who's not afraid of getting his hands dirty," Mr. Stark said. He slapped his together. "Well, I'd better get started now that the snow has stopped. I'll be picking up your father in an hour, so I'd better get the driveway passable," he added as he stood.

"Where's my mother?"

"Maids couldn't show up, so she's in the doctor's office hunting down the defiant dust," Mrs. Marlene said, rising. "Dillon had an omelet. You?"

"You already had breakfast? What time did you get up?" I asked him.

"About an hour ago."

"Yes, thank you, Mrs. Marlene. I will have an omelet," I said. I poured myself some juice and sat across from Dillon. Mr. Stark left, and she went into the kitchen. "You never told me you worked on a farm."

"It was a couple of years ago. We haven't really told each other too much about ourselves yet, Fern," he said, and smiled. "Got to leave something for tomorrow," he added. "I was just fourteen. My father got it into his head that I should be earning my own allowance, and he knew Mr. Gibson's brother. I had to take a bus and walk two miles. You know who Woody Guthrie was, right?"

"A folk singer, part of the labor movement. He wrote 'This Land Is Your Land.' "

"I am impressed."

"I did a report on him for history class. He was one of the choices. I guess you slept all right. Afterward," I added.

"Conked out. Everything all right?" he asked.

I poured myself a cup of coffee and buttered a roll. "My mother knows you came to my room," I said. "I thought I'd better warn you. Unless she said something already."

"No. Am I in trouble?"

"Not yet. We'd both be, anyway."

"I'd better get to my car, dig it out, scrape the ice off the windows, and make my escape."

"I'll help," I said. "After I have my omelet."

He laughed. "Where's Little Miss Muffet?"

"Complaining and pouting. Probably waiting to see if my mother will bring her curds and whey."

"Will she?"

"I don't know. Not if I can help it, but I usually can't help it." I sipped some coffee. Suddenly, the lights came on.

"Civilization again," Dillon said.

I rose and blew out the candles. "Let me check on my breakfast," I said.

Dillon poured himself more coffee.

I returned with my omelet just as my mother stepped into the dining room.

"Morning, Ms. Corey," Dillon said immediately.

"Good morning." She paused as if she was

going to say something intense. I held my breath, but she just nodded at me and went into the kitchen.

"So is that mad?" Dillon asked in a whisper.

"Worried," I said. "I'd better find you a pair of boots. You're not going to shovel snow and scrape off ice in those loafers. Are you about a nine?"

"Yes. What, is there a shoe store here, too?"

"No," I said. "I took a guess. My brother's a nine and a half, but you should do all right in them." I finished my omelet and got up. "I'll be right down."

"Okay," he said, and surprised me by beginning to clear off the table. "Got to work on your mother." He winked.

When I got to the top of the stairway, Samantha stepped out of her room.

"Is Dillon still here?"

"Yes, but we're going to clean off his car so he can go home."

"I knew it," she said. "I knew he wouldn't stay to play checkers like he promised."

"Some of us have important things to do, Samantha. Get dressed and go down to breakfast so Mrs. Marlene can work on other things."

She scrunched up her nose.

"If you want, come out and help us clear off Dillon's car," I said.

There was a flicker of interest in her face.

"You'll be done before I get out there," she decided.

I shrugged. "If you had gone down to breakfast instead of sulking, you'd be ready."

"Who cares?" she said.

Yes, I thought, and walked away. *Who cares?*

I went into Ryder's room slowly and stealthily like a thief in the night. Of course, it was still in the wrecked state it had been in, something my father had ordered to be left that way. Why was a question that I thought was haunting my mother as well.

Avoiding looking at it as much as I could, I went to Ryder's closet to look for a pair of boots Dillon could use. Ryder had a few different pairs. I took the ones I thought were most functional and had started to close the closet when something I saw froze me.

There in the opposite corner, crumpled up, was what looked like my prom dress, the dress that had belonged to Ryder's mother, Samantha, the dress we had found together in the attic. My mother had had it tailored for me. Hesitantly, I knelt and reached for it. When I held it up, there was no question. It was the dress. I'd had it practically buried at the far left corner of the rack in my own closet. Since I had moved back to the main house, I had looked at it only once. In my mind, it was part of all that was forbidden now.

How had it come to be here?

Could Samantha have brought it to him? Would she ever confess to it?

Had my father seen it? My mother?

What should I do with it now? Should I tell my mother about it?

I knew my father still suspected me of giving the framed picture to Ryder. Why wouldn't he suspect me of doing this as well?

Because of my father's orders, no one had been in this room to organize and straighten out things, especially the clothing. The chances were very good no one except the one who put it here knew the dress was in this closet.

I made an instant decision, hoping it was the right one. I stuffed it under my arm, checked to be sure Samantha wasn't out in the hallway, and then hurried to my room. I put the dress back in my closet, took a deep breath, and went downstairs, where Dillon was waiting in the entryway.

"Hey," he said. "Thanks." He put on the boots and nodded. "Mr. Stark's plowed out a lot around my car, but the windows are caked with ice," he said. "He gave me one of these." He showed me the scraper. "I have one of my own in the car, just not as good."

"Let's go, then," I said, and reached for my coat and put on my boots.

We stepped into the brisk, just-above-freezing morning with a partly cloudy sky and a diminishing wind. Mr. Stark was just about finished with the driveway. He had already shoveled out the front walk. I started on the side windows while Dillon worked on the windshield. When we looked at each other, our breaths seemed to want to join in midair. He laughed at my determined efforts to get the ice glaze off. I was using both hands now.

He had started the engine, and the heater was doing some of the work for us. Mr. Stark left his tractor for a few minutes to help us do Dillon's back window and then said he had to go for my father.

"I don't think my mother's going to let me go anywhere today, Dillon."

"Not all the roads are even plowed yet," Mr. Stark said, overhearing me.

Dillon nodded at him. "I'll call you and we'll practice some lines over the phone," he told me.

We watched Mr. Stark drive off.

"I'll go in and thank your mother again," he said.

When we entered the house, he started to take off the boots.

"You can hold on to them if you need them," I said.

"Those are Ryder's," we heard, and turned to see Samantha standing there.

"That's fine. I don't need them now. Just driving straight home," Dillon said, smiling.

"Are you coming back?" Samantha asked.

"Someday," Dillon said. "Hold the checkers."

"You won't come back, and if you do, you won't want to play checkers with me or pool or anything," she said with the air of a biblical prophet. She turned and walked toward the dining room before either of us could respond.

"I thought I had a bitter view of things," Dillon said. "Now I feel as happy as one of Santa's helpers."

My mother appeared in the hallway. She had stepped out of my father's office.

"Thanks again, Ms. Corey," Dillon called to her.

"You just be careful on those roads. I'm sure they're far from perfect," she said.

"Will do." He put on his shoes and opened the door.

I looked back. My mother had gone into the dining room.

"I'll call," he said.

We kissed, and he walked out. I stood in the doorway and watched him get into his car and drive off.

After I closed the door, I looked up at the stairway. The dress, I thought. How did it get from my closet into Ryder's closet?

The answer to that would surely reveal another secret.

12

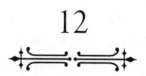

My phone was ringing the moment I had stepped into my bedroom a little more than an hour later. I had helped Mrs. Marlene clean up the kitchen. I smiled, imagining it was Dillon letting me know he was home safe and maybe telling me how much he missed me already. But I was wrong.

"How was the pizza? Did you get home safely? What about Dillon? Was he upset that I couldn't come? You're still trying out for the play, right?" Ivy asked, firing her questions at machine-gun speed.

"Are any of those questions multiple choice?"

She laughed. "I'm just going a bit crazy locked up. We're still waiting for our driveway to be plowed. My mother and I shoveled our walkway. My Internet was down as well as our cable TV. Were yours?"

"I never checked, but late last night the electricity went off for quite a while. So, a review and summary: We didn't get pizza. My mother wanted me home because the storm was flying in, and when we got to Wyndemere, it was wild, and the roads were already impassable, so my mother invited Dillon to stay over, and we had dinner here."

"What? Stay over? Did he do it?"

"He had no choice, but I think if he had, he would have chosen to stay," I said, my voice full of suggestion. "Did you know that Dillon once worked on a farm?"

"No. To be honest, Fern, as I told you, I really don't know all that much about him. Whenever I asked him questions about himself, he would just shrug or smile and say, 'What's the difference?' I just stopped asking."

I wondered if she even knew he was adopted but quickly decided that anything Dillon had told me about himself would remain a secret. Considering where I lived, keeping secrets wasn't a problem.

"Well, what did you two do all night?"

"We had a nice dinner, and then he played checkers with my brat sister and pool with me until it was time to go to sleep."

Enough said, I thought.

"You probably can never be bored in that house. Nothing else happened?"

"I told you, the electricity went off."

"I was hoping to hear about it going on," she said, and giggled.

"You know, I haven't done any of my home-work," I said, moving to change the subject. "I'm lucky we have the snow day. Better get to it.

I'll see you tomorrow. We're definitely going to audition for the play. Practice your lines."

"Okay," she said. " 'Byeeee." Her voice drifted off like that of a deserted little girl, desperate for a friend.

Loneliness had a way of inserting itself into your life in so many ways from the day you were born, I thought. There were many times when I was left alone like Ivy with few lifelines to friends. Did that make me stronger, more independent, or more insecure? Maybe what attracted me most to Dillon was his complete indifference about navigating friendships. I could easily envision him brushing off Ivy's personal questions. With a simple shrug, he handled so many questions and comments. Understandably, that would bother most people. If he was depicted in a cartoon, the balloon above his head would have the word *Whatever* and nothing else. Maybe because of all the tension in Wyndemere, his lack of concern made him even more attractive to me, made me more envious. There was power in indifference. At minimum, it illustrated self-confidence.

I really did have homework to do, so I went to my desk and began. I had no idea how much time had gone by until I heard a knock on my door and saw that I had dived into my work more than an hour and a half ago.

My mother stood in the doorway looking in at

me. There were so few times in my life when her face had taken on this same deep expression of gloom and doom, so deep that it seemed to freeze into a hard ceramic mask. Whenever I did see her like this, it was easy to believe she would never smile again. I held my breath, my heart as taut as a bowstring.

"What's wrong, Mummy? Something about Ryder?"

"Your father needs to speak to you. He's waiting for you in his office."

"Is it about Ryder?" I insisted.

"Of course," she said without hesitation.

"Did something more terrible happen to him?"

"He's the same. It's about you as much as it is about him, Fern. I want you to promise me that you will be completely honest with your father, that you will tell him anything he wants to know."

"What does he want to know?"

"This is a conversation that you have to have with him, Fern. It's best that I not be present, nor should I interfere. Go on," she said, stepping back. "He's waiting . . . anxiously."

I rose slowly. Why anxiously? I wondered. Why didn't she want to be there? Interfere with what?

"I didn't do anything, Mummy," I said. It was the child in me. I regretted it immediately, because it sounded so guilty, so immature.

"It's not possible to live this life without having

your own secrets, Fern; but a mature woman, or man, knows when she or he must reveal them, or some of them. Dark thoughts, actions, can be so heavy they weigh down your very soul. The only relief comes with honesty."

What was she talking about? Was it because she had realized Dillon had been in my room? Had she told my father? The last time I felt myself trembling this hard was when I was watching the paramedics work on Ryder after Parker had brought him up from the lake.

"Go on," she whispered.

I started out, my head down, my mind reeling with possibilities. Had Samantha spread another lie? Surely, both my parents knew how deceitful she could be. I looked toward her room. Her door was closed. If she had done or said something that would get me in trouble, she wouldn't hesitate to be standing there, gloating.

My mother followed slowly behind me. I glanced back at her. She nodded, and I started down the stairs, not unlike someone who was descending toward her own execution. I felt like one of the darker upstairs shadows was clinging to me or I was at least dragging it along behind me.

It was possible to count on the fingers of my two hands how many times I had been alone with my father in his office. There was something about the floor-to-ceiling bookcases with their first editions of medical texts and leather-bound old novels, the vintage hardwood floors kept as immaculate as the day the floorboards were laid, the framed diplomas, framed pictures with important and powerful people in the community and the state, as well as framed pictures of his first wife, of Ryder, and the large portrait of my paternal grandparents leering down, something about all of it that gave his office an air of regality. Sitting behind his oversize desk in his plush high-back leather chair, he always looked taller and truly very important to me.

No one, not even Bea in the old days, raised his or her voice very much in this room. Whenever I had entered it, I practically tiptoed and always paused at least six feet from his desk until he had beckoned for me to come closer. Most of the time, the curtains were drawn open on the tall paneled windows behind him. They looked out on the undeveloped acreage of the estate, the forest pristine. It was peaceful, a view that would encourage you to think or just relax, meditate. This was my father's escape, where he came to comfort himself if he lost a patient or perhaps where he simply contemplated his life.

Right now, the door to the office was partially open. I knocked and heard him say, "Come in, Fern." I remembered him doing that a few times before. It was as if he could look through walls, especially these. When I was little, there wasn't much that I thought he couldn't do. He was "the Doctor." He saved lives, held the heartbeats of his patients in his very hands. He could frustrate death.

However, I was surprised to see that he wasn't behind his desk. He was sitting in the rocking chair across from the black leather settee, his fingertips pressed against one another in cathedral fashion. His jacket was off, but he still wore a tie. He looked very tired, his shoulders sagging a little. His usually neatly brushed hair looked a bit messy, like the hair of someone who had been running his fingers through it when he was frazzled.

"Please, close the door," he said after I had entered.

He nodded at the settee, and I quickly went over and sat. I didn't lean back. I sat forward, my arms crossed over my breasts. I couldn't recall him ever looking at me with more intensity.

"As you know, following Dr. Seymour's wishes, we've been very careful about discussing your and Ryder's relationship during that period right before you two went out on the lake. We've made it very clear to you that you should do the same. Perhaps we waited too long to begin that important discussion with Ryder, but Dr. Seymour was concerned about how the impact of that, along with the rush of terrifying details relating to his near drowning, would affect his fragile psyche. I understood completely and agreed with him.

"When I was younger, interning, I was on duty one night at the hospital when a car accident involving four teenagers occurred. The driver was under the influence, way over the alcohol limit, and the two passengers in the rear, one the best friend of the girl in the front seat, were, along with the driver, instantly killed. The girl I treated had all sorts of broken bones, concussion, near-fatal internal trauma, but she survived. It took two operations and months for her to recuperate, over ten weeks in the hospital, actually.

"Every day during those ten weeks, she asked anyone who visited if he or she had seen her best friend. Clearly, she was wondering why she hadn't visited her. The doctors insisted that no one, not even her family, tell her what had happened. She had no memory of the accident, and the belief was that information would be too shocking and would impede her recuperation. It could have lasting psychological damage if it wasn't handled properly, slowly and carefully, which it eventually was. She went on to physical therapy, was released, and, last I heard, went to college, married, and had two children."

Tears seemed to freeze in my eyes, but it was my father who looked like he was close to them.

"I didn't tell Ryder anything you or Dr. Seymour didn't want me to tell him," I said, but he didn't seem to hear me. He almost didn't recognize my being there. Throughout the recollection of that car accident, he seemed like someone talking in his sleep.

"We, meaning Dr. Seymour and myself," he continued, "were very aware of the fact that as Ryder's condition improved, his feelings about you became confused. He had many memories of you stored, memories that went back to when you and he spent time as youngsters in Wyndemere, but there was that gap when he grew apart from you and you lived in the rear of the mansion.

"As you know, both your mother and I blame ourselves for not realizing how that all had begun to change. It took the event on the lake to drive it home. My hope and your mother's was that you would accept the reality of who you and Ryder were to each other, as shocking as it was, and move on. I did urge you to do that. I know your mother did, too. I would never say, however, that I did enough. I'm aware of my shortcomings when it comes to my family, my children. I'm absent even when I'm here. When I discovered that Ryder had that picture of you and him on prom night, I was very upset. I know you knew I was."

"I didn't give it to him," I said. "I didn't lie to you." My throat was so tight that I wasn't sure I had spoken loudly enough. He ignored what I had said anyway.

286

"I returned home late the night before Ryder's breakdown, and as I always did, I stopped in his room to see how he was. He wasn't there."

He paused and stared at me expectantly. I shook my head. What was he telling me? Was he asking if I knew where he was?

"I had started to go back downstairs to search for him when I heard him walking in the hallway. He was coming from your room."

"No!" I said, raising my arms, my hands in fists. "He was never in my room at night, never."

He shook his head at me as if I was to be pitied. "I stood there and watched him come out of your room, Fern."

"If he was there, I didn't know it."

"He saw me. He looked like he was sleep-walking. His look was that vacant. I followed him into his room and made sure he got into bed. Then I pulled a chair up beside him and asked him why he was in your room. He said you were having nightmares, and he had gone to comfort you. He had slept beside you; he had held you."

I shook my head. "That never happened. He must have dreamed it."

"He said it kept happening, and he knew why. You were afraid he didn't love you, and I don't mean like a brother and sister. He said he could see that in your eyes."

"No, Daddy. That's not true. I never said or did anything to get him to believe that," I said as

287

forcefully as I could. I could feel the heat in my face.

"He said he told you that of course, he still loved you. How could he not love you? Then he pulled back his blanket to show me."

I couldn't move. He was staring at me now with such accusation in his eyes.

"Show you what?"

"He slept with your prom dress beside him in the bed. He had it laid out as if it was being worn, as if you were beside him."

Was that thunder or my heart pounding like a closed fist against the inside of my chest to accompany the scream building inside me? I shook my head. *The dress, oh, no, the dress,* I thought.

"The picture was one thing, Fern; the dress is quite another. What did you hope would happen when you gave it to him?"

"I didn't . . ."

"I made a quick decision and told him the complete truth, all of it, including the accident. I was afraid of where this was all going now. It was like a runaway train. I confessed it all without first conferring with Dr. Seymour. To be sure, I wasn't confident I had done the right thing, and sure enough, it probably wasn't. The following day, he had his breakdown."

I was shaking my head so hard that my eyes ached. "I didn't give him that dress."

"When your mother called me about Ryder's breakdown and I arrived at the house with Dr. Seymour, I saw that I had forgotten to take away the dress. I was so angry that I balled it up and threw it into the closet. That's where it was left . . . on that floor."

The chill that traveled through my body was probably close to the chill of death. I trembled in anticipation of what he was going to say next.

"When I looked for it earlier, it was gone. Did you take it back?"

"Yes, but—"

He put up his hand like a traffic policeman, sat back, and just rocked a moment, looking out his window and not at me.

"You don't have to tell me anything or try to explain anything, Fern. When I was only twelve or so, I used to dream that I set this house on fire and watched all the shadows of death and unhappiness go up in the black smoke, dissipating in such a way that they could no longer trouble anyone."

He turned back to me and smiled, but coldly.

"Silly, of course, to blame anything we do on the leering portraits and statues, empty rooms still echoing with sobs, and corners clutching tragedies, entrapping them in shadows, but as intelligent and as scientific as I am, I can't shake the idea that this house has a mind of its own, a power drawn from its inhabitants, yes, but perhaps something far more primeval. My mother certainly believed it.

"I have no doubt that you are inherently a good girl, Fern. What's happened to you, around you, would be too overwhelming even for those much older and experienced than you are. I don't deny that you are a victim, too. It's all happened in this house. So," he said, slapping down on his knees, "your mother and I have discussed this somewhat and agree."

"Agree about what?"

"We think you should attend a private school that has dormitories, a private school where you can be away from all the dark places of the past that promise to do you more harm, more harm than we've already done to you ourselves," he said. "I will thoroughly research the school. It will be the best private high school available. You'll make new friends, get a fresh view of things, develop your outstanding talents, and grow into a fine young woman."

"You're not listening to me, Daddy. What you think happened between Ryder and me did not happen," I said. "You're making a mistake. I took the dress when I saw it there because I was afraid you would see it and have these exact thoughts. Samantha . . ."

He smiled and nodded like he had been waiting for me to mention her. "Samantha needs a different sort of private school, one that resembles a tough love camp or something. We can blame many things on her, but unless you described in clear detail the events that occurred before you and Ryder were caught in that storm, she has no idea about the . . . about it. After all, how else would she know anything like that?"

I looked away. Denial was futile.

"What about Ryder?" I asked. "What's going to happen to him now?"

"He'll have to remain in the clinic for a while. He's almost catatonic. As I said, I blame no one but myself for the current situation. In time, we'll start again, easing him back, hopefully once again to a life with some promise. This is best for everyone, Fern. I'm sorry I wasn't a real father to you. Even after you were settled here in your proper place as my daughter, I failed you. I've failed with all my children. Whatever good there is in them is because of your mother. I don't think I ever truly appreciated how important she is to all of us, especially me."

"How long before you send me to this private school?" I asked, resigned to my fate.

"Not long. As I said, let me investigate. I have some very important friends who will know what should be best. For now, carry on the best you can where you are."

"Will it be far away?"

"I don't know. I don't expect so, no. Your mother wouldn't approve of that. Look," he said, trying to insert a lighter touch, "I'm right here but couldn't be farther away if I tried. Right?"

"No," I said. "You cast a long and deep shadow. It doesn't leave with you."

His eyes widened, and I thought he came the closest to a warm smile that I had ever seen from him.

"I have no doubt you will be very successful in whatever you choose to do, choose to be, Fern."

"That's the problem, isn't it, Daddy? I never had a choice when it came to who I would be."

I stood up and looked as firmly at him as he could look at anyone. I was, after all, his daughter.

"You have misjudged me," I said.

Where I got the courage to continue, I did not know, but continue I would.

"I never thought I would think it, but when it comes to what's happened here, you're myopic. I just learned the word today with some homework I had to do, but it fits you so well that it's true serendipity. The problem with specialists is they see only the one organ and not the whole person. That's probably been your problem your whole life."

I didn't wait for his response. I walked out of the office, closing the door behind me. My tears didn't break free until I reached the stairway. Before I started up, my mother stepped out of the living room and called to me. I looked back at her and shook my head, and then I ran up the stairs. Samantha opened her door to peer out at me. When she saw me, she closed her door again.

Lucky she did. *She just saved her life,* I told myself.

I hurried on to my room, shut the door behind me, and practically dove onto my bed, burying my face in my pillow. I felt like smothering myself. I expected I would cry until my chest ached, but surprisingly, I was too stunned and saddened to cry. I turned over instead and glared at the ceiling, anger rushing in over sadness.

Wyndemere, I thought, *why are you doing all this to me?*

My phone rang. I wasn't going to answer it, but when it went to the answering machine and I heard Dillon's voice, I practically tore the receiver off the cradle.

"Dillon."

"Hey," he said. "I thought if you weren't busy, I'd read some lines to you and you could—"

"I'm not going out for the play," I said quickly.

"What? Why not?"

I thought for a moment.

"Did something else happen, something to Ryder?"

"Yes, something else happened," I said. I thought for another second.

"Well, what?" he asked.

"Never mind. How bad are the roads?"

"They aren't bad now. Why?"

"I want you to come over to take me for a ride. I need to talk to you."

"Really? Sure," he said. "I'll be there in about a half hour."

"Don't rush, and don't dare get into a car accident," I warned. "That would be like putting the last nail in my coffin, vampire or not."

He laughed. "I'm on my way," he said.

I got up and went into the bathroom to wash my face and fix my hair. When I looked at my image in the mirror, I squinted and said out loud, "My father is wrong. I will not be a victim."

Quietly, I put on a cable-knit sweater and a pair of shoe boots. Then I scooped a sock hat off the shelf in the closet and went to the windows to wait and watch for Dillon. He pulled into the driveway just about when he said he would. His eagerness buoyed my courage. I turned and rushed out and down the hallway and then practically bounced down the stairs.

I heard my mother and my father coming down the hallway from his office. I was shocked. They were holding hands but let go and paused when they saw me.

"I'm going for a ride with Dillon," I said.

I didn't give my mother a chance to respond. I did hear her call my name when I opened the door, but I closed it behind me before she could call to me again.

Dillon had stepped out of his car. He was standing beside it as I hurried to him.

"Drive," I ordered, and got in.

He looked back at the front door, gave that typical shrug, and got in. He didn't ask anything once he looked at me. Probably afraid to speak, he started the engine and drove out slowly. I didn't look back. He turned left, and we were off.

"So?" he finally said. "What's this all about?"

"If you keep going another mile or so, you'll see a road on the left that takes you down toward the lake. It's a public beach, and there's a dock for boats they rent."

"No one's probably there. The lake's frozen over."

"Just find a place to park," I said.

He was quiet. Neither of us spoke until after he had made the turn.

"Never knew about this, but then again, I didn't spend any time at the lake," he said.

I said nothing until he found a plowed area reserved for parking. He pulled in so that we faced the lake, but he didn't turn off his engine.

"I'll keep the heater going," he said, and sat back.

I leaned forward, looked down, and then sat back and began without turning to him. "You're quite familiar with what happened after the prom last year at Shane Cisco's after-party?"

"As familiar as I care to be."

"You know what happened to my date, Paul Gabriel?"

"I know he was expelled. I haven't followed his career," he said sardonically.

"My stepmother, Bea, I guess I have to call her that, was still living at Wyndemere and made it a federal case, claiming I was responsible for all the negativity now aimed at Wyndemere and even her family name. My father didn't do much to defend me. He rarely challenged Bea. He left the running of the house up to her mainly. That's another story. What happened as a result, though, was that he wanted Ryder and me to spend less time together. His way of putting it was 'until things calm' or something. Neither Ryder nor I appreciated that."

"So you spent more time, not less, together," Dillon said as if he had to fill in the blanks.

"Yes. What you have to understand is we had no idea at the time that we were related, that Dr. Davenport was in fact my father."

He stared at me. Was he going to fill in these blanks? "You're saying you didn't spend time together just to defy your father?"

"No."

Cool Dillon finally looked a little shocked.

"We didn't know who we were."

He nodded. "How far did it go?"

"Not any farther than you and I have," I said.

Maybe I was imagining it or hoping for it,

but he looked like he was relieved. "And now?"

"After the lake accident, which resulted in Ryder's memory loss, my father and Ryder's therapist, Dr. Seymour, emphasized how important it was for me not to restore those memories directly. They wanted Ryder to sort of ease into it, into his memory of the accident. For these past months, I've been walking on eggshells. As far as he knew, I was Emma Corey's daughter and not much else. My sister Samantha enjoyed that and did her best to keep me as that person only. It was the way Ryder had known me most of his life. He was in the accident before Dr. Davenport had come forward to tell the truth."

"So he's never actually been told the truth."

"Not until now," I said. "And now only because my father believes I was secretly trying to revive our short romance."

"What gave him that idea?" he asked, with expected suspicion.

"A picture Mr. Stark took of Ryder and me the night of the prom was found in Ryder's possession, as well as the dress I wore, which was his real mother's dress altered and tailored to fit me."

"How did he get all that?"

"I think Samantha did it to stir up trouble. I did something that only helped her along."

"What?"

"When I went up to get you that pair of Ryder's

boots, I discovered the dress was in his closet. I was afraid my father would find it and think I had given it to him, so I took it."

"And?"

I looked away for a moment. It was so hard to say these things. "He had already seen the dress, had seen it beside Ryder in his bed."

Dillon stared, his mouth slightly open. "In his bed?"

"Spread out like someone was there wearing it."

"And then . . . and then you had taken it?"

"Yes."

He nodded.

"There's more. The night before Ryder had his breakdown, my father went to check on him, and he wasn't in his room. He was about to go looking for him when he saw him coming from the direction of my room. When he asked him where he had been, he told him he had to comfort me, embrace me in my bed. I told my father Ryder was dreaming; it never happened, but there is that lingering doubt."

"Whose doubt?"

"My father's."

"He thinks it really happened?"

"Yes, but it didn't. I swear."

"Wow. Now what?"

"My father felt it was necessary at that point to tell Ryder the whole truth. It had the result

Dr. Seymour feared; it was why he reacted so violently and why he was set back in his recuperation. My father blames himself, but . . ."

"But he blames you, too."

"Yes. Even my mother does, I'm afraid."

"So what happens now?"

"My father wants me to attend a private high school, live away from Wyndemere. That's why I told you I'm not going out for the play tomorrow."

Dillon's balloon containing his usual *Whatever* was gone. He looked genuinely stunned and unhappy. "Oh?"

"I wanted you to know everything, Dillon, but I want you to help me do one more thing."

"Sure," he said, without even waiting to see what it was. "What?"

"I want you to help me get into the clinic to see Ryder."

13

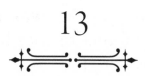

Dr. Seymour's clinic was not a psychiatric hospital for the criminally insane. There weren't bars on the windows or high fences around it, but it still had serious security. You couldn't simply visit someone there whenever you liked; you had to be approved, be on a list authorized by Dr. Seymour himself.

There was no doubt in my mind that neither my father nor my mother would like me visiting Ryder, especially now. I was even unsure of what would happen when they found out. Would I do further damage to my relationship with my parents, damage that would take years to repair, assuming it could be repaired? Did my mother love me enough to withstand the storm of disappointment and blame that would surely follow? Even Mr. Stark would be devastated. He was very fond of Ryder and practically worshipped my father. My being sent to a private school, ostracized from this family, as fragile as it was, was probably the least of what would result.

I had never been to the clinic, but I knew where it was located. I had made it my business to learn about it after Ryder was originally sent there.

About five miles outside Lake Wyndemere, the squared U-shape building sat on a small knoll, high enough to give the residents and staff a very good lake view. It was a relatively new complex. A billionaire named Daryl Fenton had donated the money in the memory of his granddaughter, who had committed suicide when she was a year younger than I was now. He had chosen Dr. Seymour to design and head it. Aside from a plaque with his granddaughter's image embossed over the words *A thing of beauty is a joy for ever—Keats,* there was no other reference to the Fentons.

The clinic had beautiful grounds, rivaling any estate or mansion, with lush gardens blooming in the spring and summer, fountains, and walkways. Contact with nature was considered therapeutic. It was no secret that the clinic was expensive and catered to the very wealthy. I had heard that even celebrities suffering from addiction resulting in some mental issue were often patients there. However, I also learned that Mr. Fenton had left an endowment to help finance the treatment of teenagers in desperate need who were less able to afford it.

I had no idea whether Dillon would help me get in to see Ryder. I feared that once he had learned that I was being sent to a private high school, which would make it very difficult for us to see each other during the remainder of this school year, he might decide it was better to make a clean break in our budding relationship. Why suffer with it? I certainly wouldn't blame him if he decided that was the best choice to make. Ironically, at the start, I thought he was the one bringing along all sorts of complications. As it turned out, I was the one nearly crushed by them.

"Why do you want to see him now, Fern?" he asked.

"I want him to understand who I am, who we are. I think it's the only way he'll really find himself again. It breaks my heart to think how lost he is. I'd like to do that before I leave."

"But you said your father admitted that he told him everything and that's why Ryder became so upset, had the breakdown. He blamed himself."

"I'm sure I contributed to that reaction. You have no idea how I've treated him since he's been home. At times, I forced myself to be indifferent when we were together at the dinner table or in his room, in the game room, anywhere in the house. I acted disinterested in him, barely talking to him most of the time. I let Samantha dominate our conversations, and I avoided going to his room without her or someone else present. I was afraid I'd be accused of exactly what I'm being accused of now. I gave him a Christmas present but had to be sure it wasn't anything very personal. It was just a funny shirt. I was even afraid to show my father too much affection in front of him, and I am sure my father, who rarely showed it anyway, avoided showing me any whenever Ryder was present. It's been pins and needles. Believe me. I understand what soldiers face when they go through a minefield.

"But I want him to understand and believe that I will love him still, as his sister, and I don't blame him for anything that's happened. I can't just leave it all as it is," I said, my throat so tight with emotion that it ached for me to speak. "Neither my father nor my mother will permit me to do that now. They'll just send me away, and the dark thoughts will linger in Ryder's mind. I can't imagine what it will be like for him to return to Wyndemere with those added shadows woven like cobwebs only he will see."

Dillon nodded. "Nevertheless, you're taking a big risk. You might set off a hell of an explosion in your family."

"Yes, I know. I'll admit I'm afraid."

"You could just leave and put it all behind you. Start over."

"Like some Etch A Sketch and redraw my life?"

"Which doesn't make me happy," he said. "I was beginning to believe I might enjoy my last year here before heading off to college and then stay in touch with you, come home as many times as I could."

"I'm hoping we'll still be able to see each other

most of the remainder of this school year, maybe on some holiday weekends."

"Unless he sends you across the country or overseas."

"He won't. My mother wouldn't permit it."

"Maybe she would after you do this."

"She won't," I insisted. "She won't be happy, but she knows what it means to be separated from your family by great distances, and I don't mean just in miles."

"Yeah, I imagine she does." He was silent, thinking, and then he nodded. "Okay. Give me some time."

"What are you going to do?"

He put the car into reverse and started to back out of the parking area. "Reconnaissance," he said. He smiled. "I finally have a real challenge."

He drove me home.

"We might have to cut classes to do this, Fern," he said when we pulled up to the front of the mansion. "Timing could be very critical."

"Two days ago, that would have terrified me," I said. "Right now, it's about what a sneeze is to pneumonia."

He laughed. "I'll call you later."

"Thanks for trusting me and caring for me enough to want to do this, Dillon," I said.

We leaned toward each other and kissed. After I got out, I watched him drive away, wondering if I had started something I couldn't stop. I

304

could hear Mrs. Marlene warning, *You can't put toothpaste back in the tube.*

But maybe that was the only way I could get myself to go through with this: get on the plane while it was moving. I could regret it all I wanted, but I couldn't stop the takeoff and being on that flight.

My mother stepped out of the living room the moment I entered the house. The way she had her shoulders hoisted like someone who just had an ice cube dropped down her back and the way she was pressing her lips together, creating those tiny white spots at the corners of her mouth, told me she was angrier than ever. It wasn't something I had often seen, but it took only once to embed it forever in my mind.

"You never leave this house without my permission," she said through clenched teeth. "Why did you do that?"

"I'm sorry, Mummy, but I needed to leave and breathe fresh air. I'm being accused of things I didn't do."

"Go up to your room and stay there, Fern. Right now, I'm too upset with your behavior to discuss it."

I walked toward the stairway. When I looked back, she had already returned to the living room. I could hear my father's voice, but he was speaking too low and softly for me to understand anything he was saying. When I entered my room, I went to my windows and stood there with my arms folded under my breasts, gazing out, remembering happier times.

Once, to defy Bea, who had refused to permit me to ride in the limo to school, Ryder refused to go to school in the limo and boarded the bus with me. He loved "getting her goat," as Mrs. Marlene would say. I recalled our snowball fights and sledding in the winter, biking around the lake together, and playing badminton and tennis. There was a point when Ryder was into his friends, and doing anything with the younger daughter of the head housekeeper diminished to almost nothing. Those were the more difficult days for both my mother and me. Bea was still the reigning queen and patrolled this mansion with a riding whip at her side, snapping it at her servants and especially at me.

One day, Ryder took a longer look at me and saw that I had moved from childhood to adolescence. I couldn't remember a time when I didn't think of him romantically. Something happened, especially the night of the prom, when we danced together and then he was chosen king and I was chosen queen. We let things continue to develop. I told him I felt like a commoner in England having an affair with a royal.

"There's nothing common about you," he told me.

I brought his words and his kiss along with me

into my dreams every night. And then all that had come crashing down around us in that spring storm. It was as if what we had been doing was so forbidden that even nature was outraged.

"Why is everyone mad at you?" I heard Samantha say now, interrupting my reverie. I turned around, poised to pounce. She even took a step back when she saw the look in my eyes.

I smiled coldly, my lips surely resembling two streaks of ruby-tinted ice. "Aren't you happy about it, Samantha? Aren't you so pleased?"

She shrugged, called on some courage, and came in a little farther to lean against the leather chair, running her fingers up and down the arm of it and avoiding looking directly at me. She was acting strangely, which ironically calmed me.

"Why should I be happy about it? It's like a morgue down there, and as soon as I say anything, they tell me to stop shouting and go find something to do. They won't let me invite anyone over, either. Whatever it is, it's not fair! Why are they punishing me, too?"

"Please, Samantha. I'm not in the mood right now to hear your silly complaints."

She didn't move.

I thought for a moment and stepped toward her. "Why did you say what you said to Dillon? Why did you tell him Ryder would be upset if Dillon was my boyfriend?"

She looked at me guiltily and then looked down.

"Why?" I insisted.

"Ryder always asked me more questions about you than anyone else when you weren't there. I thought maybe he liked you more than he liked me."

"What do you mean by always? When exactly did that start?"

"After he came home from the clinic."

"Soon after?"

"Yes," she said. "He didn't ask questions about me as much, and when I told him things I was doing, he looked bored."

"What did he ask about me, exactly?"

"Stuff."

"What stuff, Samantha? Please be specific. Give me an example or two."

"Who were your friends? Did you go on dates? Did you have a boyfriend? When I told him about your going to the movie, he wanted to know if you would be going with a boy. I said I didn't know, but then, the next day, you were going to a lunch date with a boy, so I told him. I said the boy's name was Dillon Evans. I told him I'd heard that he was weird, but that was before I met him."

"How did you know about my lunch date?"

"I heard you tell your mother and Mrs. Marlene before I went to Raegan's house. That's when I ran upstairs and told him about Dillon."

"What did he say?"

"Nothing, but I could see that he wasn't happy. I told him I was going to my friend's house and couldn't do anything with him. I was sorry he would have to be alone. I guess he was just upset he had to stay home all the time. He liked me to tell him things," she added adamantly. "You didn't tell him much. He even asked me why you hardly spoke to him."

"He asked you that? When?"

"I don't know. A while ago. I told him not to worry, I'd tell him stuff. And I did!"

"That's why you gave him that picture, right, Samantha?"

"I didn't." She paused, stopping herself from saying something else.

"You gave it to him because, as you said just now, you thought you could get him to remember things, and then you would be so important, be able to brag and make our father proud of you. I'm right, aren't I? Aren't I?" I shouted.

"No," she said. "I mean, yes, I tried to remind him of things all the time, and sometimes he did remember. And he thanked me, too. I was helping him more than you were. You only made him sad."

"That's why you gave him the dress, too, right?"

"What dress?"

"Never mind. I think I've learned enough. You have a mean heart, Samantha. Someday all this jealousy will eat you alive. You'll be horribly alone, because you'll drive away anyone who would even dream of liking you."

"I will not." She smiled. "You're the one being punished now. What did you do? Why won't anyone tell me?"

"I suppose you're right about that, sly Samantha. I am the one being punished, not you." I sat on my bed. "But the biggest punishment might be the biggest gift I could receive after all."

"What? Why would you get a big gift? That's not fair. What's the big gift?"

"The gift is that I'm not going to be living here all the time."

"Where will you be living? Back in the help's quarters? That's not a gift," she said, smiling. "I used to tell my friends it was once a dungeon."

"Mentally, I suppose it was. No, I won't be living anywhere in Wyndemere, Samantha. Sorry to disappoint you."

She looked suspicious. "Was your mother fired? Do you have to move away?"

"If she was, you'd be the most miserable person in this mansion, Samantha, and the sad thing is you don't realize it. You don't realize how she has cared for you, protected you, even when I wished she didn't all these years. How many mothers do you think are like her? Certainly not your real mother."

Her face softened. "I'm not saying I want her to be fired and made to move away."

"I'm sure you don't. You're not that stupid. You know you'd be the loneliest person in the world."

She looked remorseful, even a bit frightened. "So what's your big gift, then?"

"They're sending me to a private school where you sleep in a dorm. I'll be here only on holidays and maybe the summer. Maybe not. I don't know. Sometimes there are summer programs at these schools. Sometimes they send you to Europe with a group. I could be gone for years."

She genuinely looked stunned and upset.

"Why aren't you smiling? Doesn't that make you happy? You'll be queen of the roost, Samantha."

"What roost? No, it doesn't make me happy. I don't have a brother here, and now I won't have a sister."

"You still have your friends, Samantha. You can probably have them over more frequently once I'm gone."

"My friends don't like sleeping over here that much," she admitted. "They like coming here to do things sometimes, but they would rather go home after dinner."

"Why?"

"I don't know."

"You know," I said. "You're afraid to say it. I don't blame you. They think this place is haunted."

"It's not!" She looked at me sharply, back to being Bea's daughter. "You're the one who's happy my friends don't stay over. You hate me," she said, her eyes tearing.

I shook my head and sighed as if I had reached down for my final breath. "I don't hate anyone. When you hate someone, he or she usually doesn't care anyway, and you walk around with oil boiling in your heart. You'll learn that it robs you of smiles. Sometimes," I said, looking out the window, "you can't even appreciate a sunny day. You end up hating yourself, hating what you've become. Take my advice for once, Samantha. Don't hate anyone. Just . . . ignore him or her. Use your eraser."

"What eraser?"

I smiled. "You have to find it yourself, Samantha. It's in your head and your heart."

"There's no eraser in my head or my heart. That's stupid. You're crazy," she said.

She looked around, glum again. Despite her clawing jealousies and envy, she had spent a lot of time in this room with me, asking questions, talking about boys and school, sharing her little secrets, and, despite her personality, struggling to find a sister. Wyndemere House was already filled with empty rooms in which echoes went to sleep in the very walls. Now mine would be added.

"Don't worry. I'll make sure no one bothers

your room when you're gone," she said. "Just in case you come right back."

"Don't bet on that, Samantha. Our father is too determined that I don't, especially after Ryder comes home again."

She looked down, pondering. Then she looked up quickly. "Are you going to take your dolls?"

"I might," I said.

She looked even sadder.

"Thanks for reminding me."

"You're welcome."

She stared a moment. "It's still not fair," she said, then turned and left.

That was probably her pathetic way of saying something nice to me, I thought, and for the moment, at least, I had someone else to pity besides myself, but that moment didn't last long. My mother wasn't ready to forgive or forget, as she was about to demonstrate.

I thought it was some sort of holdover from the days when she lived in England. When either she or her sister did something her parents thought wrong, she was sent to her room. At dinnertime, food was brought to her. Part of the punishment was to eat alone. Those were the days when being with your family kept your heart warm and hopeful. It was painful to be denied it. Truthfully, it was painful for me now, too. I was quite unlike many of my classmates, who thought nothing could be more boring than family dinners when they could be with their friends hanging out at malls or in friends' basements and bedrooms while everyone texted everyone with the same question: *What are you doing now?*

My mother inflicted her parents' punishment on me tonight, but she looked like she was in far more pain about it than I was. She brought the tray in and placed it on my desk.

"This is your dinner. I will return in an hour to pick up your tray, Fern."

"This is silly, Mummy, and unfair," I added, hating how I sounded like Samantha. But it was unfair.

"I want you to spend time alone, thinking about everything. Tomorrow, after you return from school, we'll talk. Eat your food before it gets cold." She started out and turned in the doorway to look back at me. "No one is happy about this," she said, and left.

No one was happy about this? What did she think I was? Ecstatic?

I'm trying to swim up a waterfall, I thought. The more I protested and the more I denied the accusations, the worse things were. I picked at my food and then sprawled on my bed and dozed. My mother came in nearly an hour later and saw how little I had eaten.

"You know he wants to send me to a private school, don't you?" I asked as she started to pick up the tray, avoiding looking at me.

She paused and turned to me. "Under the circumstances, it's probably the best thing," she said. "Come right home after school tomorrow. Your father is working his schedule so he can come home early, hopefully with information, and then we'll have a full discussion about it all."

"My father," I said disdainfully, and turned away.

She picked up the tray and left. I was going to return to my homework but thought, *Why bother now?* Instead, I took a shower and got ready for bed. A little while later, Dillon called.

"You still want to do this?" he asked immediately.

"More than ever."

"Okay. I found a way to get you in," he said. "Because of the schedule there, we'll have to leave during the school day. We'll pretend we're going to lunch, and then we'll leave through the door in the west wing. It opens closer to the parking lot. Less chance of being seen."

"You're going to get into so much trouble, too, Dillon. Are you sure?"

"My parents will barely notice. See you soon," he said.

I hung up, but my heart was pounding. How would I fall asleep tonight? My mind was spinning like a roulette wheel. Would it stop on a lucky number?

If Dillon really did get me in and I found Ryder, how would he react? Would he have another tantrum? Would he hurt himself? Would the police be called? Exactly how much trouble would I have gotten Dillon into, too? We both would have cut school. He and I would probably be suspended. What would his parents do? Would it affect his attending college? Couldn't we get criminal records for breaking into the clinic?

I didn't fall asleep until it was almost morning. It was the first time in a long time that I needed my alarm clock to wake me on a school day, too. And when I awoke, the questions that were on my mind when I had gone to sleep were still there. I was in something of a daze while I dressed. Fortunately, my father wasn't at breakfast. I dreaded feeling his anger. He had already left the house. Neither my mother nor Mrs. Marlene said anything much to me, nor I to them. It was like eating after a funeral.

All this was true for everyone except, of course, Samantha. She complained about not being able to have just a doughnut for breakfast. Mrs. Marlene gave her a good lecture on nutrition. I ate what I could. My mother was watching me with side glances but said nothing except to remind me to come home right after school. I imagined she thought my avoiding looking at her was a result of my guilty feelings. I was simply

316

afraid she'd realize I had other intentions. She had always been keen when it came to how I felt and what I thought.

When we got into the limo, Samantha rushed to tell Parker about my being sent off to a private school. She was still feeling sorrier for herself and surprised both Parker and me by complaining that she wasn't being sent off to the same private school. I wondered if she had spoken to one of her snobby friends, maybe Raegan Kelly, who probably told her I would be in a better place that cost a lot.

Parker said nothing, but when he looked at me as I got out of the car at school, I could see the sadness in his eyes. Chances were that he'd be another person I would disappoint today. He was the one who had dived into the lake and saved Ryder's life. Everything that happened to Ryder since was very important to Parker.

Maybe Dillon was right yesterday, I thought as I walked into the building. Maybe I should just leave and not look back. Maybe I should become someone else. Twenty years ago, my mother had walked out of her house and changed her life, practically changed her identity. She was in deep emotional pain doing it, I was sure, but she was determined to follow her dream, and she didn't look back. It wasn't a dream of mine to leave the only life I had known, but I was losing the freedom to choose anything for myself while I lived in the mansion now. I couldn't even choose my dreams.

Dillon met me in the hallway by my locker. He was carrying a shopping bag.

"What's that?"

"Our key to getting in," he said, and he reached into the bag to bring out two T-shirts with the words *Sasco's Food Products* in bold letters across their fronts. He showed me two black caps as well. He put them back in the bag and walked with me toward my homeroom. Ivy was waiting for us by the door.

"I don't understand what those are for," I said.

"I found out the clinic gets deliveries from Sasco's. There's an entrance for deliveries at the right rear of the building. I bought two cases of soups that we'll bring in as a supposed special delivery. If anyone at the clinic asks, you and I work at Sasco's part-time.

"But," he said, holding me back before we reached Ivy, "the best is yet to come."

"What?"

"Remember the hostess at Nature's Ways, Maya?"

"Yes, so?"

"Turns out her sister works at the clinic. Maintenance. A fancy name for cleaning girl."

"How did you find that out?"

"I went to Nature's Ways last night, and Maya

sat with me. It wasn't very busy. We had more conversation than ever. She wanted to know about you. Were you my girlfriend, etcetera. When I explained who you were, she was excited. She knows Wyndemere House. Of course, she knows who your father is. She knew all about your brother's accident and told me that her sister Toby works at the clinic."

Ivy, now curious, started to walk toward us.

He continued to speak but more quickly. "She texted me this morning with your brother's room number and the schedule he follows. That's why I told you we have to leave around lunchtime. I went on the Internet and got the layout of the place. I know exactly how to go."

"What are you two talking about so intensely?" Ivy asked.

I looked at Dillon. His revelations and plan had whisked away my hesitation.

"Where to go for dinner this weekend to celebrate," Dillon told her.

"Celebrate what?"

"My birthday."

"Your birthday? But . . . I don't know why, but I remember it was in July."

"It is, but I don't have to wait until July to celebrate it, do I?" he asked, then winked and hurried off to his homeroom.

"What am I missing?" Ivy asked me.

"You said he was unpredictable. Why are you

surprised at the outrageous things he says?" I smiled and started for our homeroom.

The only question was whether I could hide my absolute terror about what I was planning to do.

"I'm looking forward to the audition so much," Ivy said as we entered our homeroom. "Aren't you?"

"Oh, yes, but put it out of your mind. You'll make yourself too nervous."

"Like I could do that," she said, and we took our seats.

I looked at the wall clock. In a little more than three hours, I would either commit to Dillon's plan or back out. Either way, I was sure I would be changing my life. Every minute would be different.

When you watch a clock, it seems like time stands still. Most of the time during my morning classes, my mind was off somewhere else. I almost got caught ignoring the lesson in math when Mr. Brizel asked me to work out a problem. He liked us to do it aloud so he could evaluate our thought process. I did okay, and he moved on to someone else, but I could feel the ring of sweat at the base of my neck.

Ivy, who noticed I was behaving differently, said she attributed it to the auditions coming up. "You're looking more nervous than I am," she said between classes. "You were the one who told me to put it out of my mind, too."

"Do as I say, not as I do, remember?"

"Ha, ha. That's an excuse for hypocrisy that some of our teachers use, especially those who still smoke."

When the bell rang to break for lunch, I felt my heart stop and start. For a moment, I wondered if I would faint as soon as I stood up. Ivy waited for me at the door. Unlike me, she couldn't stop rushing the day.

"Go on ahead, Ivy. I need to go to the bathroom."

"Nervous Nellie," she said. "Maybe I should go with you."

"No. Get our table for Dillon and me. I'll be right there."

"Don't throw up or anything," she warned, and smiled.

If she only knew how close I was to doing just that, I thought. As soon as she moved off, I hurried to my hall locker, got my jacket, and then walked quickly, my head down, to meet Dillon at our rendezvous in the west wing of the school. He was already there. This was it. We were starting with a major school no-no, cutting classes and leaving the building without permission.

"Are you really sure you want to do this, Dillon?"

"Mentally, I'm already gone," he said. He took my hand, instinctively knowing I needed him to do just that. Then he opened the door, and we slipped out of the building. It was pretty cold, which was fortunate. No one was hovering around the parking lot. Neither of us looked back.

We got into his car quickly. He started the engine and backed out of his parking space. A number of spaces were reserved for seniors. I looked at the rear seat and saw the cases of soup with Sasco's name and logo on them.

"You want to get the T-shirt on," he said, and opened his jacket to reveal he already had put his on.

I took off my jacket, then took off my blouse and put on the T-shirt.

"Look all right?" I asked, turning to him.

He smiled. "Best-looking part-time worker they'll have," he said. "Take one of those caps, too." He nodded at the bag.

I dug in and found a black cap. I found the other one and handed it to him.

"Ivy's probably freaking out waiting for me in the cafeteria by now," I said. "She'll go looking for me in the bathroom, thinking I'm sick with nervousness about the audition or something. When she can't find me and doesn't see you, either, she'll really freak out."

"She'll be upset we didn't bring her along."

"I doubt that. Cutting class? Her mother would have heart failure. Literally. How are your parents going to take this? Really, Dillon?"

"My mother won't have a nervous breakdown,

but she'll badger my father about it. He will probably take away my car privileges."

"For how long?"

"Until he forgets. A few days," he added, smiling. "It's been sort of this way all my life. Actually, I think they've been grateful that I didn't turn out to be Jack the Ripper."

I sat back. Dillon made a turn and sped up. He figured it would take just about the same time as lunch hour at school for us to get to the clinic. Some of my classmates might ask Ivy where I was and note that Dillon wasn't there, either, but that would be the extent of their interest.

However, a little while later, our teachers for our first classes of the afternoon would notice our absence, and messages would be sent to Dean McDermott's office. The dean and his secretary would check the bathrooms first. They might search other places in the school, and then they would return to the office and inform our parents that we were missing. Probably the police would be notified, and a search would start to find Dillon's car. There was nothing to be done about that now.

As Mrs. Marlene might say, the die had been cast.

There was no turning back. When the clinic came into view, I began to consider what I would say to Ryder when I confronted him. What would I ask? Would I try to find out if Samantha had been lying about him? Was that even a wise route to take? *No,* I thought. *Skip all that, and simply tell him how much you still care for him and how you don't blame him for anything.*

The real question was whether he would even realize I was there. The words *almost catatonic* loomed. The potential for this being a disaster or futile was pretty high.

Before Dillon turned into the entrance from the highway, he reviewed the layout of the clinic. I think my whole body was on fire with fear as he spoke. Was I breathing? It was hard to swallow. As soon as we drove through the entrance, he bore right to go to the far corner and the delivery entrance.

"Just about there," he said.

"What if it's locked?" I asked when he pulled near the door.

"There's a buzzer, but it's not usually locked until late in the afternoon, Toby says."

"Won't she get into trouble for giving us all this information?"

"We won't mention her name, Fern. We never spoke to her. That's not a lie. Everything I know came from Maya. I promised we would never give away Toby if we got caught, and we won't give away Maya, either, or it would lead to Toby. This was something we did entirely on our own. I'll admit to the research on the Internet, and they'll believe us. Agreed?"

"Absolutely."

He looked at the door. "Ready?" he asked, and then turned to me, not touching the door handle. He was giving me a last chance to back out.

"No, but let's do it," I said.

We got out of the car, and he went to the rear and brought out the cases. They weren't terribly heavy.

"Remember," he said, "this is a special delivery if anyone asks."

"It is that," I said.

He smiled. "C'mon. It's going to be a piece of cake," he said. "You'll be in and out, and we'll return to school and face the music."

"I'll face the music in more places than that."

He laughed and then kissed my cheek. I wondered, was he really doing this to please me and help me, or was this simply some needed excitement in his life? He approached the door and looked at me. I nodded, and then he turned the handle and pulled.

It opened.

"Here we go," he said. "There's this little entry. To the right is storage, and to the left is the kitchen. We'll go through the kitchen. That leads to the corridor I described. You're just going to keep walking until you reach room one-oh-two. It will be on your right not halfway down that hall. I'll watch you go out of the kitchen and then slip back out and wait in the car. We don't want me to be noticed loitering," he explained.

We stepped in. We could hear people talking, but no one was in the hallway.

"I'll do the talking and distract as much as I can when we're in the kitchen. You keep moving slowly."

We turned into the kitchen. There were four people working, two preparing food and two cleaning dishes, glasses, and silverware. A man who seemed to be the head chef stepped away from the counter. He looked like someone from central casting, the stereotypical image of a chef, big, with rolling-pin forearms, wearing a full apron and a white hat.

"What's this?" he asked gruffly.

"Special delivery," Dillon said.

"Who called for that?"

"I don't know, sir. We're part-timers who were sent to another location nearby and asked to drop this off on our way."

He stared at us. I held my breath. The two men cleaning dishes and glasses lost interest quickly and returned to work and their conversation.

"Drop it on that counter there," the chef said, nodding at an empty space on a counter close to the door. We moved to it. The chef watched us and then turned back to what he was doing. Dillon nodded at the door. I didn't look back. I went to it, opened it, and slipped out, expecting someone from the kitchen to start shouting.

No one did.

I closed my jacket to hide the T-shirt and stepped to my right. A nurse or nurse's aide came out of a room, carrying a tray of some patient's lunch. She didn't look in my direction. I waited until she turned a corner and then started again. I didn't want to run and attract any attention, but I couldn't help nearly jogging until I reached room 102. The door was slightly open. I glanced back, and then I entered and closed the door behind me.

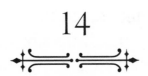

14

Ryder was sitting in a teal-cushioned chair, his eyes closed and his right hand over his left in his lap, both hands resting on that book about birds he had received on Christmas. He wore a familiar blue long-sleeved shirt and jeans with a pair of matching blue loafers and white and blue socks. His hair was neatly brushed. Just looking at him, you couldn't tell if he was a patient or a visitor. He looked quite relaxed. I hoped he wasn't on some sort of sedative. That possibility hadn't occurred to me until this moment. He might not even realize or remember that I had come. I wished it wasn't so, but for the moment, it was hard to imagine that a short time ago, he had devastated his bedroom.

When he sensed I was there and opened his eyes sharply, I took a deep breath and braced myself. Was he going to shout? Jump up? What?

He stared at me silently, unmoving, suggesting that my initial fear might be right. He might be drugged. He didn't seem to recognize me.

"It's Fern. I came to say good-bye, Ryder," I began.

He blinked as if he had something in his eyes

but still didn't speak. I imagined that if he wasn't under the weight of some drug, he was thinking I might be a figment of his imagination or he was still in a dream.

"I can't stay here long. I cut school to come here and snuck in."

I couldn't stand the way he was staring at me with that blank expression. I had to look away and gazed around the room. Everything appeared new in it, polished and clean. There were artificial red roses on a desk. The walls were panels of light oak with thin black swirls. Two large prints hung on opposite walls, both of rural scenes, one with deer at a small pond, looking up as though startled. The windows faced Lake Wyndemere. I imagined they wanted him in a room that had that view so he would feel more comfortable. The bed was queen-size, with a light blue comforter and matching pillows, in a dark brown frame with a padded light brown headboard. There was a square digital clock on the table beside the bed on the right and just a box of tissues beside it. There was nothing on the table on the left.

Right now, the simplicity of the room disturbed me. I couldn't imagine Ryder being happy about it. Drugged or not, this had to bother him. He had grown up in a house with classic works of art, beautiful paneled windows, elaborate molding, chandeliers, and furnishings with character, heritage. Of course, he wouldn't have that when he went someplace else, especially to college someday, but no matter how kind they were to him here, I was sure he felt lost. He was on some stopover from amnesia to confusion in a place that seemed deliberately created to be bland and anonymous so it could fit almost anybody.

I turned back to him. "I've come to say good-bye to you, Ryder, and to apologize."

He continued to stare at me without a sign of any emotion in his face. If he wasn't under the weight of some drug, then this was probably what my father had meant by telling me he was almost catatonic.

"I'm sorry it seemed that I wasn't interested in you or only vaguely interested when you were brought home. Believe me, I was like a horse chafing at the bit. Remember when we were younger, how Mr. Stark always accused one of us of that, being impatient all the time?" I smiled.

His eyes did seem to get brighter.

I heard voices in the hallway and thought, *Oh, no, they've already discovered I'm here, and they'll get me out before I've said what I need to say.* Ryder seemed conscious of it, too, and looked expectantly at the door. Whoever it was went past us, however. I let out a breath and continued.

"We were all warned about what we could and couldn't say to you, especially when it came to the storm on the lake and what happened to you. Everyone accused me of defying the orders and telling you things I wasn't supposed to tell you. I didn't, but unfortunately, no one believes anything I say anymore, not even my mother. Now I wish I really had told you everything, especially about us.

"I think our little sister had a lot to do with what's happened, but she's good at covering up her lies and stirring up trouble to make herself feel more important. Remember, she's also Bea's daughter, which is reason enough to feel sorry for her."

I waited a moment to see if the mention of Bea would stir up memories, but Ryder continued simply to stare without much expression. Frustration and disappointment began to build inside me. It was like talking to myself, practicing the speech I was going to give him.

"Dr. Davenport is convinced that I gave you that picture of us Mr. Stark took just before we left for the prom. Remember? You talked me into going with Paul Gabriel and helped me find one of your mother's dresses to have altered. I found that prom dress in your room after you were brought here this time, and I thought I'd get it out before Dr. Davenport saw it there and accused me of giving it to you. Little Samantha and one of her conniving plots was responsible for that, I'm sure.

"Of course, that's exactly what Dr. Davenport

did do, accuse me. I didn't know he had already seen the dress. I sort of indicted myself by taking it back to my room and hanging it in my closet again, even though I was purely innocent.

"So I was called to his office so he could tell me that a decision had been made. I'm to be sent to a private school, a live-in private school. It could be some time before we see each other again. I want you to know how sorry I am about what's happened to you. Please believe me. I never wanted to do anything that would hurt you, even in the smallest way. I'm sorry you're back here.

"Now, thanks to Dr. Davenport, you know most of what I was supposed to keep hidden, what I was forbidden to even suggest to you. I imagine you're still having trouble digesting it, and it was that frustration you felt that caused you to do what you did in your room at Wyndemere. Dr. Davenport blames himself for that, for rushing to tell you who I really am, but I do think he blames me as well. He's convinced I was working against his and Dr. Seymour's plan of treatment for you and he had no choice. The abruptness was surely like an overload of information for you. You blew out like a computer."

I paused again, searching his face for some sign of awareness, recognition. It wasn't there yet, but I smiled at my own words.

"Listen to me going on like this. I guess I

sound like an amateur psychiatrist or something, diagnosing your behavior. Anyway, now that Dr. Davenport has told you the truth, you can probably imagine how I felt when my mother and then our father revealed the truth to me. This is probably horrible to say, but to me at the time, it was as if you really did drown that horrible day."

His lips began to tremble a little. *Get it all out,* I thought, *get it all out quickly.*

"However, time's gone by. Of course, I'm happy you survived, and I pray that soon you'll get all your memory back and go on to do wonderful things. I couldn't get myself to say it for so long, Ryder, but I still love you. As a sister should," I added. "The Ryder Davenport I knew while I was growing up, the Ryder I went out with on the lake that dreadful day, is gone. Forever. Our father's and my mother's confessions drove him off.

"But my brother Ryder is here, and I want him to know that I will always love him. Someday we might be able to spend time together again, maybe even walk down to the lake and talk about our new lives, share things the way a brother and sister do. All these years, that was denied us, but I'm hoping we'll be able to care about each other and think of each other as family."

I waited a moment. He was still looking at me the same way. Tears came into my eyes. All I had said was probably lost like a scream in outer space. I pressed down on my lower lip to hold back any sobbing.

"I hope you understood some of this, if not all of it. I don't think anything's more important to me right now than your understanding what I've told you. You've lived in the darkness too long. I wanted to be sure I came here and gave you some light. I don't know if I dare call it hope." I smiled. "Listen to me. Me giving someone else hope? I suppose that's a laugh. I haven't enough of my own to last another hour, much less the days and months ahead."

I sighed. This felt so futile.

"Okay, Ryder. I'd better go."

I stepped forward, hesitated, and then leaned down and kissed him on the cheek.

"Good-bye, Ryder. Please get well. I'll be far away, but you'll always be on my mind, always be next to me."

My tears were free now to do what they wished, which was to trickle down my cheeks as I walked away.

Just as I reached the door, I heard him say, "Wait."

I turned, surprised. There was a new look on his face, an expression without confusion, a face more like the face of the Ryder I had known, perceptive, smart, and self-confident.

"It's my turn to confess," he said, and he said

it so clearly that I was the one thinking I was imagining things.

I walked back as he sat up. "Confess about what?" I asked.

"Samantha didn't bring anything to me," he said with a clarity and firmness I hadn't heard from him since the accident. "I went into your room while you were at school, and I found our picture in the drawer. While I was looking at it, I remembered the dress well; I remembered us going up to the attic and searching my mother's things until we found it.

"I went into your closet and discovered it hanging toward the rear on the rack, and I brought it to my room and kept anyone from seeing I had it for as long as I could. It was like having you beside me."

I stood there, gaping at him, looking dumb, I'm sure. Then I felt myself smile. "You remembered all that? The prom, our being together afterward?"

"Yes. My memories were coming back to me, trickling at first and then streaming back in waves of images, voices, and places. At night, after everyone had left me, I would lie there and wonder why I was thinking about you so much, why I was eager to see you."

"Were you?"

He nodded. "Dr. Seymour helped me work through some of my dreams. The lake especially. In one dream, you were with me in the rowboat, but I always woke up before I understood. What I didn't understand were my feelings for you. When I asked about that, Dr. Seymour would tell me to wait, the answers would come. You have to spoon-feed your memory back to yourself, he said. It's less damaging. I was always a little suspicious about it, and then, just as you said, my father rushed all that along. I'm sorry about what I did in my room, but you were right. I was frustrated and angry, very angry at him.

"Suddenly, there was my father, a liar, deceiving, hiding the truth, the great Dr. Davenport, who never backed away when it came to telling me what I should do, what I should think. Always forcing others to face the truth, the famous diagnostician who would never permit loved ones to face the reality of his patients' sickness, was lying to himself and to us all these years.

"Think of it, think of how he permitted Bea to treat you and your mother. I realized that even when she wasn't present, he never treated you as he should, but then in minutes, his solution was to take away my feelings for you, the feelings I wanted to have, I was hoping to have. You are right. I was so . . . frustrated. I hated where I was, what I was. I couldn't stand looking in the mirror. I wanted to beat on the image until he disappeared. That's really what I was trying to do."

"Oh, Ryder," I said. "I'm so sorry."

"You have no reason to be sorry, just as I don't. You and I, we're the real victims. I have yet to tell them what I think, what I've done, but I will now. You're not going to be anyone else's scapegoat, least of all my father's, or I should say, our father's. Thank you for coming here, Fern. Thank you for risking so much for me."

"For myself, too," I said.

He smiled. It was the smile of the Ryder Davenport I had known all my life. He really was coming back. Maybe rage was good. Maybe it forced him to drive away his amnesia, to stop wondering about the meaning of small things and grasp the biggest truth of all: who he was and who I was, too.

He stood up, and we embraced each other, held each other for a long moment, a moment I had dreamed so many times since he had been brought home.

"I wasn't pretending completely," he said. "There was so much that just didn't connect in my memories, but until they did, I wanted things to stay the way they were. I felt safe with all the attention I was getting. I guess I was being deceptive, too."

"I'll never blame you, Ryder. I hated myself for behaving so indifferent to your struggle," I said.

"You were there, tantalizing, tempting me to remember it all. That's all I cared about."

We both heard the sound of many footsteps.

He backed away. "I'm so glad you came," he said.

"So am I. No matter what," I replied, just as the door was thrown open.

Two nurses and a security man entered quickly. "Out!" the security man told me. "Now."

I looked at Ryder. The nurses were trying to get him to sit. He wanted to resist, to help me, but I smiled at him and said, "It's all right. I'll be all right, Ryder."

He smiled back. Then I walked out and was led down the hallway to Dr. Seymour's office. Dillon was already sitting there, a security guard standing beside him.

"They came out and found me in the parking lot. We forgot about the video cameras." He shrugged. "We're television stars. So how did it go?" he asked.

"Perfectly," I said. "Thank you."

I was practically pushed into another chair.

"Hey," Dillon said. "Watch it."

"Relax," the security guard next to him said, and put his hand on his shoulder to keep him down. "The police are on their way, big shot."

Dillon smiled. "Maybe we'll claim loss of memory and move in here," he said.

That was my Dillon Evans, defiant, ironic, sarcastic, and very creative. Being with him was like riding a wild horse, but when he was relaxed and on a gallop, you never felt excitement as wonderful.

Of course, our boldness or, as my mother would say, "cheekiness," was quite short-lived. Looking stunned, Dillon's mother arrived right before my mother appeared, and he was led to another room with her. My mother entered and asked the security guard to please step out for now. She said Dr. Seymour had said it was all right. He shrugged and left.

"Explain yourself, Fern," my mother said after she sat on the settee across from me.

Where should I begin? I wondered. Although I was in more trouble than I had ever been in, I felt strangely satisfied, even happy. Maybe I had caught Dillon's carefreeness. I was amazed at myself, how I wasn't at all afraid, even knowing what awaited me in school as well as at home.

Except for the truth about my father, my mother never lied to me. Like most mothers, I'm sure, she held back on other things, tried to get me to do what she wanted by unfairly emphasizing the dangers and discomforts of the other choices. It was always all in my best interest. But this was different. Oh, how different this was.

It was not in my nature to connive, to rationalize and twist facts and events for my benefit and make others, especially my mother, feel guiltier. Despite our second-class citizenship at Wyndemere for so many years of my life, I had grown up with the love and affection of those who mattered to me the most. I bore the burdens that came with being a fatherless child, that "illegal" child Enid Austin had accused me of being as long ago as first grade.

Even during the years when the parents of other children in my class warned them not to associate with me, not to invite me to their parties, I somehow didn't feel as meaningless and despicable as Bea Davenport and her snooty friends tried to make me feel. My mother, Mr. Stark, Mrs. Marlene, and many others who grew to love and respect my mother insulated me. I grew up strong. I had an ally in Ryder, too. As children, we did much together. It was inevitable that I would have a crush on him and then eagerly pursue something more with him.

Within this fragile world, I grew stronger and bolder, pushed back on prejudice until I was more and more accepted. But I was always aware of the possibility that this delicate bubble I lived within could break. When Bea was at Wyndemere, she never let me forget it.

And then, one day, it did come crashing down around me. The Revelations were that heavy. So here I was about to take advantage of it, yes, conniving, but in my mind justifiably so.

"I'm here because you lied to me, Mummy. I'm here because you let me grow up under a shadow, one of those heavy ones at Wyndemere. You and my father decided a long time ago that the truth was better kept trapped in one of the cobwebs. You're responsible for bringing me here as much as Dillon Evans is, as much as I am myself, you and my father."

My mother looked away. She nodded to herself and pressed her lips together before making a big sigh and turning back to me. "Why didn't you come to me first and ask if you could come here?"

"Would it have really helped, Mummy? You accused me; you wouldn't believe me. Everyone was against me seeing Ryder, unfairly against it."

She looked down. I felt terrible making her feel terrible, but it seemed so right to do it.

We both looked up when my father entered the office. He closed the door softly behind him and leaned against it. There he stood, the mighty Dr. Davenport, around whom I had tiptoed most of my life, whose look could freeze me and whose occasional smile could fill me with the light of heaven. It wasn't a terrible exaggeration to think that I had once worshipped him. He loomed that great in Wyndemere and in our lives.

But right now, the moment he said something in the way of condemnation or criticism, I was ready to fight back with more vehemence than he'd think I was capable of.

"I have to apologize to you, Fern," he began, which took my mother by surprise as much as it took me. "Dr. Seymour and I have just spent fifteen minutes listening to Ryder confess about that picture and the dress, about a number of things, actually."

"Oh, Harrison," my mother said to him. "Ryder did those things?"

He nodded. "I once told Fern that when you make a big mistake in your life, it resembles throwing a rock in a pond and watching the ripples, each ripple becoming some other problem as a result. I think we threw quite a rock into that pond, Emma, years ago. It was mostly my fault," he said.

"I'll never let you believe that, Harrison," my mother said.

This short exchange was the most intimate conversation I had ever witnessed between them.

"I've just spoken for a few moments to your young man's mother," my father said, turning back to me. He looked at his watch. "Your mother and I will return to the school with you. My office has contacted Dean McDermott, and he is setting aside time to see us. Dillon and his mother will follow us."

"Why?" I asked.

"We all have some explaining to do. I'll take the lead on that," he said.

It occurred to me immediately that my father, the famous Dr. Davenport, had never acknowledged me as his daughter in public with me present. He had never gone to a parent-teacher conference at my school, and although he once came to see me in a play, he came under the guise of someone interested in the daughter of his head housekeeper. No one would have particularly congratulated him on my accomplishments, certainly not with the anticipated pride of a parent.

"Dr. Seymour will not pursue any legal action against you or Dillon Evans for breaking into the clinic," he said. He almost smiled. "One benefit was that you identified a security weakness. Okay. I think it's best we all leave for the school immediately."

My mother stood. She reached for my hand, and I rose quickly. Still a bit stunned, I walked with her behind my father. Mrs. Evans was waiting in the parking lot. Dillon had gone around to the right and brought up his car.

"Can I go with him?" I asked.

"Yes," my father said before my mother could respond. He walked with me to Dillon's car and opened the door for me. "Drive carefully behind us," he told him.

I got into Dillon's car quickly.

"I don't know what's happening, exactly," he said. "But I'm not asking any questions."

"Neither am I," I said.

We followed his mother and my parents out of the clinic parking lot and onto the highway.

"Feels like a funeral procession," Dillon said.

"Hope not," I replied.

We drove on. As we did, I described what Ryder had told me and how my parents had reacted to the realization that I wasn't guilty of the things my father especially had accused me of doing.

School had just ended moments before we all drove into the parking lot. Dillon parked in his reserved spot. His mother and my parents went to guest spots. We sat in his car for a few moments, waiting for most of the student population to get on buses and into their cars.

"Ready to face the firing squad?" Dillon asked.

"As long as it's with you beside me."

He smiled, and when we got out of his car, he reached for my hand. Most of the students still leaving saw us and stared with curiosity. Some who were in our classes paused to watch us enter the building through the front and join our parents in the lobby. I tried not to look at anyone as we made our way to the dean's office.

My father asked the secretary to request that he, my mother, and Dillon's mother meet first with the dean. He nodded at some chairs, and we sat. Dean McDermott came to his inner office door. We saw that Principal Young was in his office as well. He closed the door when everyone but us entered.

"I wonder if capital punishment is still in effect here," Dillon said, deliberately loudly enough for the dean's secretary to hear. She glared at us and then returned to her paperwork. We sat back to wait. I suddenly realized we were still wearing the Sasco's T-shirts.

"What's so funny?" Dillon asked, smiling, astonished that I wasn't sitting there crying.

I pointed to his T-shirt.

"Oh. I hope they don't sue us for impersonating deliverymen."

Nearly a half hour later, the door opened, and our school principal stepped out. He barely glanced at us before leaving for his own office. The door remained open. Dillon's mother appeared next. She still looked quite dazed. For a moment, I thought she was going to leave without saying anything, but she paused and looked at Dillon.

"I'll see you at home," she said. "I've called your father and told him everything. He's away on a job, as you know, but he'll be calling you tonight."

She continued out of the offices. I looked at Dillon.

"He's always away," he said. "Even when he's home."

We both looked up when my parents and the dean stepped into the doorway. The dean and my father shook hands, exchanging some words we couldn't hear. My mother was looking down and then turned to look at me as they started out.

"You'll go home on the late bus," she said. "We'll talk more after dinner."

I watched her leave with my father. The dean beckoned for us to enter his office.

"I'll always remember you," Dillon joked when we stood. The astonished look on the dean's secretary's face nearly made me laugh at what was clearly the wrong time.

We entered the office, and the dean closed the door behind us. He told us to sit in the two chairs in front of his desk, and then he went around and sat behind it.

"I asked the principal to be present for this meeting with your parents," he began, "because I was aware that there were special extenuating circumstances. Extenuating, not justifying," he quickly added. "Cutting classes and leaving the school grounds without permission are among the most serious violations of our code of conduct. We take on a legal responsibility for you when you enter this building. All sorts of things could have happened to you. I'm sure that by now, most of the student body knows what you did, too.

"However," he continued, "thanks to Dr. Davenport, Principal Young and I are aware of the family crisis you're suffering through, Fern. We're not without compassion. As for you," he said, looking at Dillon, "under any other circumstances, if you pulled this, I'd render the full extent of punishment. For now, I'm going to believe you were motivated by compassion, too." He looked at me. "Or maybe other things. Whatever. The fact that neither of you has ever had a discipline problem during your school life does matter to me, but again, it doesn't excuse what you've done. So . . .

"First," he said, "you'll both serve two days' after-school detention. Dillon, you will lose your driving privileges to and from school for the remainder of your senior year. Fern, you will be denied driving privileges until your senior year, at which time the situation will be reconsidered.

"Second, you will both write out formal apologies to the teachers of the classes you missed. How each teacher handles that is at his or her discretion. They can assign zeros to your class averages, additional homework, whatever."

He looked at his watch and then at Dillon.

"You are not, I repeat, not, to drive Fern home today. You do not have permission to take any student from this school or to this school in your vehicle. We require parental consent for that, and you've lost your driving privileges here anyway. Is that understood?"

"Yes, sir," Dillon said.

"Don't let me regret not suspending the two of you for a week outright as well," Dean McDermott said. "Okay. You'd better leave to make the bus, Fern. Dillon, you remain here. I'm not quite finished with you."

"Thank you, Dean McDermott," I said, standing.

Dillon looked at me. "If I'm not back by sunrise, call the FBI," he said.

I bit down on my lower lip, this time to stop a laugh, and hurried out of the office.

I had forgotten about Ivy. She was standing at the door to the parking lot.

I shook my head as I approached her. "I don't want to talk about it now, Ivy," I said.

Her face nearly overflowed with disappointment. "Will you call me later?" she practically begged.

"Yes. After I have a chance to catch my breath."

When I got home, neither my mother, Mrs. Marlene, nor my father was there to greet me. I was anticipating another, more severe lecture. I went right up to my room. No one, not even Samantha, came up to see me. She was probably unaware of it all anyway. The silence was as painful as any verbal chastisement. I couldn't stand it and decided to call Ivy and talk to someone after all.

Ivy was in the three classes I had cut when I went off with Dillon, so I wanted her to give me the homework anyway. I felt it might go a long way toward my redemption if I kept up with the work, surprising all my teachers, I'm sure. I still had to live here for a while until my new school was arranged.

When Ivy mentioned the play again, I finally told her my parents were seriously considering sending me to a private school.

"Oh. Really?"

"That's why I did what I did today, sneaking into the clinic. I was afraid I wouldn't see Ryder for a very long time."

"But why did you have to cut class and sneak in?"

"I'm not on the approved list of visitors."

"Why not?"

"It's complicated, Ivy. Anyway, Dillon was a great help. Actually, he thought up the plan to get us inside."

"Everyone thought you'd be suspended," she said. "But the school has changed its policy a bit on that. Some kids were being suspended so much they missed too much work and were almost forced to fail." She added, "Your friend and mine, Denise Potter, has come up with another theory she's spreading." She sounded reluctant. "Marcia Green told me a little while ago."

"And what's that?"

"Special favor to your father. He saved the principal's older brother's life with a bypass last year."

"Did he? I didn't know, but I don't keep up with

what he does, who his patients are, and whom he saves."

"What do you think?"

I didn't want to explain any more, to reveal that my father had told both the dean and the principal details of Ryder's condition. I wasn't sure myself how much or what he had told them. I was confident that whatever he told was enough to get them to do just what the dean said, consider extenuating circumstances. I certainly wasn't going to ask my father.

"I don't know, Ivy. Dillon's pretty upset about losing his driving privileges for the rest of the year. I think he'd rather have been suspended."

"And he'll be even more upset when he learns you're going to a private school."

"He is. I told him."

"Oh."

"Tell me more about the audition. How did you do?"

"I don't know. Mr. Madeo smiled when I went up to read and saw I had drawn a mustache on my face, just the way Dillon did it. And I did that little nasal thing you suggested."

"He must have been impressed with that."

"He told me to be sure to come back and read again."

"That's a good sign, Ivy. I'm so happy for you." She was quiet.

"I am. You'll be sensational."

"Maybe. The auditions run through Friday. He's going to post the cast list on the bulletin board outside the principal's office on Monday morning."

"I'm hoping you'll be on it."

"Without you two, I won't be happy about it," she said.

"You'd better be. If you're in it, I'll try to get back to see it if I can."

"Will you? I can't believe you're being sent away."

"I'd better get to my homework. I have to write three apology letters, too. See you tomorrow," I said.

"Okay." There was that little lost girl's voice again, drifting off. I almost felt sorrier for Ivy than I did for myself.

How easy the solutions for her unhappiness were, I thought. Someday she'd find another close friend, for sure. She was too sweet and intelligent not to make lots of new friends, especially in college.

If she only knew how hard the solutions for my happiness were, she'd surely be in tears.

I sat there spinning in a kaleidoscope of emotions. I was so happy with how my visit with Ryder had gone, but I was devastated by the chasm of disappointment and sadness that had fallen between me and my mother. I knew I would never have a better friend. The darkness was still here, still hanging triumphantly over all of us.

But that was soon to end. It was truly as if someone had opened a window.

Epilogue

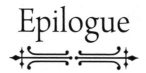

Even Samantha realized that something very important was about to happen. Rarely was our father seated in the dining room before we had arrived. My mother was seated as well. The table was set, but there wasn't any food on it yet. My father had opened a bottle of red wine and poured glasses for himself and my mother. Samantha looked at me for a hint about what was happening, but I was looking down in anticipation of a harsh lecture.

"I'm hungry. What are we eating tonight? I hope it's not that stew thing," Samantha said.

"Sit and be quiet," our father said sharply.

I looked up, poised. I would not cry.

"Ms. Corey and I have made some new decisions," he began. "We have decided first that Fern will continue her education here. She's been on the honor roll every semester. We're both proud of her achievements." He looked at Samantha directly. "You should strive to do as well, Samantha. More time on your work and less time wasted on nonsense."

"What nonsense?" she asked.

I kept my eyes down. I was happy to hear this, but I was sure there was more coming. I could feel it.

"We are going to concentrate more on Ryder's full recuperation. He has made significant progress, and we're hoping he will continue his education."

He sat back. His pause was so long that I had to look up. Then he reached for my mother's hand and spoke looking only at her.

"For a long time now, Ms. Corey and I have shared the burdens of Wyndemere and its occupants, Ms. Corey bearing the bigger share. We have known each other for over twenty years now. I can't imagine anyone more devoted to my children or to me right now. I know both of you and Ryder appreciate her more than you can say."

My mother smiled.

He turned back to us. "Life is far from a straight journey. There are many turns, many you never anticipate, and if you are to survive and do well, you have to learn how to adjust. Who is it who's always telling us that a branch that doesn't bend breaks?" he asked, looking at my mother again and smiling.

"Mrs. Marlene," she said.

"Ah, yes. Few wiser. So," he continued, "we have an announcement to make first to you two.

Ms. Corey and I are getting married. It will be a simple civil ceremony performed in this house by a friend of mine, Daniel Harris."

"The governor?" I asked immediately.

Samantha looked too stunned to speak ever again.

"He's that, too," my father said. "However, it will be a simple affair."

"As simple as Mrs. Marlene permits," my mother said, smiling.

My father laughed. "We have a great deal to do here, a lot to repair, but if we all work together, I think we can bring some sunshine back to Wyndemere. Any questions?"

Samantha surprised me. "What do I call her now?" she asked.

My father shrugged. "Mother, Mom, or, as Fern calls her, Mummy," he said.

"But I have a mother," she said, and then added, "Sometimes."

"Now you have two," my father said. "One who will always be here for you."

"I'll call you Mummy, too," she told my mother. "It's different."

"Yes, it is. Often," my mother said.

"Good," my father said. "Now, it's time to eat. I agree with Samantha. I'm hungry."

My mother got up and went into the kitchen.

"So, Samantha," our father continued, "tell me about this mediocre math average you've been

355

carrying. I was pretty good in math. You should be, too."

She looked to me for help.

"She'll improve," I said. "I'll make sure of it, Daddy."

My mother, our mother, reappeared with a bowl of salad. She began to serve it.

"After dinner tonight, what say the four of us play some eight ball? I hear you two have become quite good," my father said.

Samantha's eyes almost popped.

"We'll team up. Samantha and Emma against Fern and myself."

"We didn't call it pool, we called it snooker, but you're in for a challenge," my mother told him.

Mrs. Marlene appeared, beaming. Samantha was happy, too. Mrs. Marlene was going to serve one of Samantha's favorite meals, spaghetti and chicken. Our father, our Dr. Davenport, as we would call him often in the future, decided to give both Samantha and me some wine, too. Samantha was quite surprised and rattled on about how some of her friends bragged about having wine at dinner.

"Or elsewhere," my mother said, her eyes dark with suspicion.

"Maybe," Samantha confessed.

Everyone laughed.

Something happened that night. It wasn't just the four of us for the first time ever spending time together in the game room, and it wasn't simply our father being more relaxed than either of us had ever seen him. It wasn't the show of affection between him and my mother during the evening, either.

It was more like the darkness in Wyndemere had recoiled, shrunk back into the deepest corners. The echoes of past tragedies and sadness weakened and were impossible to hear, even at night when we were all in our beds and the house was its quietest. Finally, we could sleep and have the dreams that came from somewhere inside us, dreams that housed our hope. Nightmares were left outside our front door. They were swept away in the wind that dropped them over the lake.

I prayed that this was also true for Ryder, who slept at the clinic, hopefully with a new smile on his face, and that it was also true for Dillon, who would always have a place in my heart. For the next two days, he and I were probably the most well-behaved students at school. He wrote his apology letters in poetry. We did our detention, and then, at his suggestion, we went to the play auditions on Friday. I saw Mr. Madeo's face when we entered. I had the feeling he had been waiting and hoping for Dillon, at least. I gave it my best. We had practiced our lines again over the phone on Thursday evening.

Although Dillon was prohibited from driving to school, his father didn't stop him from driving on the weekends. We dated both Friday and Saturday nights. He came over on Sunday for dinner and spent some time with Samantha and me in the game room.

On Monday morning, Ivy greeted me almost the moment I stepped into the school lobby.

"We all made it!" she said, her face burning with excitement. "You're Lucy."

"My Dracula will be happy," I said. I didn't want to tell her about the playful way he had been nibbling on my neck on our dates.

By opening night, six weeks later, my parents had been married, and the community was abuzz with the news. They didn't go on any sort of honeymoon, because my father's schedule was quite full. They were making plans for one, however. We were getting periodic reports on Ryder's improvements. His return home was imminent. Both Samantha and I were excited about it. Our father talked about plans for him to continue his education, too.

Sometimes I imagined Wyndemere groaning under the strain of so much happiness. It wasn't used to it. It did seem to me that the windows were permitting more and more sunshine to stream through. My mother went at the house more vigorously. Mr. Stark began to do more repairing, oversaw more whitewashing, until even the outside looked more welcoming. He and Mrs. Marlene and Parker were coming to our play's opening night. I didn't think I was ever more nervous about anything.

And then I was told something that almost took my breath away.

Samantha came backstage while I was getting my makeup put on.

"You're not supposed to be here," I said. "After the play, you can come backstage."

"Mr. Madeo said it was all right."

"He did? Why?"

"To tell you," she said.

"To tell me what?"

"To tell you Ryder is here, and he's sitting with us."

"Don't cry," Dillon warned, overhearing her. "You'll ruin your makeup." I had the suspicion he had known.

I didn't cry, at least until it was all over and we had stepped out to thunderous applause. Dillon was holding my hand, and Ryder was standing with my family and clapping.

We were inside a theater, and it was evening, but somehow, when I looked out at everyone, I saw sunshine.

The storm was over, I thought. We were moving calmly over the great Lake Wyndemere, calmly toward the grand house.

And very soon after, we were all home again.

Center Point Large Print
600 Brooks Road / PO Box 1
Thorndike, ME 04986-0001 USA

(207) 568-3717

US & Canada:
1 800 929-9108
www.centerpointlargeprint.com